Paradis

Paradis
a novel

Mary Burke
with Natalie Burke

Living
Fossil

Paradis is a work of fiction. The names, characters, and incidents portrayed in it are the product of the authors' imagination. Any resemblance to actual persons, living or dead, events, or localities is purely coincidental.

Copyright © Mary Burke and Natalie Burke 2025

Published by Living Fossil Books, Seattle, Washington, USA

All rights reserved.

No part of this publication may be reproduced, stored, or transmitted in any form or by any means, electronic, mechanical, photocopying, recording, scanning, or otherwise, without written permission from the publisher. It is illegal to copy this book, upload it to a website, or distribute it by any other means without permission.

The authors disclaim responsibility for the persistence or accuracy of URLs for websites referred to in this publication and do not guarantee that any content on such websites is accurate or appropriate.

Designations used by companies to distinguish their products are often claimed as trademarks. All brand names and product names used in this book are trade names, service marks, trademarks, and registered trademarks of their respective owners. The authors and the book are not associated with any product or vendor mentioned in this book. No company referenced in the book has endorsed it.

ISBN 9789083513089 (paperback) | 9789083513010 (ebook, Kindle)
Library of Congress Control Number: 2025900374

First Edition

Cover photo by Mary Burke
Layout and cover design by Natalie Burke

Author's note and dedication

I, Natalie Burke, Mary Burke's daughter, have published *Paradis* posthumously. While I have rewritten some segments and made modifications in preparation for publication, I have endeavored to keep the story as true to its original form as possible.

I dedicate this book to my mother, Mary Burke, and her profound appreciation for the Florida wilderness. I love you, Mom, and miss you every day.

Paradis

Prologue

Past the live oaks with their heavy arms, beyond the expanse of spiky saw palmettos, south of the verdant cupola housing its freshwater spring, and north of the marching mangroves, there lies a beach—a picturesque embodiment of a tropical paradise. A postcard view. An artistic swirl of teals and turquoises, framed by two palms gracefully leaning toward one another, sharing a secret. An elusive horizon blends seamlessly into the vastness of the sea, and the sand is pristine, delicate, porcelain-white. The soothing soundtrack of the ebb and flow of the waves coaxes the observer into a reflective and tranquil state of mind.

However, beyond this idyllic haven, in the depths of the Gulf of Mexico, a low-pressure system develops above unusually warm waters…

Mary Burke

◆ ◆ ◆

"Your house is so exotic; our viewers are going to love it! Oh, and the fact that you have to take a boat to get here, well, isn't that just the cherry on top? Mwah!"

Clarice pauses a moment to take it all in. The cracker-style house is painted in shades of orange, yellow, pink, and red. One wall appears ablaze, glowing so strongly in the sunlight. Wooden lizards morph in and out of the foliage, their tongues lolling out and mouths smirking like tricksters. Abstract metal concoctions emerge from overflowing kudzu vines, twisting into benches and solar lamps.

Gary and Mike point out some of their favorite art pieces as they walk Clarice to the screened-in porch of their island home. The white shell path leading to the stairs crunches under their shoes. Clarice instructs her fly-film drone operator to continue capturing the area as she conducts her interview. At the top of the porch, she pulls up a hot pink chair, and Gary takes a seat in a shocking orange chair. Mike excuses himself; he doesn't like being on livestreams.

On the table, Clarice places a small geodesic orb on a stand. She swipes a few times in the air and then smiles at Gary. "Ready?"

Gary amiably laughs and nods, signaling his approval.

"Hello, off-grid home lovers! We are sitting with Gerardo Díaz Hernández, who goes by Gary. Wave to our audience, Gary!" Above the table appears a miniature holographic image of Gary sitting beside Clarice. To the right of that, the live footage from the fly-film drone plays.

Gary waves enthusiastically at his own image.

Paradis

"So, Gary, this is your lovely oasis—"

"Mine and my partner's, Mike Henderson. He may stop by later. He's a little shy, unlike me."

Gary's cordial laughter causes the stream to flood with hearts and smiles. Comments cascade across another screen, situated for Clarice to easily read.

"Tell us about yourself, Gary."

"Well, I'm a third-generation Colombian American. I've lived in Florida my entire life. I just love the heat here. I'm a scrap-metal artist, and my husband is a woodworker. Together, we built and decorated our perfect island getaway." The footage from the fly-film operator expands to fill the entire image.

"It is spectacular, and our fans agree." The screen is plastered with positive expressions, stickers, emojis, and exclamations. "So, what made you two decide to move off-grid?"

"Well, it's complicated." Gary leans forward in his chair. "See, my identity was stolen—"

A gasp. Clarice rests her hands on Gary's hand. "That is just terrible."

"I was selling art all over the world at the time. Someone must have gained access to my accounts: private key, retinal and facial scans, all leaked into the ether. I lost over five hundred thousand dollars, and my digital credibility was destroyed. It became impossible to make purchases; my credit score was irrecoverable, catastrophic."

"Did you already know about living off-the-grid?"

"Nope, I was a privileged city boy." Gary's laugh again sends hearts cascading through the stream, as he continues,

"Learned everything from Neuron Streaming. Not a sponsor, hah. But seriously, it was easier than I thought. After the hacking stress, Mike and I decided to retire early. Did some research and ended up buying this land from that wacky Kicklighter family. You know them? The ones with that Netflix show?"

"Of course, the Kicklighters are very well known, though not for their decorating sense." Clarice winks at the camera, and links about the Kicklighters briefly flood the stream.

"They helped a lot, though. Coordinated most of the building logistics, hauled in the supplies we needed, and we worked with the same contractors they used for their house. Tobias Kicklighter and his sons even hand-built our chickee hut." The fly-film operator quickly directs the drone toward a large, raised picnic shelter with a palm frond roof. "Of course, we took care of all the decorations and painting ourselves."

"I must say, this is certainly a paradise you've built here."

"Well, almost. Paradise without the *e*."

Clarice shoots a quizzical look.

"The name of the island is Paradis. Get it? Paradise without an *e*!"

A drizzling rain starts. Heavy and dark clouds materialize on the horizon.

"What a great name!" Clarice touches her ear, and the fly-film operator cuts the footage. "Well, I think the weather just decided that this is the end of our interview today. Thank you very much, Gary. This was wonderful. And thank you to our viewers. Make sure you all subscribe to see more great off-grid homes!"

Paradis

Once the livestream cuts off, Clarice gathers her equipment and meets the drone operator at the base of the steps. Together, they ride ATVs to the shore, where Clarice loads her equipment into an aerocar and takes off.

Gary and Mike return home. Together, they sit on their porch and watch the rain until no more light can be seen.

The next morning, it is still raining.

♦ ♦ ♦

"I'm not leaving."

"Come on, Ma. The house is gonna flood. It's been two weeks straight, and those news reporters say it ain't gonna stop any time soon."

Cici glares at her son and puckers her face. "Let the waters take me, then. I've lived here my whole life, and I'm not about to leave now."

"We're just gonna go stay with Jimmy, you remember, my friend? You like Jimmy, and his kids, and his wife!" Jerry is pacing, throwing his hands in the air with exasperation.

"I like it here in Snug Harbor." Cici remains still, her hands folded in her lap, her face stern. "Hon, I'm ninety-three. It isn't so easy to just up and leave when you get to my age."

Jerry storms into the kitchen where his wife, Hilda, is watching the weather channel, attempting to ignore the commotion from the other room.

He takes a seat next to her. "She's so stubborn."

Hilda holds his hand. "She's old." She looks at her husband. "Do you want to evacuate?"

"Hell no, I'm not leaving Ma." Jerry gets up and grabs a beer from the fridge.

"Then we'll hunker down. Hell, we've done it before, and you know our neighborhood is on high ground, at least by Florida standards. Remember Hurricane Eugene? That turned out just fine."

The lights flicker. Jerry heads outside to check on the generators.

When he returns, he shuts off the lights and screens, all of which have been repeating the same weather report: rain, then more rain. "We ain't getting to the store any time soon. We've got to preserve what power we still have."

Hilda and Jerry join Cici in the living room. They take a seat on the tropical plant-upholstered couch, while Cici sits on her La-Z-Boy. They look through the window framed by floor-length brocade drapes. Together, they sit silently and watch as the last patch of visible road goes underwater.

◆ ◆ ◆

"Have you talked to your mom?" Liam stands in the doorway of Amber's office, fiddling with his iGlass.

"Not since yesterday. What's happening now?" Amber looks frazzled, her eyes showing signs of exhaustion. She slept terribly last night. Florida, where her mom lives, is in total shambles, and her mom's communication has been spotty at best. On top of that, the project she had been super excited to work on just became the subject of a lawsuit by the American Psychiatric Association. Now she'll have to work on one of Quench's other projects, probably creating digital vacations for the super wealthy, unless her team can figure out some way to placate the APA.

"Check out this stream." Liam projects a holographic image on the wall next to her. She watches as a large group stands in water up to their knees, yelling at what appears to be a politician on a stage. The image becomes sharper, revealing the politician as the Lieutenant Governor of Florida. The Governor of Florida flew to his second home in Michigan three weeks after the rain started and hasn't been seen since. The Lieutenant Governor is speaking, but his words are drowned out by the screams from the crowd. Suddenly, three bangs ignite total chaos. The crowd surges to the exits; people are running, stumbling, and splashing into the water. The Lieutenant Governor collapses, shot directly in the head. Guards rush into the confusion of swimming people, water sloshing everywhere. Police apprehend a screaming man flailing a gun and wearing mouse ears. The stream's comment section goes wild.

Lmmmmmaaaaaaaooooo the mouse did it

Haha Florida Man strikes again

I read that he wasn't a resident, just some stranded tourist. Poor guy

What a shit state

Amber looks away. "I can't watch this." Liam shuts off the projection as Amber swipes in the air. "Call Mom," she says, then looks at Liam. "I'll try again, but you know she never has her iGlass... Mom, hey Mom... Wait, are you okay?" Amber sighs loudly. "Come on!" she exclaims.

Liam stares blankly ahead, clearly watching more streams on his iGlass.

"Can you believe it?" Amber throws her hands in the air. "She hung up on me, said she was busy and would call back."

"Whoa, look at this stream. Some guy got his LiveCam in his bedroom to turn on, and there are, like, eight alligators just chilling in his room." He projects a new hologram. Alligators are floating inside a room. Only bed posts and the top of a door give clues to the fact that it is a bedroom.

"Here's another one." Liam projects an image of Miami. People are using boats to ram storefronts, while others swim out of stores, hauling full racks of clothes behind them. He projects another image. "Look at this one—these people just commandeered some huge yacht, and now they're all just dancing and drinking. This is nuts, modern pirates."

Amber sighs, feeling overwhelmed by all the holographic images. Her iGlass pings, signaling a call from her mom.

"Oh, thank God... Mom, Mom, are you okay? What is happening?"

There is a long pause, and Amber's face turns white.

"YOU DID WHAT?!"

Another pause.

"What are you thinking?! Come to Issaquah, now! You can live here—" She flashes a look at Liam. His eyes are wide, and he mouths, "Are you crazy?" Amber ignores him. "You'll like living here! Cute coffee shops, boutique stores, good food, ME!!!" Her voice is especially loud at that last note, and she notices the iGlass's automatic volume adjuster kick in.

She sits, chewing her lip. Liam waves his hand in front of her face, begging to hear what is happening on the other end of the line.

Paradis

"What are you talking about?" Amber continues. "Washington has so much nature—huge trees, multiple mountain ranges. Freaking Mount Rainier is right there on the horizon—"

Amber pauses and slowly exhales. There is defeat in her voice. "Yeah, yeah, I know... Look, I've got to get back to work... How about I just call you later... Yup, okay... I love you, Mom."

She hangs up, tears welling in her eyes.

Liam shuts down the streams. "What happened?"

"She bought a house on some barrier island named Paradis. She says she's going to live there off-the-grid."

Amber sets her work status as AWAY. She goes to the bathroom and splashes her face with water. Liam follows.

"I just don't understand her sometimes. It's like she hates civilization. Doesn't she realize *I'm* part of civilization?"

Amber dries her face, and Liam gives her a giant hug.

💧 💧 💧

Emergency Broadcast Announcement:

Attention all residents in Florida State's Central-West, Central-East, Southwest, and Southeast regions. This is a mandatory evacuation notice issued by the Florida State Office of Emergency Management and National Guard. Due to unprecedented heavy rainfall and severe coastal flooding, a state of emergency has been declared. All residents in the highlighted areas must evacuate immediately. Evacuation must be completed no later than Monday, September 15.

Mary Burke

This message will be continuously broadcast on all major networks until September 15. The following major counties are included in this evacuation notice: Miami-Dade, Monroe, Broward, Palm Beach, Charlotte, Manatee, Hillsborough, and Pinellas. Additional affected counties can be found on the scrolling marquee below the highlighted map.

Your personal electronic devices will notify you and provide evacuation guidelines if you reside within the affected area. If you do not possess a device or require assistance, please proceed to the nearest FEMA shelter or contact local authorities for support. Effective September 15, water and power services will be terminated in all counties under evacuation notice. Emergency personnel will be unable to provide further assistance beyond this date.

Emergency services, including FEMA and the National Guard, have deployed boats to aid individuals who require assistance during the evacuation efforts. Boats and buses from various locations nationwide have been dispatched to facilitate the transportation of evacuees to Orlando. Additional transportation options will be available from Orlando. We kindly request that you limit your belongings, as these buses will be operating at maximum capacity. Rest assured, reinforced barriers have been constructed along I-75 by the army to ensure safe passage for all evacuees.

Please note that the duration of the floodwaters and the likelihood of their receding are currently unknown. Your safety is our top priority, and we urge you to comply with this

Paradis

mandatory evacuation notice. Stay tuned to official updates and follow the instructions of local authorities for further guidance.

Paradis

Paradis

Fall

*Two roads diverged in a yellow wood,
And sorry I could not travel both
And be one traveler, long I stood
And looked down one as far as I could
To where it bent in the undergrowth;*

*Then took the other, as just as fair,
And having perhaps the better claim,
Because it was grassy and wanted wear;
Though as for that the passing there
Had worn them really about the same,*

...

- Robert Frost

Chapter 1
Mangroves

I paddle my kayak into the mangroves where the tannin-stained water stands only a foot deep. Little fish dart and splash. It rains lightly, bringing forth the intermingling odors of rot and life. Here, nature reveals its secrets within labyrinths of deep green tunnels.

There was a time when I would have sped through these mangrove tunnels, eager to escape into the open waters, finding the tunnels claustrophobic, thinking their roots were menacing, ugly like mop strands, and smelling just the same. But now, my perception has transformed. I regard these trees as majestic mothers, nurturing and protecting marine life and the coast. I perceive their roots as delicate fractals, nature's careful basketry, skillfully holding back the surge of salty waters. I take my time through these tunnels, pausing to watch larvae gape below the water, snapper and shrimp swim below, crabs and lizards skirt across the roots, and egrets and pelicans perched in the leaves above. Life thrives everywhere, even in hidden worlds I cannot see.

I pause to watch a snail traverse the arch of a root and imagine a life slowed down to his speed. How quickly we race through life; how challenging it is to slow down and notice that other creatures have their own agendas on this planet. For thirty years, I taught high school biology, but only now am I starting to understand how little I know. I could spend endless hours learning from these mangroves, eagerly and carefully observing life. However, today I am on a mission—collecting oysters. My destination awaits: a mangrove island situated about fifty feet from the Paradis coastline. There, the trees are encrusted with oysters—good ones, not too small, with hard, sturdy shells.

As I navigate through this mangrove arcade, I indulge in a daydream: My late husband Mark paddles ahead of me. Naturally, he is shirtless, his back muscles flexing with each revolution of the oar, sweat glistening in rivets down his strong arms. He glances back at me, frozen in time, not yet old, no longer young. A few strands of gray hair sweep across his forehead, his smile etching subtle creases that only enhance his handsomeness. I am young again as well. My arm muscles can stretch the oar further, the soreness of past days lifting, and I can paddle smoother with renewed vigor and exuberance.

These days, I allow frequent visits from Mark's ghost. Paradis Island, my new home, reminds me of him. Just like Mark, Paradis brims with vibrant life. It is flavored with beauty and danger. Mark belonged to nature, thrived on its challenges, undaunted by python-infested swamps or ninety-degree angled cliffs. His strength was my safety net and I believed he was invincible. Until I learned that nothing—and no one—truly is.

I arc around a bend in the tunnel of trees. Two groups of ibises and roseate spoonbills scatter in a boisterous flurry; it's difficult to tell who startled whom. I watch their graceful motion with awe and their path reveals the opening to the Snug Harbor sound. Smoothly, I glide into the bright open waters beyond the passages and head toward the tiny mangrove island. I circle close, my kayak's wake lapping against the matriarchal guardian roots, frightening a raccoon family also out collecting oysters. Most of the oysters pull right off, but for those that don't, I carefully wedge my chisel, trying my best not to hurt the roots. It's slow progress as the repetitive motion tires my arms, serving as a reminder of my sixty-two years. Mark's ghost has departed, and I find myself back in the present, longing once again for his strength and companionship.

On the other side of the mangrove island is a small beach, spacious enough for me to bring my kayak ashore. I search for clams, but no matter how much I dig, I find nothing but mud and plenty of fiddler crabs. A splendid breeze blows away the mosquitoes, so I decide to sit and rest, careful to avoid the fiddler crabs busily digging their tunnels. Across the sound, the supposedly inhabited mainland town of Snug Harbor shows no signs of life—no vehicles or boats. My ears anticipate some mechanical hum of human activity, but all I hear are the waves. Even the birds sit in quiet contemplation.

Paradis

I allow my mind to wander, a potentially dangerous activity, but one that must be occasionally indulged. How long have I been living on Paradis Island? Three weeks? A month? It feels longer. I am still in the honeymoon phase of my new home, the wonder of being in a new place powerful enough to mask the emotions I should be feeling about the Florida Floods. Perhaps I am in denial, postponing an inevitable emotional breakdown. Maybe I've become skilled at mental compartmentalization, neatly filing this grief alongside the others. It's possible that this is a skill that has come with age. Or maybe it is the island itself, the inexplicable healing power of nature. Regardless of the reason, however illogical it may seem, I find myself happier here than I have been in a long time. At sixty-two, I am finally living out my childhood fantasy: a free-spirited and self-sufficient life on a beautiful, secluded island.

My thoughts are interrupted—a mechanical hum, a change in the pattern of the waves. A boat? This disturbance corrects my last thought. *Mostly* secluded island. I scan the Gulf's horizon—a solid, blinding white in the brightness and haze, until it is interrupted by a shape: a fifty-foot electric yacht christened *Kickback,* property of my island neighbor, Tobias Kicklighter.

I hope he will continue on, but the interruption on the horizon only grows larger. Eventually, I can see the shapes clearly—two figures, one of which is gesturing. Tobias Kicklighter enthusiastically waves, and his eighteen-year-old son, Toby Too, stands stoically.

I am spotted. The yacht comes to a halt; the engine turns off. It is still a distance from the shore, but in the silence of the day, Tobias's voice comes through clearly. "Mornin' lit'le Addy, how's da oyster huntin'?"

His disruption has scrambled my thoughts. I respond with a silent stare, frozen, as if only motion and sound will betray my existence. The glare off his boat is harsher to my eyes than the water has ever been.

"Hey lit'le Addy!" he calls again, followed by a high-pitch whistle.

I succumb. Offering a bleak smile, I wave in their direction.

"Are ya still comin' by da farm dis afternoon?" Tobias asks, his voice thick with his Wisconsin accent.

I mime an inability to hear, eager to encourage his swift departure.

Instead, Tobias manages to raise his voice louder. "FISH FRY?!"

"Yup, see ya there!" I yell back.

"What?" he shouts.

Apparently, returning to my meditative beach musing isn't going to be that easy. I stand and wade out a few steps in the surf, cup my hands around my mouth, and raise my voice. "Yes!"

"Dat's great!" He smacks the top of the wheel, grinning his toothy smile. "We're about done catchin' 'dem fish!"

I stare, feeling uncomfortable. This clearly isn't the easiest way to hold a casual conversation.

"Well, we gotta get." Perhaps the feeling is mutual? "Only a lit'le time before da next downpour. Ya know how it goes dese days. See ya at da farm, lit'le Addy!"

I force another smile and wave, feeling relief at seeing Tobias's boat turn away. For a few minutes, I observe the

Paradis

Kickback churning the waters of the bayou before returning to my spot in the sand.

The encounter has left me uneasy. Nature doesn't expect small talk. A few weeks alone can clear the mind, but it doesn't necessarily make one good company. Tonight, I will be joining Tobias, his family, and my other island neighbors for a dinner. This will be my first island dinner since settling here, and it was the catalyst for my oyster-collecting mission today.

Before I came here, I read all about Tobias Kicklighter online. He is the majority property owner of Paradis Island. He sold me my fifty acres of land, complete with a raised shotgun-style house, for $300,000 cash. Paradis is a barrier island, once protected as a state park and only accessible by boat. Shaped like a cayenne pepper, the island spans approximately two miles east to west and eighteen miles north to south. It suffered little from the flooding that devastated much of Florida. Even before the mass Florida exodus began, Tobias was able to purchase the property from the parks department for a "super cheap" price, whatever that means to a multimillionaire.

Tobias started out as a humble sales associate for Recreational Equipment, Inc. When he and his wife inherited a few thousand dollars from her uncle, they purchased five acres in the Wisconsin wilderness where they spent weekends and holidays living off-grid. When their eldest son, James, started streaming the family's experiences, it quickly garnered a large following. Several tabloids detailed the couple's turbulent relationship, Tobias's DUIs, his membership in AA, and his sporadic brushes with the law. These events seemed to captivate even more followers, and when streaming viewership skyrocketed, a lucrative deal from Netflix soon followed. *The Kicklighters' Off-Grid Prepper Program* aired for seven years. Hasbro even made a Tobias action figure.

Apparently, I had been living on some other planet because, before his advertisement for the property, I had never heard the name Kicklighter. I attempted to watch the show—an intro packed with entertaining off-grid antics, family interviews with thick Wisconsin accents, and then, a loud crack, a dead buck, pooling blood. I quickly closed the video app. He is a hunter; I am a hiker. We both are experienced and resourceful, but our perspectives on the wilderness differ. But now he is my neighbor. He, his wife, and their children live five miles south of my neck of the woods. Thinking optimistically when I bought the land, I thought perhaps I could learn from Tobias, hone some off-grid skills, or strike up a friendship with his wife, who knows about canning and quilt-making, useful non-suburban housewife stuff.

There are two other neighbors on the island as well: Gerardo Díaz Hernández and Michael Henderson. They live about four miles north of me, and they stopped by to welcome me right after I moved in. They also helped me check the connection of the solar inverter to my power-node and added a water pump, faucet, and showerhead for my outside rain barrel-fed shower. They refused any payment, so I treated them to lunch, and we talked about gardening. They showed me an *Off-Grid Houses* stream that showcased their homestead's beautiful gardens, where they artistically mix the exotic with the mundane. I haven't seen it in person yet, but I can't wait to visit.

Paradis

New home, new neighbors. Excitement and anticipation for tonight's dinner building with the tide. Anxieties popping into my thoughts like the cumulus clouds overhead. It is time, I decide, to paddle back home and clean up these oysters for the neighborhood fish fry.

Chapter 2
A KickAss Fish Fry

Household chores fill the afternoon as I await this evening's chauffeur, Toby Too. I clean the oysters and bake cornbread. I sweep out debris and droppings from my chicken coop with a thick-bristled broom. My chickens are a joy to watch. Myla, Becky, ShawnRee, Marla, Karen, and Maggie, flamboyant ladies who dance a chaotic rhythm of foraging, preening, and digging in the sandy soil. From some underbrush leaps my cat, Dandelion, a short-haired orange tabby. He recklessly scatters the chickens, but Dandi means no harm. He rolls at my feet, begging for pets. I drop the broom and sweep him into my arms. Almost immediately, however, my Dandelion snuggling time is interrupted by the cacophony of shattering logs and branches beneath the wheels of a jacked-up, solar-plated GM Armadillo truck. Toby Too has arrived.

Paradis

With his assistance, the oysters and cornbread tins are collected, and the oven fire is extinguished. As soon as I'm sitting in the passenger seat, we're off. Toby Too is a blonde, six-foot-tall, earbuds-wearing country boy. After some half-hearted attempts at conversation go nowhere, I decide it's best to concentrate on keeping my cornbread tins balanced on my lap and my body upright during the bumpy ride to the Kicklighters' Farm.

I would have enjoyed some mindless chit-chat. My stomach is vocal with apprehension about this gathering—it flutters with nerves and rumbles with hunger. Up to now, I've only had brief contact with the Kicklighter family, and each time we were focused on specific tasks: finalizing paperwork, moving furniture, Tobias calling his oldest son, James, to help me troubleshoot the power-node. From those interactions, I discovered that I don't much care for Tobias. He is crass and loud, his presence always interrupting some moment of island serenity. But he and his family are skillful and wealthy, and in case of emergency, they will likely be my greatest resource. It doesn't seem wise for an old lady out here to ignore her neighbors.

Shortly, we are passing through the posts marking the entrance to the Kicklighter farm. Large bold letters spell "KickAss" in red, while a small cursive "Farm" is daintily scribbled below. I wonder what witty name I should give to the Adeline Thorndyke estate.

The smoky aroma of fish on the grill grows stronger as Toby Too parks on a grassy patch next to a pair of ATVs, about thirty feet from a large Seminole-style chickee shelter. Mosquito netting protects the chickee's platform, and through it, I see a buffet table, picnic tables, and benches. In the pines behind it looms an ultramodern house on twenty-foot-high concrete piers. This minimalistic arrangement of glass cubes, all glare and hard edges, seems out of place amidst the irregularities of nature. Solar panels line the tops of the cubes, and cypress slats sit on the sides. The slats stand partially angled, presumably to provide protection for the huge solar-paned windows. It's a clever design, essentially giant vertical blinds, allowing for cross ventilation and energy efficiency.

Toby Too, my earbud-bedecked chauffeur, is already out of the truck. He unlatches the tailgate and lifts my buckets of oysters from the truck bed. I'm about to get out when I spy a pack of pit bulls trotting toward the truck. They surround him, barking, sniffing, and salivating at the buckets of oysters that he holds aloft as he walks away. From my interactions thus far with the Kicklighters, it seems fitting that they would own pit bulls. I open the door slowly and quietly, but one of the dogs immediately turns and pricks his ears toward me. Knowing that dogs can smell fear, I decide the best course of action is to close the door and remain seated in the monster truck. Tobias looks my way, waves his spatula, and shouts the mantra of all dangerous dog owners: "Hey, lit'le Addy, doncha worry, dey're friendly!" His words provide no solace; I sink deeper into the seat and wonder if dogs can open car doors.

Luckily, Tobias's wife, Marmalade Mae (more commonly called MaMa), comes to my rescue. "Down, Eenie, go on now." With that encouragement, the largest of the pit bulls bounds back toward two of Tobias's sons who are throwing a football. With cornbread tins in hand, I take a deep breath and climb out of the truck. It's time to get to know the neighbors.

I hand MaMa the cornbread tins when I reach the chickee. MaMa is an ample, athletic woman. She sports a camouflage maxi dress with matching flip-flops. Her light brown hair is styled into waves and her makeup is impeccable, which is no small feat considering tonight's humidity. My petite stature and rugged styling feel pronounced in her presence. I have let my hair grow out gray, cutting it myself to keep it short and comfortable in the Florida heat. Instead of makeup, my skin has the sheen of zinc sunscreen, which has discolored nearly all my shirt collars. Approaching the buffet table together, we must contrast sharply: a mouse and a panther. As if only to enhance our size difference, giant, burly Tobias joins us. He is slurping down a raw oyster doused in Sriracha. His tangled ponytail and beard mimic the Spanish moss that drapes the oaks. A deep crease at the top of his nose brings attention to his bushy eyebrows and slate-colored eyes. He shouts toward where two boys are tossing their football, "Lit'le Addy's here, so we can eat now. Kids, come on, wash up!"

The two kids immediately abandon the football and retrieve a third brother, who purposefully wanders in his iGlass and haptic gloves.

The food looks amazing. Mindy, the Kicklighters' extremely freckled and lanky fourteen-year-old daughter, is working the grill. She plates each of us a fine red snapper. Toby Too stands alongside his sister, busily coating oysters in cornmeal. I take stock of this large family comfortably living among the Florida wilderness: three young boys, a young girl, and Toby Too towering above them all. Only missing is their eldest son, James, now an adult living his own adventure back in Wisconsin.

Massive Tobias leans over me. He laments that they found no grouper fishing. "Hard to come by nowadays," he says, then informs me that my place is at the "adult" picnic table.

I pile my plate until it is overflowing: grits, pole beans, mango, papaya, cornbread, crackers, and fish spread. I can eat a lot for an old lady. Grabbing a red Hog's Breath beer from a washtub of cold water, I find a spot at the "adult" table. It's raining now—a fine, drizzling rain.

Across the table from me sits Gerardo, who everyone calls Gary. He enthusiastically motions toward the rain with a hush puppy. "Looks like you got here just in time."

Michael, Gary's partner, who we all call Mike, takes the seat next to him. They are attractive guys whose mannerisms mirror one another. Mike has blonde hair with flecks of gray, his bright blue eyes framed by large circular glasses in an identical shade of blue. Gary is of the salt and pepper variety with dark eyes that sparkle with constant enthusiasm. His smile is crooked and mischievous, and his laugh is deep, hearty, and sincere. Both are artists; Mike works with wood and Gary with metal. Their outfits are a hodgepodge—paint-splattered shorts paired with clean guayaberas. Mike's right cheek is speckled with bold yellow paint.

Tobias asks if I'm enjoying my "vittles," a word honed from his TV show, I'm sure. But he has a point—it is the best red snapper I've ever tasted, the grits the creamiest, and the beer immensely refreshing. He's plopped his largeness down next to me, with a huge helping of steaming cornmeal-dusted oysters scooped onto his plate.

Paradis

He spits saliva my way, along with squirts of lemon wedge and Sriracha, calls me "lit'le Addy," and asks if I have a hollow leg. I feel the blood rise to my face and grimace at his nickname for me. Is it a remark about my five-foot-three stature? My bony, narrow shoulders or rather elfin physique? Is it his attempt at backwoodsman charm? I only find it condescending.

Gary lightens the mood, however, with his signature convivial laugh. "We're hoping we can do this once a month, taking turns at each of our places," he says. Then, he asks what brought me to Paradis.

This prospect of talking about myself revives my earlier anxieties. I plan to only tell them about the reservist at the National Guard shelter in Orlando who had sent me the property link, maybe quote some lines from Frost's "The Road Not Taken." But instead, my whole life story starts to spill out. I start talking about my childhood, growing up in the Kenwood neighborhood in St. Petersburg. I mention how I graduated from St. Pete High, attended the University of Florida, and met my husband, Mark, while hiking the Appalachian Trial—two gators far from the swamp.

"R.I.P. St. Petersburg," intones Mike, reverently.

My mind is full of Florida—land of the flowers, freshwater springs, fountain of youth, senior citizens, golf carts, rocket ships, South Beach, alligators, Disney World, cracker cowboys, Seminoles, Okeechobee, super-UV-plus-blue-light-blocking sunglasses, Everglades...

Ah, the Everglades. I tell them about Mark's first steady ranger gig at Everglades National Park. About how I taught biology at Miami-Dade's Homestead High School. I mention the purchase of our first house and the birth of our only child, Amber.

Gary interjects, "Were you there the summer of the four hurricanes?"

I nod. "That was the year the Everglades closed and Mark lost his job. We ended up moving to Tacoma, Washington, where Mark got a new ranger gig at Mount Rainier National Park." I examine my fish, thinking of dissections in my biology class. I strategically isolate some remaining flesh, take a bite, and hope someone else will speak.

Gary's exuberance fills the silence almost immediately. "That was when Mike and I met! We were both evacuees at a Best Western in Punta Gorda."

Mike takes Gary's hand. "Love at first sight."

Gary beams.

Tobias looks slightly amused.

MaMa interjects, "Thank goodness we were livin' in Wuh'scahsin."

"What does your daughter do?" Gary asks me.

"She's a virtual world designer at Quench in Seattle."

Tobias scoffs. "Is she makin' dem video games?"

"Kind of. I don't really know too much about her work. I think she mostly creates vacation packages or something."

"I've heard of those." MaMa nods her head excitedly. "It lets people visit exotic lands, explore ruins that normal folks can't even access. I saw it on the news."

Tobias harrumphs loudly. "I hate those damn games. My boy Richy's crazy about dem. Dat's all he wants to do all day. Goddamn plague on the planet, if you ask me."

Paradis

Although brashly stated, I don't totally disagree with Tobias. I had always covertly questioned Amber's choice of pursuing her field. I was, of course, proud of her accomplishments, but I couldn't help but wonder if she had given up on the real world. I have always believed her generation should be focused on finding ways to fix the existing reality, but instead they seem intent on building artificial ones. I've read studies linking the sort of experiences she created to "virtual obsessions." Some individuals are prone to becoming addicted to them. Occasional stories trend about people taking out second mortgages, losing their jobs, abandoning their spouses, or forgetting to feed their children. However, these incidents only seem to bolster sales and increase stock prices. Her company's motto: "When the landscape is changing, make your own." The whole concept sends chills down my spine.

Tobias passes me a fresh bottle of Hog's Breath, and when I start to drink, the inevitable is asked: "So, where's Mark?" I can feel the beer thick in my throat, the beads of sweat forming on my forehead. I'm used to this question. Talking about Mark does inevitably point out his absence. But I never get used to how time slows down. How strange, small details in my space start to feel so important: the tattooed beer rings on the table, the congealing Sriracha around the bottle's top, the cornbread crumbs on my shirt. How the crest of memories suddenly crashes over me and my brain replays the events from thirteen years ago with perfect clarity.

April 23, 4 p.m. in our Washington condo. I was watching a news report outlining new strategies for mitigating wildfires when my phone buzzed. Mark's boss: "Mark hasn't checked in." He had been out checking on a trail in Mount Rainier National Park, the Paradise Trail. I "shouldn't worry yet," but they were "sending out a search party." I shouldn't worry. His boss went on about how Mark was savvy enough to survive a few nights in the wild. By the end of the week, the search party included helicopters, dogs, and the news media. Six weeks went by, six weeks during which time had no place or meaning. When the news came, I actually felt relief. On June 4, a party of hikers spotted what was left of him downstream from the Paradise Trail.

"He died in a hiking incident thirteen years ago," I muster out. "Believe he stepped through an ice bridge, was probably swept downstream and suffocated under the ice." My throat goes dry as I say the words. These words, rehearsed and repeated so many times, are still so difficult to say. "The Park Service held a very nice ceremony. My daughter kept the flag and we scattered his ashes on Mount Rainer."

MaMa draws her hand over her mouth, and Tobias, with a mouth full of cornbread, suggests, "Must be hard bein' alone here without a man's help." As if someone snapped their fingers, I'm brought out of my daze. What an inane response. Or was that just Tobias's version of offering *deepest sympathies?* Feeling flustered, exposed, and a little confused, I quickly wrap up. "When Amber enrolled at the University of Washington, I decided to return to my roots. I came back to St. Petersburg, reconnected with some old acquaintances, retired from teaching, and for a while, all was pretty good. Until, well, you know." I take another swig of Hog's Breath and gesture around us.

"The flooding," Mike answers.

Paradis

"We came down here for the sunshine," says MaMa. "Wuh'scahsin winters are brutal, ya know."

"With all dat climate madness, insurance companies up and leavin', land was cheap, bein' sold by the Parks' Department, 'n so..." Tobias shrugs. "Anyone else needa 'nother drink?" He gets up and leaves the table.

Gary leans forward and his arms gesture widely. "But why here, Addy? Why Paradis?"

It dawns on me that I didn't actually answer his question. Why Paradis? Why not somewhere else? Why be alone? Why not move in with my daughter? The recent cataclysm of events that brought me here unfolds in my thoughts like a series of blurry, water-stained photos.

Rain. Rain that covered the state and never relented. Rain that overwhelmed. "It's just rain!" "It has got to stop!" Eventually, the water had nowhere to go but up our streets, into our yards, and eventually our houses. Then things only got worse—sewage systems broke, the grid fizzled, bridges and roads literally washed into the sea. Bloated bodies started surfacing. Politicians harangued. People shot each other. Alligators ate people, poisonous snakes took over bathrooms, opossums with their babies commandeered bedrooms, Zika was rampant. The rain continued. Finally, the government made the call—half the state was instructed to evacuate. Eighteen million Florida residents took to the crumbling highways. South of Orlando turned dark; congressional districts were redrawn.

But why Paradis?

A lone word spills out of my mouth: "Romanticism."

Gary's mischievous smile fills his face.

To me, it was an obvious answer. Who hasn't dreamed of running away from the turmoil of civilization to live the rest of their days on a tropical island? Well, I guess many people haven't. People caught up in the mayhem of civilization, tempted by technology, money, and material possessions. Suppressing and tempering their dreams of adventure, deeming them unrealistic, too difficult, too dangerous. Don't they realize the abundance nature supplies? How much richer life can be! How much more *intensely* one can live! I can't help but think of Amber, so entrenched in the modern world.

"I briefly considered moving back to Washington, but Florida... There is just something special about Florida..." My mind wanders. Something watery. Something soft and slippery as swamp moss on a cypress. Something hard and sharp as the beak of an alligator snapping turtle. Even the sky has attitude here—soft as a babe's bottom in the morning and hard as an anvil cloud at night. I keep my answer simple. "Florida is home."

Closely, I observe my island neighbors. Is everyone traumatized in some way, profoundly altered by our changing world? Storms, floods, hurricanes, landslides, droughts, heatwaves, blizzards, fires. Death. Are we fighting back by living here? Being stubborn? Refusing to leave when everyone else did? Or are we just taking advantage of the situation—cheap land in a tropical paradise that lost its *e*? Maybe we are all running away from civilization by running to a place society deemed too dangerous to bother with. Too broken to fix. I wonder if I was twenty years younger, would I be out building dikes? If I was forty years younger, I'm sure I would be radiant with naïve hope. But now, I revel in nature's victory

Paradis

over the virus of man. I selfishly envelop myself in nature, letting it wash over me, hoping to forget all the problems of the mad world.

And on that thought, as if to mock our frail human existence, nature lets loose with a colossal clash of lightning and thunder. Those of us at the table freeze for a moment, as if victims of blinding flash photography.

When my eyes readjust, I see Tobias and the five kids are already pulling down plastic sheets attached to the edge of the chickee's roof. MaMa's up and over to the platform's edge, peering through the plastic, checking, I assume, that their house is not on fire. Tobias's youngest son, Tommy, squeals and points to a nearby smoldering pine.

"We came here to be free." Gary is leaning forward to be heard over the driving rain.

Gary and Mike are holding hands on top of the table.

Mike adds, "We came '*because it was grassy and wanted wear.*'"

Excitement spreads through me. I too had been contemplating Frost's poem since making my decision to move to Paradis. I respond flawlessly, "This is definitely the less traveled road." A mutual understanding passes between us, like a secret shared between close friends.

Tobias and MaMa return.

Sweating profusely in the humid air, Tobias pours clear liquid from a jug into a collection of shot glasses he's procured from a bag. He laughs robustly. "Damn loud Florida thunder calls for a bolt of white lightnin'! Can't stay on a sinkin' island without a still, ya know." He raises his cup. "To Addy's husband, Mark."

I find his toast to Mark unexpectedly comforting. I watch as he empties his glass in one smooth swallow. MaMa follows suit. Mike and Gary stare at their cups, as if deciding what to do. Tobias refills his cup and welcomes me to Paradis, giving me a friendly pat on the back. My eyes feel slightly watery, but I can't discern if it's from the surge of emotions or the strong smell emanating from the glass in front of me. With a gentle smile, I raise my own glass in a salute to my tablemates. I take a sip, and I cough. "White lightnin'" is an apt description.

The rain settles into a typical Florida downpour, and the white lightnin' diverts the conversation from my life and arrival in Paradis to lighter topics. MaMa, who has downed at least a couple shots of the lightnin', is intent on sharing with me the story of when the Westby High School football team won the state championship and Tobias proposed to her with his championship ring. She takes another hit of the lightnin'. I manage to slowly nurse mine. I push away Eenie's big, black, wet nose from my crotch. From out of the corner of my eye, I observe a raucous holographic casino game being played at the kids' table. Mike and Gary engage in a discussion with Tobias about an excursion they are planning to Joey Pelagro's—the combination post office, internet café, and hardware, grocery, and feed store near Snug Harbor. Gary's tone sounds annoyed about the trip, while Tobias is repeatedly commenting on his respect for the operation Joey has running. Mentally, I make a supply list as MaMa continues her tale about her high school days. I interrupt her and ask about the location of the bathroom. She directs me to a cabana area up a path to the house.

Paradis

Since the opportunity to ask about going to Joey's with the guys doesn't immediately present itself, I wander up the path to the cabana. It is lined with solar-powered tiki torches and hammocks swinging in the damp breeze. The cabana has a homey feel, with a couch, a coffee table, solar lamps, spare propane tanks, and a house battery on the wall. A small door leads into a bathroom with a concrete floor. Behind a shower curtain and a raised tile rim, a wooden rain barrel funnels water into a shiny gold showerhead. A composting toilet sits at the end of the room with Japanese-style smart bidet controls. It too is gold-chromed.

On my way back, I hear a ruckus coming from the chickee. Tobias is over at the kids' table, shouting commands. I can make out snippets: "makin' coffee" and "bringin' over dem fellas' pies." The holographic game has vanished, and the kids are all but tripping over themselves as they clear the tables, start the coffee, and grab pies and new utensils.

"Lazy kids," he harrumphs, but then quickly transitions to discussing plans for Halloween at the guys' and Thanksgiving at my place.

I'm quick to inform him that I don't have enough chairs, let alone space. I gesture at his elaborate chickee setup.

He swigs back another shot of lightnin'. "Dat's no problem," he says. The Kicklighter children arrive with plates, forks, and slices of mango and lemon pie. "Me and dem kids," he continues as his arm flails outward, loosely grabbing Toby Too around the shoulder, "we'll come by and build ya a chickee." Toby Too rolls his eyes and shifts his shoulders, releasing his father's grasp. He puts down the plates of pies he is balancing and quickly walks off to the house without a word. Mindy brings cups and pours out coffee, while the wiry, glasses-wearing boy, who I recognize as the one that sported the iGlass and haptic gloves earlier, brings the milk and sugar. MaMa introduces him as Richy.

I look back at Tobias. I'm apprehensive about his offer, but I also see it as an opportunity to learn some building skills, if he even remembers this exchange tomorrow. "Well, if you're offering," I say, "but only if I get to help and you teach me how to build it."

"Woont have it any other way!" Tobias exclaims. His speech is noticeably slurred at this point, and his largeness is swaying.

In what appears to be a well-rehearsed exchange, MaMa reaches over and, in a single swift motion, takes the lightnin' bottle and covertly passes it to Mindy, who quickly vanishes. Did some signal pass between them? Tobias almost immediately attempts another grab for the lightnin', but, seeing it gone, he shrugs and turns his focus to the pie.

I too look at my pie. Dissecting a piece with some mango, I take a bite. The pie is surprisingly good.

I decide against staying for s'mores. It's getting late, and the rain has stopped. But before I take my leave, I ask Mike and Gary if it's okay to accompany them on their supply trip to Joey Pelagro's. They smile excitedly, and we discuss plans until Toby Too is ready with the GM Armadillo. The drive back is similar to the ride there—Toby Too and his earbuds, not a word spoken. At least this time, I'm not hungry.

Chapter 3
How I FaceTime with Amber

The only person I regularly communicate with in the outside world is Amber, and we do so once a week via FaceTime. To achieve this electronic miracle, several trees donated their lives so that the dish on my roof can enjoy unobstructed communication with a satellite in geosynchronous orbit 22,000 miles above the Earth. Joey Pelagro, Snug Harbor's favorite off-grid supply guru, coordinated the installation of my satellite internet equipment and application software that would permit his store (of course) to debit my online wallet whenever I make purchases.

I pluck my iGlass from its solar charger and put it on my face. "Amber, FaceTime," I say.

"Hey, Mom! What's up?"

A young, oversaturated version of myself appears. Amber, wearing her iGlass, is seated at her desk in her Issaquah home.

Her deep chestnut hair is cropped short, her skin rosy and dewy. Her upturned hazel eyes, which look almost identical to my own, are barely visible behind her iGlass. In the corner, my image hovers like a personification of time. I gesture, full screening Amber and hiding my own image from view.

"Do you still look this good?" I ask.

"Filter-free." She smiles, and for a moment she reminds me so much of Mark. "Is your place presentable? I've been looking at the pictures you've sent me."

I answer, "Do you have time for the threepenny tour?"

"Penny? Haven't seen one of those in ages. Let me just log off from work."

She logs off, and I commence the livestream of my house—the paneled walls of island pine and oak, the dust motes that float in the sunlight across the table, the built-in shelves holding books, a rattlesnake skull, and a horseshoe crab molt gleaned from the island, as well as a family photograph of Mark, myself, and Amber. Amber's two stylized oil paintings of the Cascades and the Gulf of Mexico hang juxtaposed on opposite walls.

"You hung up my paintings!" Amber beams.

I step close so the brush strokes become visible, Amber's impressionist landscapes contrasting in subject and color. The Cascades are rendered mostly in grayscale, except for some careful strokes of deep green. The Gulf of Mexico is painted in neon tones, so recklessly bright that looking at it for too long pains the eyes.

I move into the kitchen area dominated by my La Nordica stove, where two pans of dough are warming. Canned and

Paradis

boxed foods, along with a first aid kit, fill the shelves on the opposite wall.

Amber, always a tactile learner, makes a motion as if to poke a mound of dough. "I miss your bread."

"Fennel and regular white."

"Mom, write down your recipes and I'll e-book them. It could generate a little extra income for you and make everyone else in the world a little fatter."

"Maybe." I hesitate. Amber is always thinking up some way to make money. I change the topic before she becomes too attached to the thought. "I have to tell you about the fish fry I attended."

"The dinner at the Kicklighters'?"

"Yup, appropriately named KickAss Farm."

"Well, was it a kickass fish fry?" My daughter giggles, and it's like the tickle of a light breeze through wind chimes.

"Yeah," I say, considering the evening with a smile, "the Kicklighters are quite the characters! Living 'off-grid' on a Florida barrier island with a whole lot of expensive stuff. Can you believe they have a golden, Japanese-style composting toilet? Guess they've got the money. We ate in a chickee and had fresh red snapper. They own a pack of pit bulls." I stop myself. Am I babbling like a newly unclogged drain or what?

"Japanese-style toilet? Pit bulls! Sounds like some bizarre vacation getaway. Mom, are you sure you're happy there? Are you safe?"

I brush off her concerns. "You should smell the fresh air here!"

An interesting word—vacation. Does my daughter think this is only a vacation for me?

"Well, promise me you'll stay away from packs of pit bulls, snakes, and sharks." Amber sighs. "I just worry about you there, all alone. You know, the invitation to stay with me and Liam—"

"Amber, don't worry," I cut her off. "Between Mike and Gary and Tobias the backwoods cowboy, I'm surrounded by brawny men." I peek up to the loft where Dandelion purrs on my bed. "And most of all, I've got Dandi here to protect me."

Amber reaches out as if to stroke the cat. "Oh, Dandi, I wish I could pick you up and squeeze you."

I wish I could squeeze my daughter.

I continue the tour into the kitchen and through to the bathroom, my mind full of Amber. Her at two years old running in the surf. Her at five years old climbing the branches of a live oak. "I've thought of a name for my place. What do you think about Addy's Wedgie? It's my little slice of Paradis." I laugh at my own joke.

"Catchy name, Mom. I love it!" She laughs as well. "I want to send you a housewarming gift. It's a 3D60 camera so you can record what you're experiencing on the island."

"Isn't that what we're doing right now?"

"Not really. It's the latest thing, called the Chameleon," she says. "It has a drone attachment and a solar charger. It's super easy to use, and it has all sorts of machine learning artistic applications." She pauses, and her eyes move back and forth as if reading something. "I wanted to send the camera by UPS, but they won't let me send it to your island. No personal drop-offs to unincorporated barrier islands, they said." Her eyes stop their motion and focus on my face again. "Guess you couldn't just live somewhere normal," she jests with a slight smile, but her voice suggests a bit of annoyance. "Is there any place in Snug Harbor where it could be safely dropped off?"

"Joey Pelagro's. It's where UPS delivered my La Nordica stove. But aren't you coming in December?"

"Yeah, but that's three months from now." I can tell she is making a VoiceNote. "Joey Pelagro's," she repeats slowly. "Also, the Orlando Share-A-Car said they charge extra insurance for driving anywhere southwest of Orlando." Annoyance clear in her voice. "Basically, they said the car would be broken into if I sent it back by itself or left it sitting around in Snug Harbor. Any suggestions?"

I shrug and shake my head. "No, it's early. We'll work something out, and I don't need a camera."

"I'm sending the camera." A wry smile on her face.

I stand on the back porch, letting FaceTime transmit a panorama, wanting to steer the conversation back to the tour of my new home.

"You sure have a lot of firewood lying around," she remarks.

Success.

"It won't stop raining, so I've been stacking it inside and on the back porch," I reply.

I briskly descend the back steps, proud of my spryness at sixty-two years old. Not too many senior citizens are buff enough to still split wood. In the yard, the chickens forage, and behind their fence, the vegetable garden blossoms. Puddles steam beneath the oaks.

"Wow! I forgot you can actually see the heat!"

My mind envisions Amber at eight years old, looking for tadpoles in the puddles.

Before I can bring my thoughts back from puddles and tadpoles, I hear, "You want to see Sparky and Barky?" Wiry hypoallergenic dogs, resembling the stuffed toys Amber carried around as a child, spring into view before my eyes.

"Hello, fellows," I manage to say, raising my voice to be heard over the exuberant dogs. "How's Liam?"

"I think he's still in a meeting in his studio."

With the dogs yapping along, she leads me through their house. The furniture is contemporary, and Liam's guitars are mounted on rust-toned walls patterned with projected overlays. One pulses as an indicator to remind her she is FaceTiming. At another wall above her desk, instant messages from colleagues ping for attention. These screens that augment her home, leaping out everywhere, discomfort me. I am unplugging myself from the modern world just as my daughter is Wi-Fi-ing and Li-Fi-ing into it. She percolated. I dripped.

A soundproof glass door communicates Liam's meeting status with white images of vibrating sound waves dancing across the pane. They remind me of sunlight rippling through water, and through them, I can see Liam working at his mixing console. He appears to be teleconferencing with members of a band dressed in 1960s attire.

"He's putting together the music for a rock and roll documentary for Amazon. He's real excited about it, but I hardly see him anymore." She frowns. "At least I have the dogs and all his guitars on the wall."

"Tell him hello from me."

"Will do, Mom."

Paradis

Back at the entrance to the kitchen, a MopBot has just finished polishing the floor. Amber pauses to release dog snacks from the Speciesbar dispenser. While the dogs crunch pleasurably and quietly, Amber shows me the view through their kitchen's sliding glass door. It's a lovely day in Washington—the air is clear and tall evergreens frame the blue-tinged Cascades. "Are you sure you don't want to move out here? Fewer mosquitoes, and Issaquah has great coffee shops."

The view is alluring, but Amber's question isn't a matter of trading one sort of nature for another. All nature is beautiful. This is a question of access to wilderness and self-sufficiency. Do I trade these for safety and convenience?

"Tempting view," I admit, pausing to consider my words carefully. How do I explain my disdain for civilization to someone so entrenched in it? "But living there, well...that's all make-believe."

"Make-believe?" Her expression is at the intersection of insulted, crestfallen, and confused. "What do you mean by make-believe?" I have apparently chosen the wrong words. "I assure you, Mom, this is reality. And I'll have you know, Washington State is one of the most environmentally sensitive places on the planet. The government here won't let climate change destroy it like Florida. They care here. They are taking *real* action!"

"Maybe," I say, but in my head, I hear the words of Everett Ruess: "I have always been unsatisfied with life as most people live it. Always I want to live more intensely and richly." I study her and no longer see that little girl from my memories. Instead, I see a woman in front of me, all grown up. My little bird flown away. Living her own fulfilling life. Married to a nice man who wooed her at the University of Washington by strumming his homemade acoustic guitar beneath her dorm window.

"I'm getting an urgent ping from work." She looks askance toward an overlay, now pulsing orange. "I love you, Mom."

"Talk to you next week. Hugs to Liam." Sparky and Barky thump their tails. "And hugs to you two. I'll keep you posted on my adventures in Paradis."

"I'll keep you posted about stuff here." She looks at me seriously. "Stay safe."

I understand now that we each have constructed our own definition of what the world should look like. Our own paradigm of paradise. Like Amber's paintings on my walls, paradises in juxtaposition.

"I love you," I say.

Amber blows a kiss and FaceTime shuts down.

I take off my iGlass and sit down at my table. Out the window, on the branch of a massive pine, an osprey tears at a fish it holds in its talons.

Chapter 4
Thoreau Stops by Tierra del Fuego

The FaceTime with Amber leaves me unsettled—a queasy, peach-pit-in-the-stomach feeling. My daughter's path in life has deviated so far from my own. She is leading a successful life adapted to today's environment. And what am I doing? Sweating out puddles on an evaporating barrier island. How could I have been so presumptuous as to imply that my reality is any more or any less real than my daughter's?

I knead the dough and put the two rounds in pans to rise a second time, then put the cat out, sweep the house, clean out the composting toilet, and mix the contents into the outside composting pit. The chores do little to dispel the feelings of unease.

Outside the wildness encroaches, overwhelms.

I am so small in this reality. In all realities, the individual can become lost, but here it is just so in your face—the Brazilian parasitic vine strangling the palm in my yard, the armadillo skeleton stabbed repeatedly by vulture beaks. Maybe she's right. Maybe I should move to Issaquah. What if I catch some mosquito-borne illness? Fall down the stairs? Get bitten by some venomous snake? And it's so hot. I think about how Mark died alone, surrounded by dangerous nature. Was it an iniquitous or a veracious way to die?

I shower in rainwater pumped and filtered from the outside rain barrels. The chilled water feels good but does nothing to cool my bothered thoughts. All that computer stuff overlaying Amber's walls like demanding Post-it notes bothers me so much. I think about what Henry David Thoreau inferred about the technology of his day: "We have constructed a fate, an Atropos, that never turns aside." And he was writing about the railroad. Today, the tendrils of technology plumb far deeper. How isolated one must become to escape the technology of today.

I roll the dough into tins, let it rise once more, fire up the oven, and hang the thermometer from the rack. Again, Thoreau invades my thoughts: "Our life is frittered away by detail... Simplify, simplify." Isn't this a simplified life surrounded by nature? An alternate universe of Thoreau's bucolic Walden Pond? The power-node hums; the iGlass blinks blue lights. Perhaps not completely.

I remember reading on the internet that it is now possible to stay overnight in a cabin at the pond where Henry David Thoreau wrote his famous *Walden*. $10,000 a night. I wonder what Thoreau would think of that? If he popped up from his grave, would he Whac-A-Mole some pudgy pond tourist, or would he just appreciate them staring up at the pines?

Again, Thoreau interrupts: "Distinguish the necessary and the real. Probe the earth to see where your main roots run." Well, is this it? My roots? Or is living here just some sort of grief-driven stubbornness against adapting to actual reality? Oh, Henry David, what is necessary? What is real? Only silence now from the philosopher ghost. Well, Henry, if you ever want to chat more, you have an open invitation for Bacardi and Coke.

An afternoon coffee reenergizes me enough to fry onions and heat up a can of beans. When the oven reaches 375 degrees, I place the bread tins inside. As I wait, I look at the framed family photo. Am I wrong for living here? Did I make a mistake? Am I overthinking things? This time, my questions are directed at Mark, but he also doesn't reply. I look out the window to see if his ghost is about. But I only see Dandi chasing chickens in the yard. Being alone can either clear or clutter the mind, and I'm not sure which I'm experiencing. If Amber ever mentions me to her coworkers, they must give her the once-over and wonder if my craziness has rubbed off on her. I hope I don't embarrass her too much.

The exhaustion of loneliness presses on my shoulders. Not exactly a loneliness based on human proximity, but a loneliness based on belief. I put on my iGlass and bring up a projected keyboard display. I text Mike and Gary: *If the weather holds, could I visit tomorrow? FaceTimed with my daughter and am feeling a tad lonely.*

An almost instant voice reply arrives from Mike. "Why don't you come today and spend the night? We're eating opossum and sweet potatoes with glasses of Chablis. We always pair our opossum with a fine white." Laughter. "We can meet you at The Eye. Look for the red fairy on the northeast side of the lake."

I hesitate. Red fairy? Outside, clouds cotton-balled. Three hours until sunset. I text back: *I would prefer tomorrow, though I'm sorry to miss the possum.*

Gary's follow-up text corrects: *Florida has opossums not possums.* Another ping, Mike again. A holographic map of the fairy's location pops onto my iGlass. Mike's voice narrates, "The fairy is Gary's creation. It's a metal sculpture painted red, about three feet high, and points out the trail to the house. The Eye is a large freshwater spring about a half-mile from the house. We should be able to GPS track you from there."

Messaging with Mike and Gary has lessened my tension. I assume it is due to both busying my mind with making plans and the anticipation of being with new friends. A glance out the front window shows cumulonimbus clouds mounting against the horizon. I go down into the yard and direct the girls to their coop and whisk Dandelion up into my arms. White bread and beans satisfy my dinner appetite. I pour an extra shot of Bacardi and set the cup aside, but Thoreau never drops by. I would have enjoyed his presence, if only to have the company of a philosopher ghost, to share the thunderous dance of rain upon the roof.

Paradis

♦ ♦ ♦

Ahead of me on the winding trail, little Amber sits up on Mark's shoulders. Deer peek between tall firs. I pause to snap a photo. A cry from up ahead makes me turn. Mark and Amber have vanished. I hurry up the trail. Around a switchback, an algae-choked sinkhole gapes precipitously. My heart pounds. I stare into the hole. A second cry, and I open my eyes to see Dandi's orange paws bawling on my chest. My dream disturbs me. I stroke the cat, and gradually, my heartbeat slows to normal. Twilight streams in a soft blue glow through the loft's windows.

♦ ♦ ♦

After morning chores, I latch the cat door and secure Dandi inside with food and water sufficient for a couple of days. I send a quick email to Mike and Gary and review the path to the red fairy on my iGlass before setting it back on its charger stand. I strap on my backpack, packed for the hike and night, and head down to the beach. The beach is an indirect path, adding a mile and three-quarters to the total journey, but at low tide, exposed sandbars create shallows filled with shorebirds breakfasting upon nurseries of young fish and crabs. The banquet of birds is a brilliant sight, and the breeze and breadth of the sand keep nasty things like sandflies and snakes inland. Offshore, brown pelicans glide and plunge. Around a mile up the beach, I remove my backpack and my shoes and wade into the surf. Sand washes out from under my heels. It is that time of day when the sun kisses your shoulders with gentle warmth, a barefooted time when waves wash away bad dreams.

Approximately three miles and three-quarters down the beach, I crest a sand dune and scan the line of stately tall pines that form the ridge of the island. A young coconut palm has sprouted in the dune. I salute its ramrod straightness. Fifteen years ago, wild coconut trees were uncommon this far north in Florida. From my bag, I grab electrolyte water and my inland hiking attire. Waterproof snake boots, mosquito netting that pulls down over my sunhat, a long-sleeved shirt, and a collapsible machete complete my transition from beach attire to inland trekking. My compass heading is at sixty-eight degrees east-northeast, which, according to the directions sent to my iGlass, is the direction toward the island's heart, the spring called The Eye.

I amble up and down the dunes until I reach tea-colored waterways buttressed by mangrove roots tangled in Escher-esque complexities. Between these is an iris-dotted saltwater marsh abundant with life—fish, crabs, sea snails, shrimp. Little white butterflies and iridescent dragonflies glisten above it. I swamp-walk, taking the second step before the first step hits the bottom. A half-mile later, the land lifts to acres of nothing but pale green saw palmettos. Their fan-shaped leaves exuberantly point to the sky, and many tower above me in height. Their namesake stems are covered in fine, sharp spikes, requiring the use of my machete to safely traverse multiple areas. I keep a lookout for white-tailed deer, raccoons, gopher tortoises, and the other animals that typically live among these palmettos, including the antagonistic varieties. As I whack at the palmettos, I sing little ditties such as "snaky, snaky, stay

Paradis

away-ee" and "gator, gator, see you later." In the dampness beneath a palmetto frond, a bloated cottonmouth rests, white mouth open, singing its own song, I suppose.

Increasingly the palmettos become interspersed with scrub oaks, slash pines, cabbage palms, red cedars, deerberry shrubs, and a multitude of ferns and grasses. Frogs and crickets sound from the undergrowth, and pinewood sparrows flitter in the trees. I pause to check my compass. Last night's bad dream still plagues my thoughts. Mark had been the compass expert, and I'm starting to fear missing The Eye entirely. I attempt to calculate my location on a waterproof topographical map of Paradis, but this only leads to further confusion. I continue toward the pine ridge. My boots scuff against roots and sink into mud, sometimes managing to do both simultaneously. After another quarter of a mile, I take a break to study the map once more. When I look up, a yellow-eyed bobcat is studying me. The bobcat turns and silently dives back into the brush. It seems headed in the direction of a thicker growth of trees. Perhaps it is a thirsty bobcat. I fold up my map and follow carefully.

Moving closer to the thicker growth, I finally spot it—The Eye. An emerald iris surrounding a deep, black, dilated pupil. Cypress trees and a hirsute fringe of moss and ferns hinder an easy path to the banks, so I butt-slide and branch-grab all the way down. A short distance from my place at the water, I spy the bobcat drinking. The cat pauses with ears perked, but it judges me not a threat and goes back to lapping.

Mike's map indicated that the red fairy is on the northeast side of The Eye. I wander for an hour, exploring and slicing through foliage with my machete. Where is it? I take a break on a tree limb arching over the water and nibble an energy bar. It is hot. My pores leak sweat like a sieve. Mosquitoes bite through my shirt. My smell surely must match my appearance. At last, an inch-by-inch scan of the area reveals a very lusty, yet rusty, red fairy reclining on the branch of a massive oak no more than ten feet from where I am reposed on my branch. His left arm points at the ground and his right arm points toward the northeast. Why didn't Mike say anything about it being up in a damn tree?

Over at the roots of the fairy tree, a footpath leads northeast at eighteen degrees. Excitedly, I retract my machete, return it to its spot in the backpack, and start down the trail. A mama possum—no, opossum—with five young'uns on board moseys past me on her way to the water hole. Slashes of red paint mark the trees at about twenty-foot intervals. Near the third red mark I see a different flash of red, and my steps lighten with pure joy. It's Mike and Gary in bright red shirts!

"We were worried about you!" exclaims Gary, giving me a high-five and sweaty hug.

"I couldn't find the red fairy. Why didn't you mention he was up in a tree?"

"Where's your iGlass, we tried to contact you!" exclaims Mike.

"We're supposed to be off-grid," I retort. We take off down the trail together. This area of the island is dense with vegetation, and I wonder aloud, "How on earth do you two get to the Kicklighters' from here?"

Gary answers, "We take our ATVs along a very rough, horrible, usually wet, bone-jarring road leftover from state park days." He mimes dramatic steering as he talks.

Paradis

Mike laughs. "We drive four miles to the north end of the island, and then we turn around and ride thirteen miles all the way down the beach until you meet the KickAss Farm Road."

"Did you see Old Joe in The Eye?" interjects Gary as we walk the trail. "He's our resident alligator."

"Thank goodness, no. I swear, everyone names their resident alligator Old Joe. I saw what I'm pretty sure was a cottonmouth and a bobcat."

"You probably saw either Bob or Cat," says Gary. "There's a male and female. We have to keep an eye on the chickens."

"I see you got boots," Mike says, "but you should consider some other mode of transportation. How about when we go to Snug Harbor, you put up a sign there with your email letting people know you'd be interested in purchasing an ATV? We use Kawasakis. For today, though, we'd like if you'd stay the night."

"Yay! I thought you'd never ask! And I would love a shower and that glass of Chablis."

Both men laugh.

"Well, I think we should be able to work that out," Mike responds.

"Is The Eye your water source?" I inquire after another mouthful of electrolyte water.

"Absolutely," says Mike. "The old PVC pipes from state park days run right along this trail here. Before we put any money down, we secured the rights from the Kicklighters to use The Eye as our water source. One thing we didn't want to skimp on was water."

"But those crazy Kicklighters didn't even care. Apparently, they use some sort of fancy schmancy solar-graphene desalination method," Gary finishes.

I think of my rainwater barrels. It's all I can afford, but given that Florida's response to climate change is rain, and more rain, and storms, and more storms, I'm content with my decision.

Gary runs forward a few steps on the path and excitedly points to an archway partially obscured by the branches of an overhanging oak tree. Rusty orange lettering tops a wooden archway. "Bienvenida a Tierra del Fuego," he exclaims with an exaggerated bow.

"Tierra del Fuego?"

"Land of fire," he explains. "Early Portuguese explorers rounded Cape Horn and saw natives lighting fires on the beaches to keep warm."

"Charles Darwin was interested in these natives," my inner biology teacher expounds. "They were called the Yaghan! But I still think that Tierra del 'Raino' would have better fit your little niche of the planet."

My comment brings eyebrow raises, followed by chuckles.

"Gary likes to sound smart," comments Mike as we continue our walk forward. "A while back we took an Antarctic cruise that included an excursion to Tierra del Fuego." Mike pauses under the sign and spreads his arms. "Well, we're here. Welcome to our Tierra del Fuego, where the fires of creativity burn bright!"

My boots crunch on a path of white shells. In the moonlight, it must shine like the white coals of the Yaghan, directing the traveler toward a safe shore. Overhead, an aurora

Paradis

borealis of ferns, bromeliads, and orchids drapes the dark limbs of ancient oaks. The stream I watched before coming here failed to capture the place. Interspersed amongst the beautyberry, azalea, camellia, hydrangea, wild coffee, lilies, and roses, Mike's carved and painted totems blend and blaze. A wooden anole camouflages itself in a clump of moss. A painted bolt of red glistens on a pine tree's bark. Gary's tiny Japanese wind bells tinkle high in a palm. Abstract metal concoctions twist into benches and solar lamps. I reach the end of the shell path where a great blue heron, constructed from bottle caps, cans, and pop-tops, guards the base of multicolored stairs leading up to the porch of Mike's and Gary's cracker-style stilt house. A quote stenciled on one of the risers gives me pause—Thoreau: "All good things are wild and free." I could feel at home here.

At each corner of the roof hangs a rope tied with three knots.

"Saint Francis's cords," Gary comments, noticing my quizzical stare. "The West Indian method of warding off hurricanes."

"Certainly wouldn't want a hurricane here, too beautiful." I think my words sound almost reverent.

Mike points out that each exterior wall celebrates the sun in appropriate shades of orange, yellow, pink, and red. They haven't neglected the practical, either. Solar panels on the roof provide electricity, and a satellite dish brings communication from the outside world. Under the house, chickens can roam in and out of their coop. A high bamboo fence surrounds an outside shower and a portable toilet.

I leave my backpack, boots, and hat upstairs and take advantage of both the shower and toilet facilities. Afterward, clad more comfortably in shorts and a T-shirt, I sit at the kitchen table and help cut up vegetables for a stir-fry supper. Alas, no opossum tonight. Mike said they kept nibbling last night until it was gone.

Rain comes in the late afternoon, brief and intense. We eat garden vegetables flavored with Spanish moss tips at a Spanish-tiled kitchen table. Mike says a restaurant had thrown it in the dumpster. They kept the top and removed the rusted base. He fashioned a new, rounded central base from a local oak.

After dinner, we sit out on the house's wrap-around screened-in porch and snack on slices of fennel bread, crackers with peanut butter, and mango slices. Gary's wind chimes tinkle in the breeze. The Chablis tastes crisp and cool. Gary lets me know it is true Chablis, the one with a capital C.

"See that down below?" indicates Gary. "That's where we hold our monthly eat-a-longs with the Kicklighters."

I get up from my Barbie-pink deck chair and look down through the screen to see a patio sheltered by a cluster of tall bamboo rattling in the breeze. Bamboo fencing completes the enclosure. A gate leads out to the garden, and at the rear of the porch, a stairway leads down from the house. The area below summons visions of South Florida. Even in the fading light, the place is pure tropical delight—the deck painted turquoise-blue, a hammock hung between metallic palm trees, two picnic tables painted in primary hues, a 1950s-style barbecue pit, hibiscus and bird of paradise flowers claustrophobically root-bound and in need of new homes. Directly below, I can

Paradis

just get a glimpse of the gewgaws that hang from the rafters of the porch overhang, including coconut husks masquerading as puffer fish, macramé tentacle jellyfish, and Christmas lights cast as miniaturized flying pink flamingo lawn ornaments. Certainly, I could visit every day and notice something new each time. "Sweet little enclave down there, reminds me of Matlacha," I comment on the way back to my Barbie-pink chair.

"Matlacha! Michael and I were no strangers to the art scene there."

"I thought we went for the seafood," Mike teases.

Mike picks up the wine bottle and sloshes its meager contents. He wants to know who's up for a cheaper white. He divides the rest among us, rises from his chair, and takes the empty bottle inside.

Gary leans forward in a confidential manner. "So what do you think of those Kicklighters?" Before I can speak, however, he is answering his own question. "They let their dogs run loose, the kids are on the wild side except for the techie twelve-year-old, and he is just plain odd." He gestures excitedly as he speaks. "I assume you've seen the series; you know his counseling was just for show? A load of bluster!" I start to open my mouth, but he starts up again. "We message with MaMa, check on the kids, drop by in person sometimes, and do the monthly eat-a-longs. I just hope those kids are okay, can't exactly request a surprise visit by the Department of Children and Families here—"

The screen door flies open to Mike standing with a wine bottle. He pauses and looks into the distance. Together Gary and I follow his stare and in unison ooh and aah when we spot the fluorescent orange sunset. "A postcard view!" I exclaim as Mike comes over and pours us each another round before sitting down in a fuchsia chair.

Gary takes a sip of wine and then smiles his crooked, mischievous smile. "Anyone know what today's date is?"

"Never do anymore." Mike chuckles.

I shake my head, realizing I am also unsure.

Gary laughs his deep, hearty laugh. "Don't you just love that about living here? So little to worry about!" He lets out a loud, happy sigh. "Even with an occasional alligator or snake scare, life is so much more relaxed here than in Punta Gorda."

We all nod in shared understanding, sip our wine, and savor the sunset as it washes the world in golds and pinks.

"I used to be so stressed," Gary says. "I thought it was because of daily household chores." He laughs gently, staring off into the sunset. "I was so sure the solution was automating everything. You know, I bought every smart device, thinking it would make life easier. Happier, or something." He pauses to savor some more wine. "I had this alarm—super fancy gadget. It would trigger light dimmers, play bird sounds, and start brewing my coffee every morning. Oh, and when I sat down on the couch, the TV would immediately start up whatever I was last watching. Every Thursday afternoon all my appliances would self-wash, and a conga line of cleaning appliances would parade around the house. I think I had a DroneDuster, AutoVac, MopBot, there was another one." He hums introspectively.

I think of my daughter's home—the overlays, the apps and devices managing her life.

"And then my identity was stolen."

Paradis

I gasp. "How awful!"

"Gary was famous at the time, selling sculptures all over the world. I was always beating off the paparazzi," Mike snickers, smiling at Gary.

Gary rolls his eyes. "Someone in Dubai hacked me when I sold a sculpture to one of the sheiks. My private key got leaked into the ether along with my facial scans and fingerprints. All personal information one could need was disseminated through so many different computers that it was impossible to find the culprit." He sloshes his wine dangerously in his glass. "By the time the nightmare was over, I was out five hundred seventy thousand dollars."

"Wow…" I'm speechless. I know some folks who were hacked, but not at that scale. "Terrible." I think about my own bank account, the tanking IRA, the meager Social Security deposits. Even though I may dwell on an island, these things still tether me to the real world. Trap me in a cage of modernity—that digital financial reckoning represented by squiggles of red and green on computer screens.

"But you know the worst part?" Gary says, his tone growing even more serious. "It wasn't the money lost to some stranger's shopping sprees—new cars, Mediterranean cruises, crazy VR gaming rigs, whatever nonsense people buy. It was the fact we lost control over everything in our own damn house!"

At this, Mike surprises me with boisterous laughter.

"It wasn't funny!" Gary snaps. But after a tense moment, he also starts to laugh. I stare at them, puzzled. "Okay, in retrospect, it was a little funny. I got hacked, money stolen, someone with my identity off doing who knows what, so obviously, all my accounts were frozen. But that meant everything in my house was also frozen. Locked from use. I couldn't make coffee, use my stove, open my damn fridge!"

Mike is now doubled over with laughter, tears in his eyes. "We tried calling the customer service hotline for our espresso maker, and after three hours of yelling profanity at robot voices, we finally get connected to a human, and"—he's gasping for air from the laughing—"for some reason, they needed Gary's social security number to unlock the machine. Well, since his identity was flagged as stolen, it was worthless. Gary couldn't verify it was him, and the machine had to stay locked!"

"I just wanted a goddamn cup of coffee!" Gary frowns, his expression becoming solemn. "Besides the ridiculous aspects, you know it is still a mess! I continue to get mysterious calls to verify activities that are not me. I get pulled into security rooms when I try to travel." He shakes his head. "And hacking, well, it's only more and more common, more and more difficult to trace. If you ask me, it's no mystery why it's happening so frequently. This latest tech-savvy generation, they're really struggling. Displaced by various climate change disasters, in debt from student loans, literally impossible to get insurance for anything! They're angry and desperate. I can't even blame them—"

As Gary continues, I'm distractedly calculating my remaining funds in my head and wondering about the security levels of my bank. I make a mental note to call Amber later and ask how she keeps all her accounts safe—

Gary knocks three times on a wooden beam in the porch. "Anyways," he says, snapping me back from my mental

Paradis

arithmetic. "That identity theft is what triggered our search for an off-the-grid lifestyle. Any liquid assets we have, we've been careful to spread widely."

Mike pours more wine into his glass and requests we change the subject to "funner" topics. He asks if I know the legend of Paradis.

Again, Gary rolls his eyes, but this time he is smiling.

Mike delivers a story, which is wild and cockeyed, coupled with wine-enhanced enthusiasm. To put it succinctly: Jean Lafitte, Henry Morgan, Blackbeard, Anne Bonny, José Gaspar, Calico Jack, and Cheung Po Tsai all sailed up and down the Gulf Coast burying treasure on these barrier islands. He concludes, "One of them must have buried loot here. That's why Paradis is missing its *e*. When the treasure is found, the *e* will be restored. I've got a metal detector, and one day…one day."

Gary sighs. "Mike, you sound crazy! About five years ago, we took a ferry out to the Dry Tortugas, and since then, he's all into this pirate stuff. All he finds are bottle caps and pop tops."

"Makes great recycled art," Mike interjects, giggling.

Gary nods in agreement.

I mention the odds of pirate booty being on the Kicklighter property, and we laugh—an island laugh, momentary and carefree. I stare tipsily through my wine glass at the twilight sky. The pinks and golds have succumbed to the mysterious blue of encroaching night.

"Do you know what I think?" Gary asks rhetorically, waving his empty glass. "I think we've all moved through our honeymoon phase of living on the island. We can't just pack up the tent and drive home. Correct me if I'm wrong, but I think you're a lot like Mike and me. You've chosen to build your castle on the beach. I bet you could have moved into some mother-in-law room at your daughter's house. But you traded that crowded, technology-encrusted lifestyle for a view of the stars. A chance to really see life, live off-grid." He reaches for Mike's hand.

Mike laughs and nods toward the wine. "Well, not totally off-the-grid."

Their silhouette in the twilight makes me feel a little wistful. Mark on a mountain. Mark on the beach. Mark at my side.

The guys look at me, Thoreau and Frost guiding my way.

I feel profound after a couple glasses of wine. "Civilization blotted out the stars," I lament.

"The stars here can't be hacked," says Gary.

Mike smiles playfully. "You know, in a little while, the moon will be up, and I think we should go downstairs and dance."

The bright moonlight changes the long-lost skeletons of a thousand mollusks into a promenade that sparkles like the Milky Way. We finish off the second bottle of wine while we pirouette and square dance on this crunchy stream of stars. We startle the bats that flitter overhead, but we get into the groove with the frogs and crickets that boogie nearby. When we are sated with dancing, we go up to the house. By the time I douse off my sweat in a basin of cold water and put on my

Paradis

pajamas, Gary has lit a small lamp and made up a bed for me on the living room couch. The room is lined with shelves filled with so many books—hold in your hand, spine-bound, page-flipping books. Works by Robert Louis Stevenson, Emily Dickinson, Ernest Hemingway, Tim Dorsey, Oscar Wilde, and Zora Neal Hurston. The guys peek in and say goodnight. They are off to their bedroom at the rear of the house. What kind of wonderful people possess a library on a desert island? Classics, poetry, art, architecture, and sketchbooks of personal art projects stack the bottom shelf. Secrets and wishes. Answers and questions. My finger finds what I've been looking for: *Walden*. I prop my pillow, get between the sheets, and finally have my visit with Thoreau, who offers a prayer for all things wild:

And the breeze that passes o'er;
In the hollow of my hand
Are its water and its sand,
And its deepest resort
Lies high in my thought.

Chapter 5
Revelations

"You shall love your neighbor as yourself." (Matthew 22:39). The words are carefully painted on a signpost protruding from the water between navigational buoys. Approaching Snug Harbor for the first time via my fishing skiff, I am unprepared for the biblical notices that jut out from the water in every direction. *"The wages of sin is death but the gift of God is eternal life in Christ Jesus our Lord." (Romans 6:23). "The wrath of God is revealed from heaven against all ungodliness and unrighteousness." (Romans 1:18).* They are everywhere, like little prophetic lighthouses. *"Be strong and courageous for the Lord your God goes with you." (Deuteronomy 31:5).* Who posted them, I wonder? What is the intent? Greeting? Warning? Regardless, they creep me out.

Paradis

Near the edge of a partially collapsed and dangerous-looking pier, I throttle down the outboard motor. I glance over my shoulder and see the guys' catamaran coming up behind me. We are on our way to Joey Pelagro's.

Gary calls out, "We're going to have to moor this. Mike is going to stay with the boat and get some fishing done. I'll meet you up the road in our dinghy."

"Okay," I say, coming out as barely more than a whisper. So, Mike's not going. I signal that I heard him. My boat chugs over to what was once the shoreline of a park. A wooden sign, now coated in barnacles, struggles to keep the words "Snug Harbor Park" above the lapping waves. I hit the power switch to lift the engine. The boat coasts over to the playground swings. Behind me, the guys have tied their catamaran to a mooring buoy a short distance from the end of the pier. Mike has taken out a book and some fishing gear. His feet are already up on a chair, his book open. Next to him, leaning within reach, rests a rifle. He smiles and waves, his blue eyes squinting tightly against the harsh sun. I drop mosquito netting over my face and set the oar blades into the water. It's a forward-facing rowing system that can hopefully maneuver me through the narrow canal streets of Snug Harbor. There is no breeze, and the temperature steams humid as hell. Plastic bottles and flip-flops are spiraling foam lines in the water before nestling against the hull of my boat. Another Bible verse nailed to a pole of a picnic shelter catches my eye: *"Whosoever shall call upon the name of the Lord shall be saved." (Romans 10:13).* Behind it, trees in the park spread their skeletal limbs.

At last, Gary rows his inflatable dinghy alongside; it's a forward system as well. He shields his eyes beneath a pair of UV-tinted microLens.

"What's up with all these Bible verse signs?" I inquire.

He sighs. "Joey Pelagro."

"Joey Pelagro? He didn't strike me as particularly religious when he installed my internet."

"I didn't say he was."

Before I can even ponder what he meant, Gary has rowed on ahead. Shortly, a cloud of mosquitoes finds him. He stops rowing, takes the Lord's name in vain several times (I wait for lightning to strike), and fumbles frantically in his backpack for DEET.

I catch up with him. "So, what about the signs?"

Gary looks very irritated in his cloud of spray. "What? I dunno. Pelagro's attempt to relate to the culture of Snug Harbor. You know, rural Florida, Bible Belt land." He flails his arms in a futile attempt to squash mosquitoes and then takes up his oars again.

We exit the park into a Venetian underworld of abandoned homes with shattered windows, open doors, and mold-encrusted roofs. Bushes and trees stretch gray and brittle limbs toward the sky as if to implore God, *Why me?* Unwieldy recycling bins cough out black slime. Not exactly a prime neighborhood.

On the back of a bench, a Norman Rockwell-esque American family beckons with the inscription, "The Family That Prays Together Stays Together." As I examine the painting, a boisterous flock of green parakeets flies directly in front of me. Distracted by their commotion, I accidentally

Paradis

scrape my boat's hull across the body of a partially sunken motorcycle. Above the water level, the handlebars glint blindingly. Reversing, I maneuver around the fender of a rusting sedan, only to spot yet another Bible verse hanging from a communications tower: *"Fear not, for I am with you; be not dismayed, for I am your God; I will strengthen you, I will help you. I will uphold you with my righteous right hand." (Isaiah 41:10).*

I try to imagine this neighborhood before the exodus—a Florida from another time, its heyday in the early sixties, I presume based on the architecture. Who were these time travelers that managed to sustain their traditional single-story ranch houses, with their large yards and grand, old trees? How did they fight off, or hide from, the swarm of builders that had infested Florida like ravenous locusts? Was it God that spared this place from His wrath of McMansion with two-foot Astroturf perimeters? Did He save this community, preventing the inevitable commercial sprawl, chains, and continuous parking lots that had saturated so many rural areas, drowning Florida's culture long before the flooding started? Was it the Bible verses that spared this neighborhood; left it frozen in time?

"We're almost there," Gary calls from his dinghy, pulling me back from my mental time traveling. "The name of this road is Pineapple Way. Last time, it was dry just up ahead. I'll go get the truck while you remain with the boats. The house is about a half-mile from the flooded area."

His words leave me dismayed. "I thought we were going to go together."

"No, I need you to guard the boats."

"There's no one here. Why don't we just tie up our boats to one of these signs or hide them behind a house? I brought my muck boots."

Gary stops rowing and turns back to face me. "No," he says emphatically. "I'm going to go get the truck, put one boat on the truck, go back to the house, unload that boat, and come back for your boat. We can't leave the boats unattended. Someone will steal them."

Oh, for Christ's sake, who the hell would dare to steal a boat tied up to an eerie eschatological Bible verse?

He starts rowing again.

Sudsy effluvium streams in between chunks of asphalt.

We land our boats.

Gary calls out for his friend, "Jerry Jeffery!" I hear him mumbling, "Where the fuck is he?" He turns to me and says, "I'm going to walk up there. Stay with the boats. You brought your gun?"

"What gun?"

He huffs on down the road.

I guard the boats in the ninety-degree heat. And by guard, I mean drink water under an awning on the porch of a boarded-up house. No apocalyptic sentiments are within eyesight, but a robust growth of wildflowers flaunt themselves in the yard. I daydream of times past. Children playing in the yard across the street while a father gardens. Me and Mark sitting on lawn chairs surrounded by plastic pink flamingos.

After fifteen minutes, a muddy, fuel-cell-powered Ford pickup backs up to the boats. A silver-haired, unshaven fellow waves at me through rolled-up windows. The tailgate lowers, a ramp extends and scoops up the dinghy, and then they drive

Paradis

away. I consider taking a look in the backyard while awaiting their return, but the fear of heat stroke, water moccasins, finding a dead body, and possibly more Bible sayings keeps me fixed in place. I stay in the shade, and after twenty minutes, they are back. This time, I get invited into the air-conditioning where I exchange greetings with Jerry Jeffery. His long face wears the familiar lines and spots of Florida sun damage. Silvery stubble glitters on skin that surrendered its youthfulness years ago. He tells me the autonomous truck has a bar. Nostalgic for a past time, I order an Arnold Palmer.

Within a quarter mile, we arrive at Jerry's house. The yard's swath of mowed weeds proclaims it the only inhabited house on the street. Two women stand in the yard. One is close to my age with long dark hair pulled back, showing her friendly, round face. The other is very elderly, her skin almost translucent in the sunshine. Her rounded shoulders make her a full head shorter than the other woman. I get out of the truck and retrieve my backpack and two collapsible wagons from my boat. The ladies walk over and introduce themselves as Jerry's wife, Hilda, and his ninety-three-year-old mother, Cici. While the guys safely deposit the boats into the garage, I exchange pleasantries with Hilda and Cici and study their twentieth-century, ranch-style house. It is well cared for and has clearly been upgraded over the years, currently sporting a solar tile shingled roof, satellite dish, and laser security sensors, providing both communication and protection.

Jerry and his family decide not to join us to Joey Pelagro's, so Gary and I agree to pick up Cici's medicine, dog food for their two Rottweilers, and toilet paper. The Ford bumps along the pitted road for about two miles before we become mired in traffic of Biblical proportions. Apparently, not everyone had taken the exodus out of Snug Harbor. I sit up as tall as possible in the truck's passenger seat to try to see over the vehicles.

"How is there so much traffic?" I ask.

"Joey's the only supply store for dozens of miles," Gary answers.

In addition to cars and trucks, people weave around us on everything from scooters to golf carts—even a man with an ox pulling a cart. Where have they all come from?

On a bumper sticker reads: *"Rejoice in hope, be patient in tribulation, be constant in prayer." (Romans 12:12).* On the rear window above is a huge carbine rifle decal. I imagine Moses waving his staff, leading us toward the Promised Land of Joey Pelagro's. Or perhaps it would be Joey Pelagro himself who would lead us out of this traffic glut bondage. Surely some savior will smite all these Mad Max types, revving, honking, giving us the finger, and otherwise bullying their way in front of us. What would be the point of the Bible verses otherwise? However, seeing as no deliverers have materialized, Gary and I keep the windows up and the doors locked. Really, this is no place for a senior citizen and her artistic gay companion.

After about an hour, the security checkpoint for Joey Pelagro's appears up ahead. I'm stunned at the store's size. According to Gary, Joey's had once been a Lowe's Home Improvement that shared a parking lot with a Sam's Club. The two stores were combined into a single massive warehouse. I didn't envision anything quite like this.

Paradis

Gary's clearly on edge. The entire drive, he's been atypically quiet, frowning, and anxiously drumming his fingers on the steering wheel. He worries aloud, "I hope they don't run out of water. Last time they ran out of water, people got violent." He doesn't elaborate, and I don't ask for details. His mention of water, however, makes me crave another tea, but since there's no toilet nearby, I decide against it. I turn the air-conditioner blower to my face and watch as pedestrians return from Joey Pelagro's with fifty-gallon containers of water in their wagons and carts. At last, we reach the checkpoint where armored sentries with military-style rifles divert us into two lines of traffic. Pedestrians and smaller vehicles are likewise separated into two lines of their own. Cameras mounted atop the checkpoint's support beam focus on individual lanes, and beneath the cameras, an electronic message scrolls: *The Eye of God is watching... Welcome to Joey Pelagro's... Have a blessed day.*

The truck pulls into the scanner where the helmeted sentry tells me, "Ma'am, you need to surrender your firearm."

I stare.

"Glove compartment, ma'am."

I open the glove compartment. Sure enough, a smartGlock is inside. There is also a magazine loaded with twenty-five cartridges. I hand both to Gary.

"It's not ours," says Gary as he hands the gun and magazine through the window.

"Sir, we know whose it is," the sentry responds. "You can pick it up on your exit. You are cleared to enter. Have a blessed day at Joey Pelagro's." He waves us through to find a parking place.

Vehicles park in the lot like sardines in a can. Pedestrians weave between and climb over them. Our truck immediately communicates with another truck that is leaving and rolls precisely into its spot.

I get my wagons out of the truck and couple them, then put on my backpack. Gary has his own wagons and backpack. Once outside the truck, the contrast between the air-conditioning and the humidity nearly bowls us over. With difficulty, we pull and carry our wagons through the parking maze. Beyond the vehicle point, we mesh into a solid sea of humanity. Flea market stalls encircle Joey Pelagro's like satellites, and vendors of all persuasions pursue us. Florida's new normal in perpetuity—recombinant Moses and Mad Max. I'm dumbfounded at the scale of this operation. None of this had been anywhere in the real estate brochure when I purchased my island getaway.

We join the entrance line; thirty people are allowed in when thirty come out. I sit in one of my wagons. Overhead, supply drones fly in and out of the building like swarms of giant insects. Guards with assault rifles walk up and down the length of the line. Two frayed plastic banners hang over the entrance: "*For you have need of endurance, so that when you have done the will of God you may receive what is promised." (Hebrews 10:36)*, and the phrase that has become ubiquitous these days: *Work Together 🙂 Your Neighbor*. I do my best to avoid eye contact with the hawkers, buskers, and beggars asking for money.

Gary makes me jump when he suddenly yells in my ear, "Mike caught six fish!"

Paradis

Once I compose myself, I smile politely, lean toward Gary's ear, and ask, "Where have all these people come from?"

"Not sure, I guess from all over?" He shrugs. "I don't know of another supply store quite like Joey's anywhere in this part of the state, and it's only open Monday through Thursday. In the seven months we've been here, there's always been a line. Mike and I take turns running the supplies, but I'm pretty sure it's more often my job than his. Crafty Mike." He smiles and turns his attention back to the conversation in his earpiece.

At long last, we gain admittance. Gary knows the layout and we begin pulling items from our lists. Soon, my wagons are piled high with three twenty-gallon containers of emergency desalinated drinking water, a package of purification tablets, coffee beans, tea, Coca-Cola, Bacardi, ten pounds of flour, four pounds of salt, a twelve-pack of canned evaporated milk, a large jar of peanut butter, a twelve-pound bag of rice, a ten-pound bag of dried cat food, a five-pound bag of dried nuts and fruits, five bags of various dried beans, three gallons of vinegar, a gallon of cooking oil, chicken feed, thirty rolls of toilet paper, a new cleaning brush, and a roll of duct tape. Into my backpack go twelve cans of vegetables and fruit, tuna for the cat, wood nails for poles and framing, and a bag of socks, as I do tend to go through socks quickly. The prices seem a little steep but not out of line.

Gary waits in line at the pharmacy for Cici's pills while I guard the supplies. I also pull a number for a blood pressure check and teeth cleaning at the pay-as-you-go clinic. I am still waiting to be seen when Gary comes over.

He wants to know if, after our teeth cleanings, I want a bite to eat. "Pelagro's Pizza is good, single slice with a choice of toppings."

"Sounds fabulous to me," I respond, "but I need to stop by the mail depot first. Amber sent a package." Gary projects a holographic map from his microLens that displays my route to the depot. Finally, my name is called for my cleaning.

A short time later, I am waiting in the mail line. The baby in front of me throws up on her mother's shoulder, making a mighty stink, and it is unfortunately another half hour before I make it to the front of the line. After some scrambling, the postal clerk locates my package, and we check the contents together. I sign for my camera and all its accessories and go back to wait for Gary to complete his teeth cleaning.

At Pelagro's Pizza, Gary uses his microLens to order us pizza slices, Coca-Colas, and cannoli. I watch a FoodMaker drop my Margherita mushroom pizza ingredients onto prepared pizza dough. An automated arm swings out and places it, along with other pizza slices, into an open oven. My slice comes out the other side. It's piping hot and placed on a paper plate. I retrieve my pizza slice, a cannolo, and my cup of Coke from the end of the conveyor belt and pick up a paper napkin and biodegradable knife and fork from nearby receptacles.

We chomp away on cheesy Pelagro's pizza at a small, sticky, circular table surrounded by odd-looking characters. In the surrounding alcoves, groups of every blend of fashion, race, and ethnicity sit in circular booths eating similar Italian concoctions. Cutting through all this chatter and squall, I hear

Paradis

fast-paced music vaguely reminiscent of the *Star Wars* cantina song.

"It's good, isn't it?" yells Gary, referring to the pizza.

"Delicious!" I yell back.

He wants to know what Amber sent.

"A camera that looks like a green eyeball with..." As I finish my last bite of pizza, I grab the packaging to examine the text on the front. "180-degree lenses and a pamphlet with links to an AR online user manual. It also includes a drone arm attachment with four *protected* rotor blades."

He smirks, takes a final slurp of his Coke, and mentions that I have a clever daughter who knows how to keep tabs on her mom.

I return his smirk. "I do have a caring daughter."

Before we drop our biodegradable tableware into the compost bin, I return to the conversation Gary had started on the porch the other night. "What do you know about the relationship between Tobias and MaMa?" I inquire.

He shrugs slightly, but his voice answers confidently, "It's complicated. The way I see it, she's an enabler. He's insecure and feels he has to dominate, but I think she regularly calls his bluff." He deposits his trash, and as we pull our wagons toward the storefront, he continues, "He's okay, I think. Like, I'm sure they love one another, but that family also loves drama and attention. Tobias can also be impulsive, and he thinks he's always correct. He drinks too much..."

Gary continues to excitedly ramble on. His mood has much improved.

The exit lines are very organized. When my turn comes, I wave at the exit camera, confirm my purchases, and my account is automatically debited. When Gary and I get outside, a heavy layer of clouds overhead foreshadows impending rain. The hawkers are busy folding up their flea market tents. Gusts of wind buffet us as we weave our way to the truck through an emptying parking lot. We load our supplies and stop briefly at a hydrogen pump to top off the truck's fuel tanks.

The banner at the exit side of the checkpoint reads: "*The Eye of God is watching... Joey Pelagro's thanks you for your business... Please visit us at www.joeypelagro.com...*" The sentry hands Gary the smartGlock and its loaded magazine. He crisply waves us through, and I return the pistol and ammo to their places in the glove compartment. Once on the road, the Ford's horn clears pedestrians off to the side. With the light traffic, we are crunching the gravel toward Jerry's by 4 p.m.

Mike is texting and calling about a thunderstorm warning, and he wants us back as soon as possible. A check of the weather app on the truck's console scares me. We make a quick call to the Jefferys, who are kind enough to offer us a stay in their extra bedroom.

I happily accept their offer, but Gary wants to get back to Mike and get home. After returning to the Jefferys', Jerry accompanies Gary, helping him load his dinghy and waiting until Gary calls to let him know they are safely heading back on the catamaran. The downpour begins in earnest as soon as Jerry's truck pulls back into the Jefferys' garage.

Jerry comes in from the garage through the kitchen door with a big sack of dog food over his shoulder. The two Rottweilers trot along, sniffing at the bags. Hilda pulls her scraggly, gray-streaked hair back with a clip to keep it out of the pot of black beans and rice she's preparing on their propane stove. I chop onions at the counter beneath a painting of golden rods on a black canvas.

"Jerry's mom painted it," says Hilda. She waves her spoon, her large brown eyes eager to chat. "Aren't they lovely! She's got them all over the house." Sure enough, wildflower paintings brighten the kitchen from every wall. She continues, explaining that Cici used to dry flowers and mount them behind glass, but after a while, they mildewed, so she changed to acrylics and oil. "Completely self-taught!"

Jerry takes the stirring spoon and samples the dinner. His hands are calloused and meaty. A loud "Mmmmm!" confirms the food is to his liking. He leans over to kiss his wife, returns the spoon to the cook, and goes over to the mini-fridge and grabs a beer.

"I bought Bacardi Gold at Joey's today," I say.

"I wouldn't mind a shot," he replies. He opens his beer. "Can use this as a chaser." He asks if I want one.

I decide on just the rum.

He opens a kitchen cabinet and pulls out two shot glasses.

"Don't forget about me!" calls Cici from her La-Z-Boy in the living room.

We all laugh, including Cici. Jerry looks to his wife, who says no to the rum. He grabs a third glass while I go out to the garage and rout around for the Bacardi, wondering if I'll live to see ninety-three.

By six o'clock, the rain has dissolved into a drizzle. Mike calls to say that he and Gary are safe on the island. Jerry, Cici, and I have drained our shot glasses, and we are all sitting in the living room eating dinner from tray tables. The dogs amble in from the kitchen, plop down on the rug, and occupy themselves by licking their privates.

Sensationalist news streams coat the walls, emanating from projectors not too unlike those in my daughter's home, though I suspect they are an older model. I look around the room: *Monsoons drown Indian coastal cities... Category Six typhoon devastates Tokyo... Hacked vehicle software causes fifty-four-car pileup... Micronesians chain themselves to palm trees rather than leave their home*. I swivel my chair to the left. Interviews with a refugee from New Orleans about the loss of the French Quarter and with an executive from Consolidated Water about the severe water shortage in the American Southwest. I switch my focus to wall number three: *Terrorists paralyze London with threat of EMP attack... Deaths in African famine top forty-six million... Nearly ten thousand homeless after Ransomware attack locks customers from ARCF Bank... Global bear market continues due to water and food distribution problems.* And at the bottom of all the screens scrolling: *Work Together 🌎 Your Neighbor*. A nice thing about living on a mostly deserted island is seeing less news, usually. And with that thought, I decide it's time for a second shot of rum.

I turn my attention from the streaming tragedies to study Jerry and Hilda. Their eyes and heads move in sync as if they are watching a Wimbledon final. Their hands shovel beans, rice, and raw onions into their mouths. Cici snores softly in her leather recliner with an empty dish on her tray table.

The living room looks retro, with furniture and decorations from the 1960s: a straight-lined teak coffee table with matching teak end tables, shaded lamps with glass

Paradis

columns crammed with seashells, my chair and the couch upholstered in matching patterns of large tropical plant leaves, and Cici's tiny wildflower acrylics dotting dusty beige walls. The two dogs sleep on the coolness of a green-and-orange-flecked terrazzo floor. Floor-length gold brocade drapes shade the front window. I grow nostalgic for an era I never experienced.

Jerry's voice breaks through my ruminations. "Okay if I turn off the TV? We have to conserve power. We just like to catch up on the daily news during dinner."

"Please," I say, studying my empty shot glass.

Cici awakes.

Hilda asks if anyone wants second helpings.

Cici and I decline. Jerry says yes. The dogs wake up and follow Hilda into the kitchen.

Jerry wants to know my impression of Joey's.

I respond honestly, "Joey Pelagro is lying on his mansion floor making money angels." Everyone laughs. "And what's up with all the religious signs? Even the guard at the gate with his massive gun told us to have a blessed day."

At this, Cici rockets upright in her recliner, snapping down the footrest and startling Jerry and me so much we just about leap out of our chairs. Even the dogs and Hilda come peeking around the corner in alarm. "Joey Pelagro!" Cici proclaims loudly. "I was half a century old when that trickster came crawling out of the womb!" She notices Hilda and says sweetly, "Be a dear and bring in some of those lemon bars I made. And could you put on a pot of chamomile?"

Hilda disappears back into the kitchen.

Cici is leaning forward, blue-veined hands massaging the armrests. She offers her opinion of Joey Pelagro. "Even as a boy, Joey was always raising Cain. He was fourteen when he won a seat on the city council. Hacked into the Wi-Fi and garnered one hundred percent of the votes. Got elected for real when he was just nineteen. Married the same woman four times—got divorced, married again, got divorced, remarried. The man's a trickster, I tell you."

Jerry objects, stating that he likes the man. "Joey's got a complicated personality that may be difficult for us common folk to understand."

Cici harrumphs.

Jerry turns his focus to me. "Joey's lived in Snug Harbor all his life, served on city council, county school board, and two terms as mayor, and he managed the Lowe's. When the corporations closed up shop a few years back, he bought up the property. He stayed and kept order. Can't fault him for being a good businessman."

Hilda delivers another bowl of rice and beans to her husband and sets out a tray of lemon bars on the coffee table. She says, "He's a charismatic speaker, and after his divorces, he got born again. He's even a deacon at the First Evangelical."

Cici huffs, calls the man an atheist, and takes a lemon bar from her son. "Full of evangelical ballyhooing. He's the man behind the signs and he's who hired the guards. Most likely we're under surveillance right here!" She shakes her little gnarled fist at the wall. "Voyeur!" She bites into her lemon bar.

I can't help but search for a camera as I reach for a lemon bar of my own.

Paradis

Jerry calmly spoons beans into his mouth. "I don't know what we'd do without the Pelagro store. Large companies can't get insurance coverage for individual deliveries to a place like Snug Harbor anymore."

I tell them I actually chatted with Joey a little. My satellite system was a complicated setup and he was nice enough to personally help. "Where does he live?" I inquire.

Cici answers sourly, "Who the hell knows?" She demands her tea.

I comment favorably on the lemon bars and follow Hilda into the kitchen to help clean up. While we wash dishes in hot water heated by the stove, we decide it's best to put the Joey Pelagro discussion to rest.

Back in the living room, Hilda walks over to a glass cabinet while I pour us cups of tea. "Your daughter-in-law tells me you're the artist of these delightful wildflower paintings," I say to Cici.

Cici gives a half smile as she explains how she came to paint wildflowers. "I was mowing the yard, looked down, and saw these lovely little yellow, white, and pink blossoms. Started appreciating what was under my feet after that." She continues her tale, explaining how she needed money after Jerry's father up and left her. "Got a job at Hinson's Drug Store, and old man Hinson, good soul that he was, let me sell bakery items and pressed wildflower art in his store. Anything I could do to make a buck!" Cici places her hand in front of her mouth and chews on a lemon bar.

Hilda has fetched an old picture album from the glass cabinet and sets it next to the nearly empty lemon bar tray. I gawk as if it was a museum piece. When was the last time I saw a picture album not consigned to the cloud?

Cici motions toward the book. "Don't be shy, Addy. Take a look."

I pick up the album and thumb through pages of black-and-white photos with the little corner tabs: Cici on her first day at Snug Harbor Primary School, at an Easter egg hunt at the park, and as a teenager posing with cat-eye sunglasses before a downtown movie marquee. It looks like a proud time for Snug Harbor with tailfin cars flaunting themselves on Main Street—a vibrant, silver-shadowed past of hula-hoops and sprinklers on a summer day, of rainbow-flavored popsicles and swirled vanilla Dairy Queen Blizzards. I smile at this small-town innocence fixed on flimsy squares of satin photo paper.

I observe Cici as she sips her chamomile. Her fine white hair is carefully pinned back from a face showing the stereotypical markings of the aged: ocular and dental implants, transparent skin, maturity spots of long life. A woman falling into entropy. Snug Harbor local, lived here all her life. Married and divorced and raised her son. Strange how we now mull over old photos, craving some perceived innocence of eighty years earlier. Cici's dark rheumy eyes seem to regard me knowingly, reading my soul.

"Beautiful book," I comment.

"Sure is," affirms Cici. "Snug Harbor and I have traveled down a long road together. Now, hard to say which of us will go under first."

"Ma, please don't talk like that."

Paradis

"Oh, son, stop fighting the truth." Cici puckers her mouth into a furrow set for plowing.

"What about you?" I ask, turning my attention to Jerry and Hilda. "You got any kids?"

"Just dogs," says Jerry as he leans over to rub a Rottweiler's stomach. He picks up the album, leafing through it for a moment before returning it to the glass cabinet. "I guess we should just convert all this to digital," he comments.

"I like the pictures the way they are," objects Cici, managing to furrow her entire face.

I look over the preserved 1960s room before returning to Cici. "Was it better then?"

Feisty Cici points her old tree-twig finger right at me and says in an exasperated tone, "Absolutely not. It was just ours!"

Mary Burke

Chapter 6
What the Chameleon Saw

I have been practicing filming with Amber's gift, the Samsung Chameleon, the most idiot-proof 3D60 camera on the market. I last shot 360 at Amber's high school graduation and was so sure she had smiled at me when she walked across the stage. But when I played it back, no smile. No smile at all. I realized she didn't even know where I was sitting. After that, I put the camera in a drawer, thinking memories might be best when distilled through the biological machinations of what we thought we saw.

Next to the Chameleon sits my framed family photo. I pick it up. Amber is wearing the blue dress we bought at Etsy Brick that day. After the studio sitting, we ate at Tacoma Tacos, and she spilled taco juice on the dress. I could never get the stain out. I take the photo out of the frame, turn it over, and search

Paradis

for a date. No date. Was she fifteen? Was it the year Mark died, or the year before? I can't recall. I return the photo to its frame and set it back on the shelf. No camera had snapped a picture of Mark falling through that ice bridge, but I remember that date.

I head outside and take a sit on the front steps, cup of coffee cradled in my hands. It is that impressionist painting time of day before the sun punctuates the landscape with details and colors. Chickens peck in the garden. Dandelion rolls in the dirt. Several weeks have passed in tropical serenity since my Snug Harbor adventure and visit with the Jefferys. The daily rhythm of life has been chores, hiking, and ruminating on the connectedness of all island life. But today will be different; the Kicklighters are due around 10 a.m. for day one of the chickee building. I can't think of anything I've forgotten. I cut and stacked palmetto fronds, put ShawnRee in the mini-fridge to chill, and made sure the Chameleon was charged, ready to capture the activities of the day. I assume my role today will be to feed the crew and to cut up any additional fronds.

At half past ten, MaMa calls to tell me the boys are running late. So, at half past noon, when I hear the GM Armadillo tearing through the hammock with all the subtlety of a Tyrannosaurus rex, I am thoroughly annoyed. A loud, sharp crack causes the hairs on the back of my neck to rise. A gunshot? Dandelion dives into the underbrush. All the girls fluster and flap. In comes the Kicklighter truck, barreling into my yard on its great rolling treads. It stops at the base of my steps, where I see Tobias's twelve-year-old son, Richy, dangling the skinny carcass of a young rattlesnake, freshly sniped, out the passenger window. The youngest, Tommy, scrunches in the center front. Elias and Toby Too sit in the truck bed.

Tobias opens the door and approaches the bottom of my steps. He wears heavy boots, jeans, and a grimy T-shirt advertising his TV show. His ponytail hangs limp beneath a camouflaged do-rag. For many reasons—his lateness, his appearance, the random gunshot, the giant truck, the dissonance of yammering children, the large amount of coffee I consumed waiting for his arrival—he irritates me totally in this moment. "You know your monster truck and shooting that skinny snake scared the bejesus out of my cat and my chickens!" I yell in greeting. "I don't know where they ran off to!"

"Well, sorry lit'le Addy. Got held up by the farm, and maybe you should keep your chickens and cat under control."

"Yeah, like you keep your dogs on a chain. And stop calling me lit'le Addy!" My voice sounds shrill.

He looks bemused at me. "Don't mean nothin', ya know." He rubs the back of his neck, his gaze shifting to stare past me. "Well, ya wanna do dis or not?"

We are not getting off to a good start. I take a deep breath and tune my voice to a less confrontational tone. "Sorry, I'm just a little irritated." Deep breath. "Your wife said you were going to get here around ten o'clock. I've already cut like a couple hundred palm fronds and executed a chicken for you. If you had called—" I throw my hands up in the air in defeat. "Do you want water? I've been waiting to put that fresh chicken in the oven."

Paradis

His yellow teeth line up in a grin through their fringe of uneven mustache hairs. "Dat'll be nice," he answers. He takes a sheathed knife from his belt, turns, and tosses it through the truck's window to Richy, his snake-holding son. "Richy, why don't ya take dat rattler up by dere kitchen and fillet it? We can fry it up to go with the chicken. Should give us around one good bite each." Tobias turns back to face me. "Dat okay, ma'am?"

I suppress an eye roll. "Sure."

He points to the area to be cleared of brush. "I think our goal for today'll be to get da brush cleared, trees cut, and get to da debarkin'. Looks like dere's even a couple cypress we can use for dem support poles."

He claps his hands and walks toward the area to be cleared. The four boys he has with him scurry out of the truck like insects, or lizards, or commandos. They all wear jeans and survivalist-type attire, the same stuff they had worn to the Halloween-themed barbecue at Tierra del Fuego two weeks ago. Toby Too has his earbuds in, looking the same as when he picked me up for the fish fry last month. I can hear music streaming from them. Sixteen-year-old Elias, with brown hair and a stockier build than his brothers, wears more standard ear protectors. They unload chainsaws from the truck. The youngest, seven-year-old Tommy, grabs a toolbox from the back seat and lugs it over to his dad. He is a cute boy, with a serious expression and shorn blonde hair.

"Ma'am, can I go inside and skin the snake?" asks Richy, dribbling snake blood as he climbs the steps. I almost didn't recognize him without his VR get-up on.

Mary Burke

I hold open the screen door. "You can do it out here on the table." Before following him inside, I take a good look around from the top step and see a couple chickens rustling amidst the collard greens—no sign of Dandelion or the other chickens.

I bring Richy a board to fillet the snake. I'm not surprised that he's an expert, and I gather up the meat and take it into the kitchen.

When I turn around, Richy is standing directly behind me. "Can I keep the skin and the rattle, ma'am?"

I have to grin at his demeanor. Unlike Tobias's older boys, who are stocky and muscular, Richy is wiry and bespectacled. His eyes are magnified by his thick glasses and a dusting of freckles covers his nose and cheeks. He is more of a nerdy type than a backwoodsman boy. Even his vernacular is different, his enunciation perfect. He seems to have no trace of the Wisconsin accent that is so heavy in the rest of the family. I want to ask him if he is adopted. "There's not much skin, but sure." I look through my stacked firewood for a piece the snake skin could be mounted to. "How about this one?"

He nods, and I hand it over. "I have to get to this chicken," I announce, walking back to the kitchen. It's when I'm stacking wood into the stove that I hear him scream.

I quickly walk out of the kitchen, figuring Richy has skewered himself with the knife. Instead, he stands staring at the shelving. His expression is one of awe, his smile bright. "You have a Samsung 3D60 Chameleon!" He jumps and points enthusiastically.

I have to laugh at his excitement. "My daughter got it for me." I tell him I plan to film the chickee build.

"Genius! Are you going to fly-film?"

Paradis

I mention I had not gotten to that part in the instruction manual and ask how he knows about Chameleon 3D60s.

"I've read all about it! May I hold it?" His eyes are wide and full of longing.

I smile; his excitement is contagious. "Absolutely, but only after you wash your bloody hands."

He runs to the bathroom, returning quickly with his hands clean and splayed in front of him, awaiting my approval. I give a nod, and he runs over to the charger and picks up the green, spherical camera carefully, studying its Chameleon-eye lenses. "You know the camera's lenses are modeled on the squ-ah-mate eye." He speaks the term slowly, but correctly. It's enough to make my ex-biology teacher's eyebrows rise. He continues, "It has a resolution the same as the human eye. Genius!" He smiles at me, obviously proud of his knowledge. "Are you gonna attach it to a drone, Miss Addy?"

"For today, we're just going to try it mounted on its stand."

"If you let me borrow your iGlass, I can set it up to film air-ly."

"Aerially," I correct, finding his mispronunciation charming. "How about right now you focus on pinning that narrow squamate skin to the board, and I focus on getting the plump galliform carcass in the oven?"

```
[Soft electronic tone]

> Chameleon 3D60 connected to Adeline Thorndyke's iGlass
> 11/15/42, 12:52:02
```

Mary Burke

> *Recording Started*

The roaring assassination of eighty-foot loblolly and longleaf pines, of water oaks, laurels, and cypresses. Chainsaws buzzing with destructive aplomb. Frantic evacuation of countless small inhabitants.
A small boy running hither and thither. Gathering. Raking. Dampening sweat rags.
The heaviness of treefall. The mechanical chew and spit of the saws. The spraying of sawdust. Chickens scattering. A gopher tortoise poking from his hole.
An older woman hacking palmetto fronds at the bottom with stem length of four feet.
Chicken sandwiches and tiny bites of snake quickly eaten. Boys up the steps two at a time, slamming the screen door, returning with peanut butter in a jar.
Muscles sweating beneath a tee reading *Off-Grid Prepper Program*. Netflix logos on either sleeve like a drill sergeant's chevrons. Shaving a pine, movements fluid and effortless. Falling bark cushioning beetles on the ground.
The wind rustles.
The truck roaring away with its cargo, including one tiny rattlesnake skin stretched on a board.
Two little brown birds searching hopelessly for their nest. Chickens pacing outside their coop. An orange cat pads by and arches his back. New round scratching posts good for a real thorough nail digging.

● ● ●

I sit on a partially debarked pine log, my iGlass darkened, my ears cushioned in headphones. My lips curl around a Bacardi & Coke. I am outside but inside my VR Gallery. The iCloud

Paradis

application permitting the Chameleon to interface with my iGlass has installed perfectly.

◆ ◆ ◆

At ten o'clock the following morning, Tobias slams the door of the Armadillo. Richy is at his heels. "Are you going to fly-film today?" he asks me excitedly.

Tobias laughs. "Richy, why doncha just let lit'le Addy film dis like she wants." He leans in toward my ear. "Sometimes, I think my wife was out havin' a fling when we got dis one." He looks down at Richy. "Why can't ya just behave?"

He is such an eager young lad. He follows me into the house, and I let him look through my iGlass at the instructions. Twenty minutes later, he is leaping down the steps ahead of me, my iGlass on his face, the Chameleon with its rotors attached in his hands. He runs to the clearing and tosses the camera into the air where it settles into a hover at fifteen feet above the ground. With its four spindly little arms wringing four little white hands, the camera could have starred as any one of several cute little monsters in a Pixar film.

◆ ◆ ◆

```
[Soft electronic tone]

> Chameleon 3D60 connected to Adeline Thorndyke's iGlass
> 11/16/42, 10:22:56
> Recording Started
```

Like corpses on notched logs, pine trunks resting. In pieces. Soon to be disremembered and reassembled pieces.

The older woman struggling, with hands blistering quickly.
The man in his do-rag, strong, expertly planing wood. Biceps as thick as the tree trunk he shaves.
Two squirrels mating acrobatically.
A younger man humming, listening to something in his earbuds. Shirtless and sweaty, he is smoothing bark away.
Boys vaulting over the fallen, smoothing the barks of the botched and butchered.
A timeworn monotony in this preparation of the dead shined clean as baby-wiped bottoms. A buzz saw requiem of chirruping crickets.
Footsteps on wooden stairs. A banging screen door. The cat chases circling squirrels. The tree canopy sways.
The woman follows a slumping lanky boy down the steps. "I just found him inside typing code on my iGlass!"
The large man angry, throwing down the planer, grabbing the sad boy by the shirt, lifting him clear off the ground. "You little piece of shit! Whatchudoin' to Addy's iGlass? Ya always gettin' out of work!" A full-face slap. The boy is a spindly sapling lying on a pile of wood shavings.
The man looms large. Sweat spraying from the sway of a ponytail. The world spins. Blue sky. "How ya shut dis damn thing off?"

◆ ◆ ◆

I've retreated inside, shaking. I had marched Richy down there like a teacher escorting a pupil to the principal's office. I had expected Tobias to admonish his son, but to pick him up like that and put him down with that slap? Richy had fallen all the way to the ground. I don't think the other boys even looked up. Is that Kicklighter normal? And what did I do?

Paradis

Backed all the way up the stairs, I'm languishing, my heart aflutter. What did Gary say? *He's insecure and feels he has to dominate.* Oh god, has he hit MaMa? A million thoughts race through my mind. What do I do? I peek cautiously through the screen of the front room. They are just down there working away, like nothing happened. Even Richy, planing his little butt off. I need to calm down, wash my face.

What was Richy doing on my iGlass anyway? What was he programming? Why did I just let some kid I barely know use my iGlass? He could have gained access to my retinal scan, my digital key; everything about me was just lying out in the open. I reach for my iGlass, rest it on my nose. What am I looking for? Shit, I wish I had listened to Amber's lessons on security. History? Something history, access history, usage history? Something like that. Here, menu, settings, device history. *No history?* What does that mean? Did he clear my history? I open my email. *Logged out.* Browser, recent visits. *No history?* What were you doing Richy? What are you hiding? Again, Gary's words echo in my head—*Private key got leaked into the ether... Personal information disseminated through so many different computers... By the time it was over, I was out five hundred seventy thousand dollars*. My heart pounds; I'm sweating. Panic. I go to my bank website but stop halfway through typing my login. Isn't there software that records and transmits all inputs? Is that why my email was logged off? To record my password when I logged in? I call my bank. There's an automated response: "All representatives busy. Wait time thirty minutes." I call my tech-savvy daughter. Her cheery voice answers, "Not available; leave a message." I hang up. Fuck.

I peek out the window again. Everyone still just working away. I rest my iGlass on the counter. I need to busy myself; there's nothing I can do about it right now. I'll get in touch with Amber, and she'll know what to do. With trembling hands, I light the kindling in the stove. From the counter, the iGlass blinks its blue light at me, staring. Urgently, I turn it off.

I grab an onion and start to chop it. My hands are still shaking, and the knife slices right through the tip of my finger. Fuck. I curse loudly. As I rinse my finger, I watch the blood mixing with the water funneling down the sink. Out the window, Tobias and Toby Too are positioning a log upright into a three-foot-deep hole they had dug. Richy, with his head down, is still planing away. Dandelion jumps up on the table, looks at me inquisitively, and meows. "Bad day," I tell him. My eyes are wet with frustration.

◆ ◆ ◆

The next morning, the Kicklighters splash in shortly after dawn. I open the screen door. Tobias stands at the foot of the stairs, seeming quite chipper.

"Mornin' lit'le Addy. After dat rain last night, I do think dere's a touch of fall in da air." He looks back at the worksite. "We got the four main support posts in yesterday afternoon, so I think we gonna finish the frame up today and get goin' on the palm frond roof."

I peer past him toward the truck where Richy is noticeably absent. I say, "Did Richy mention anything about the camera

Paradis

after you guys left? I checked it last night and nothing had recorded."

He shrugs. "Don't know nothin' 'bout dat tech stuff, ya know."

Yeah, I bet. What had Amber said when we FaceTimed last night? *"Ol' Wisconsin Sasquatch sure didn't want a recording of him hitting his son."* Following my gaze, Tobias looks over his shoulder toward the Armadillo. "I left Richy at home." He's facing me again, fingering his beard—he actually seems a little nervous. "I'm real sorry 'bout yesterday. Dat boy doesn't know when to quit. Here's his apology." He walks up the stairs, retrieves a folded sheet of paper from his shirt pocket, and hands it over.

I unfold the note and read the boyish scrawl:

"Dear Ms. Thorndyke,

I am very sorry for using your iGlass without permission. I hope you will forgive me. I am sorry and will never again use anything of yours without asking your permission.

Yours truly,

Richy Kicklighter"

I have this image of Tobias standing over the boy, slamming his fist into his palm while Richy cowers at his desk, scribbling the apology. I fold the note and attempt to give it back.

Tobias waves the note away.

I clench the note tightly in my palm, and, with underlying anger in my voice, inquire, "When do you think you'll be done?"

Tobias clears his throat. "We should be finished tomorrow mornin' but won't have da platform built."

"We can wait a while on the platform."

He offers a shrug, walks down the stairs, and motions his tribe to get to work. From the bottom, he calls up to me. "Lit'le Addy, think ya could hard-boil some eggs 'n so? Left sort of early, missed breakfast."

I frown and go through the house to the back porch to pick up kindling and cordwood. "An overzealous, geeky kid." That's what Amber had called him when I finally got in touch with her. She wasn't convinced he had hacked anything, but she was troubled by my story. She instructed me not to open my online wallet. "If there is any attempt to make unauthorized changes, the bank should be able to timestamp it on their digital ledger." She asked several times, "Are you sure he was writing code?" Apparently, Richy shouldn't be able to write code for the Chameleon on an Apple device without "major modifications," whatever that means. Amber had asked a lot of questions. Did I check what websites he visited? Did he download anything? Talk to anyone? I felt ashamed and foolish. I had left him in a room alone with my iGlass. I informed Amber about the cleared history. At this news, she just sat silently, looking deep in thought. Then she asked, "What other devices in the house are connected to your iGlass?" The call ended when she asked if I could use some other device to contact her. "Just in case, you know, he did hack your iGlass." Abashed, I shut down FaceTime, threw dried beans into a pot to soak, and tried to sleep. Instead, I tossed and turned until I had twisted the bedcovers into a giant origami python. I feel dreadful today.

I boil eggs, put on more coffee, and put out a tray of saltines and ripened sea grapes. I deliver the food and sit on

Paradis

the top step, cradling my coffee mug. Tobias moves the ladder from pole to pole, checking the top of each with a level. Elias works with little Tommy to prepare rafters for the roof. Toby Too notches crossbeams for placement on the poles. Dandelion comes up the steps and sits beside me. He washes fastidiously. I think after they leave, I will hike to Tierra del Fuego and ask Mike and Gary if I can borrow their device to call Amber and my bank.

For lunch I prepare a red kidney bean chili with dandelion greens, onion, and jalapeño. When the stovetop biscuits are done, I take one for myself and tell the Kicklighters to come serve themselves.

Tobias heaves himself down next to me on the steps. After dowsing his chili with Sriracha, he wolfs down his food and gulps a red Hog's Breath. He offers me some beer, and I retrieve one from the truck bed.

On my return, he is pointing at the chickee. "How you likin' it? Got dem roof ribs up and 'bout ready to start nailin' in the palm fronds."

I sit down a couple steps above him and take a swig of beer. "Will you be done today?"

He turns around to look at me. Sweat lines up on his forehead like raindrops on an awning. "I hope ya still not frettin' 'bout Richy."

I say nothing.

"Regret bringin' him here, but he needs to get out in the air. We live on a goddamn island for Pete's sake, and all he wanna do is hole up in the house playin' games."

I nod.

We eat, and I watch his sweat drip. I let him know there is plenty more food.

He calls down to the kids to inform them, and Toby Too and Elias walk around us on the way up to the kitchen. It is at this time that we hear and then see something churning up the sand trail from the beach.

"'Spectin' anyone?" asks Tobias.

I stand up on the steps. Atop their ATVs, Gary and Mike bounce into the yard. They stop under the oak where Tommy is sitting. Both men wear white tees, blue jeans, and sporty, tinted goggles. I abandon my beer bottle and plate and run down the steps and into Gary's arms.

"Your daughter called us," he whispers as he releases me.

"Ainna yous guys a sight for sore eyes!" Tobias has come up right behind. He's clapping Mike and Gary on their backs. "Ya know, I like dose sleek machines. Addy, ya know, one of dese would be great for ya."

Mike's already striding over to examine the chickee, and Tobias follows him.

Gary leans in toward me and whispers, "We have news to share, but later, after they're gone."

My heart races. I ask if they can spend the night.

He nods. "Let's see if we can get this thing built today."

Tension drains, replaced with relief. I power up the Chameleon, wanting to document whatever happens today.

"Anyone hungry for a bowl of chili?" I ask.

```
[Soft electronic tone]
```

Paradis

> *Chameleon 3D60 unable to connect to Adeline Thorndyke's iGlass*
> *Saving data locally*
> *11/17/42, 12:02:32*
> *Recording Started*

A do-ragged man climbing the ladder, straddling the roof beams.
Boys handing up palmetto fronds to the man, who positions them one by one, frond side down. Two nails to a stem, one nail to the rafter below where the frond meets the stem. The second to the rafter above, near the end of the stem. Cutting away the excess.
Percussion of hammers. The wind's soft vibrato rush.
Two friendly-looking men handing fronds back and forth. No acrobatics for the older woman, safe on the ground, handing up fronds to the others.
The smallest boy scurries with supplies.
Sun skirting the treetops. Green palmetto fronds framing the little building in a bowl cut.

◆ ◆ ◆

Tobias wipes his face with his dirty rag. We all gather under the chickee's completed roof and lift up our Hog's Breaths.

"Smell dat?" proclaims Tobias. "Like a freshly woven basket. Dat's why I love it here, ya know. Da smells: salt, palm fronds, pine." He makes a loud inhale through his nose and smiles proudly. "I was thinkin', Addy, ya can just have our old picnic tables. We'll be needin' new ones anyway." He suggests I have a Thanksgiving pig roast and points to where he could set up the spit. Then he offers his toast: "Here's to livin' off da grid!"

Mary Burke

◆ ◆ ◆

After the taillights of the Armadillo disappear into the dusk, Gary and Mike shower, and I prepare a dreadful dinner of tuna, crackers, and a can of Boston baked beans. Once we're eating, Gary and Mike tell me about Amber's call with them last night.

"She gave us a summary of what happened and said you sounded really anxious, so we stopped by to check in." Mike's voice is heavy with empathy.

"Sounds like a rough day." Gary squeezes my shoulder. "I never trusted that awkward techie boy."

They continue, letting me know Amber had run a virus scan on her own smart system and found it clear. "Which is good news!" Gary exclaims. "It means if your iGlass is infected, it's isolated to only that device."

After we finish the pitiful dinner, Mike uses his microLens to bring up a poorly lit and somewhat wavy hologram of Amber and Liam. They are sitting on the tan, faux-leather couch in their living room. Even in the undulating image, I can easily recognize their place. On the wall above the couch hangs Liam's acoustic guitar, the very one he constructed at the age of fourteen in his father's woodshop. The very same instrument he used to serenade my daughter beneath her dorm window. They both wear their iGlasses. Liam's is a sporty, vivid blue. His thick long hair is pulled back in a messy ponytail, and the flyaways have softened his head's already blurry silhouette into a fuzzy blob on the low-res image. They are eating and drinking something.

Paradis

In answer to the first thing out of Gary's mouth, Amber announces it is an Amarone, "a rich and dark red wine to pair with chocolate-covered cherries." She salutes with her wine glass as she speaks. The movement of her mouth doesn't match up with her words. The poor connection is disappointing. "I was just about to message you! Mom, sorry I couldn't call sooner, so busy with work." She takes a sip of wine and then inquires as to the location of my iGlass.

"It's sleeping on its charger, been there since we last spoke."

"Good! So, I was able to check in with your bank. I explained the situation, and as your beneficiary, they agreed to check the account. Everything seems okay." She pauses to savor more wine. "Just don't use your private key until we can have the system checked," she warns.

Liam roots through the box of chocolate cherries. "I doubt a twelve-year-old can pick your wallet. But if you want to be safe, Apple can run a diagnostic and do a factory reset, update your OS." He pops a cherry into his mouth. "It would guarantee you have all the latest security features."

Amber's voice is cutting in and out, but most of what she is saying I can follow: booking a hotel, going in person to the Apple Store and bank, her flight on North American Airways—Thursday, December eighteenth, three in the afternoon—and how she will relay her information to me through Mike and Gary.

Liam has been sitting thoughtfully, leaning back on the couch cushions, his long legs resting on the coffee table. "Addy, are you certain this kid was trying to hack into your iGlass?"

Again, I recount my story for all: Richy caught red-handed, typing code on my iGlass, and then the response from his awful father, Tobias, lifting the boy off the ground and slapping him.

Liam's tone is serious. "That sounds awful." He pauses in thought for a moment before continuing, "I have a friend in the auto industry whose job is to catch auto hackers. Maybe he knows something, can check if there is any known history of this Richy kid hacking before."

Amber is sloshing her wine and becoming riled. She's up from the couch with her fists clenched. Her image temporarily wavers, but her voice suddenly comes through loud and strong. "I don't like you living out there alone, and by that Kicklighter family. I'm going to come out now, book a flight as soon as we hang up."

The living room image returns to Liam holding Amber's hand, guiding her back onto the couch. Once Amber is sitting again, he rubs her neck. "Dropping everything and flying off to an island in the middle of nowhere isn't going to make things any better." Amber sighs loudly. Liam suggests transferring several hundred dollars from Amber's personal account to the guys' account so I can make a Joey Pelagro shopping trip to tide me over until Amber arrives for her visit in December. It's a plan everyone can agree on.

"Was anything of the incident recorded on the camera?" Liam inquires.

I tell him I suspect it had been deleted.

"Well, we should at least let the Department of Children and Families know that he's abusing his son," suggests Amber.

Paradis

"I have some of the chickee build recorded, but I don't think it shows anything abusive."

Liam asks to see this chickee that's caused all this trouble, so Mike, Gary, and I walk our virtual visitors down to the yard. Raindrops drip from the trees. Dandelion frolics in the piles of palmetto fronds. The smell of wet shaved wood perfumes the air.

"Wow, solid construction," Liam expresses in surprise.

Abruptly, their living room darkens. The microLens asserts a red flashing message, losing signal. We quickly scurry closer to the satellite dish, and holographic hugs and kisses twirl in the air before the signal fades completely.

"It'll be okay, Addy," Gary assures me. "We're here."

Mike hugs me. "Mind if I drop by later this week to comb your beach with my metal detector? I promise we can split any pirate booty I find, then we'd never have to worry about hackers again.

Paradis

Winter

*Our inventions are wont to be pretty toys,
which distract our attention from serious things.
They are but improved means to an unimproved
end.*

- Henry David Thoreau

Mary Burke

Chapter 7
I Can't Tell the Difference Between My Work and My Play

Amber was never particularly fond of Orlando. At two years old, she showed her dissatisfaction by barfing up miniature Mickey Mouse butter pats—the only thing she would eat on our first trip to the Magic Kingdom—all over the backseat of our car. When she was four, however, she didn't seem to mind waiting for three hours outside Cinderella Castle so I could pay two hundred dollars for her to dress up like her favorite character. With these memories in mind, I made a dinner reservation at the Grand Floridian for my daughter and me, and for Jerry, who was no doubt rethinking his offer to drive

Paradis

me to the Orlando airport. Her flight is due in at three; our dinner reservation is at seven. Right now it is one, and Jerry's Ford pickup is sunning itself on the Florida Turnpike with thousands of other vehicles.

"I can't say enough how much I appreciate this, Jerry."

"Don't think anything of it. It was the perfect excuse for me to get the truck out on the road. It's been telling me it needed to get out for a drive, almost as bad as a dog grabbing its leash wanting to go for a walk." He laughs. "I can tell you one thing: I'm really looking forward to dinner tonight at Cinderella's Castle."

"It's at the Grand Floridian. It's a resort hotel."

"Oh, can you see Cinderella's Castle from there?"

"I think so."

"You know, I've lived in Florida my whole life, but I never made it to Disney."

I am hoping he won't be disappointed. I thought I did well scoring reservations at the Floridian. To get reservations at Cinderella Castle required knowing someone on the inside—Cinderella herself or, at the very least, either Jaq or Gus.

A yellow warning signal suddenly comes to life on the truck's dashboard screen. Sensors show low tire pressure on the front driver's side, and GPS shows us stuck on the Turnpike just beyond the exit to Winter Garden. Jerry shuts off the air conditioning and puts down the windows. "Guess I'd better take the truck in for a checkup while you're at the Apple Store tomorrow."

I lean my arm on the edge of the open window and inhale the heat exuding from the myriad vehicles and dark pavement. Even as large swaths of Florida sit underwater, Disney World remains busy as ever. A mass existential crisis would erupt on the day the Earth gulps down Cinderella Castle. Which could happen; Orlando is renowned for sinkholes, after all. On that terrible day, Tinker Bell could no longer wave her wand and make reality disappear. But at least the traffic might improve.

Suddenly, Jerry's truck belches out an asthmatic gasp, and the indicator on the dashboard starts blinking red. An authoritarian voice, the truck's voice, commands, "Emergency shutdown."

Adjacent vehicles make way, and we coast over to the relative safety of the turnpike shoulder. Jerry calls the auto service, and the truck beams an automatic locator signal. He opens his door a crack to let in some air. "They're sending a technician. Shouldn't be too long."

I stare out at the gridlock. It is 1:15.

Jerry swivels in his seat to face me directly. "You know, I'm really looking forward to meeting your daughter. Enjoyed FaceTiming with her and her fiancé at Thanksgiving, but I can't wait to see her in person."

"Liam is her husband."

"Oh. Yes, Liam, the guitar player. Are they bringing the dogs, those little live wires?"

"No, it's just Amber," I remind him, and I wonder where his mind had been when I explained this to him the first time.

"Flight arrives at three, right?"

"She said she'd call when she gets in."

Jerry had offered the invitation for Thanksgiving dinner to Mike and Gary (apparently a budding tradition among them) and said to bring that "young lady" along—that was meant to be me. Thanksgiving with the Jefferys was an opportunity for

Paradis

me to gracefully exit the "Pig Pickin'" that Tobias had planned to have under my chickee. I felt a need for healing time between the Kicklighters and myself. Tobias's disappointment seemed allayed when I agreed to attend their Christmas Eve celebration and bring Amber along.

Unfortunately, Joey's was out of turkeys, but one of my chickens, Maggie, offered her services along with two of the guys' chickens. I supplied garden greens and pumpkin loaves. Hilda and Jerry got a fire going in their outside pit and grilled the chickens. We also grilled corn in their husks (Joey's had a special), vegetable kebabs, and baked potatoes. Afterward, Mike and Gary brought up Amber and Liam via their microLens. It was a brief conversation since Amber and Liam were just about to sit down to their traditional Thanksgiving meal of Indian food. Amber has been a vegetarian since she was seven, Liam since he was twenty, and they started this Thanksgiving tradition their first year together. Despite the briefness of the conversation, spunky Cici and my hyper daughter clicked right away.

Jerry asks why I am smiling and I tell him I'm musing about Thanksgiving. His face brightens. "Best Thanksgiving in a long time," he says. "So nice to see Ma in such a happy mood. She loved chatting with Amber." Jerry attempts a stretch. "Ma's developed a curiosity about all this virtual reality stuff. She was wondering about snow skiing in VR but said it wouldn't truly be real without a broken leg or at the very least a sprained ankle."

I laugh.

He blinks sweat from his eyes. "Gonna step out and stretch the legs." Checking for cars, he carefully opens the door and stands on the shoulder. He looks down at his wrist to the cheap Joey Pelagro-brand smartband he wears and strolls over to my window. "They're going to be at least another hour."

My smile fades with that news; I guess we won't be meeting Amber at the airport. I also get out of the truck, and Jerry and I walk back to the Winter Garden exit where there is an overpass, under which we sit in the shade and wait for the tow truck.

At 3 p.m., the tow truck arrives. We are attaching our seat belts in the truck when Jerry extends his arm with the smartband.

"Plane landed!" emits Amber's chipper voice from the watch.

I explain our situation to her, and she says she'll take a shuttle to the Grand Floridian. The tow truck driver, a congenial chap, kindly agrees to drop us off at the Grand Floridian and take Jerry's truck to the nearest service center where repairs should be completed by tomorrow.

◆ ◆ ◆

With its carved-ivory verandas, ruby-roofed gables, and billowing palms, the Grand Floridian allows us to step back into the Victorian era. Undoubtedly, Queen Victoria and Prince Albert would have puffed out their chests like stodgy frigatebirds if they ever had the opportunity to visit this mock-colonial jewel in the crown. We weave our way through the highly ornamented lobby toward the Grand Floridian Café, a restaurant that the sedan chair bearers of Victoria and Albert would have shuffled quickly by on their way to the

Paradis

royally priced and chandeliered elegance of Queen Victoria's Room. But for me, our reservation at the Café offers perfect two-year-old-Amber-eating-butter-pats nostalgia.

Precisely at seven, my daughter enters the restaurant wearing her iGlass, a huge rucksack, self-made 3D-printed shoes, distressed jeans, and a T-shirt with the quote by Atari creator Nolan Bushnell: "I can't tell the difference between my work and my play." Her Washingtonian-pale complexion contrasts against her closely cropped dark-brown hair tipped as if dipped in flames. I am so excited to see her, and we hug with the exuberance of best friends. Once our energetic reception calms, she and Jerry shake hands, and the hostess seats us at a table with a window view of gazebos, fountains, and roses.

Lush, flowered carpeting, lacy tablecloths, and Christmas place settings absorb the hum of the admittedly overbooked restaurant. Each table is silhouetted into its own candlelit bubble. The café boasts a human waiter—a charming anachronism—who wears a waistcoat and recites the menu by heart. We decide on the vegetarian ravioli, the shrimp, and the steak. We butter rolls with Mickey's face and chat about Seattle, dogs and cats, and the Victorian carolers that stroll around the tables. Amber invites Liam, Hilda, and Cici to join us virtually for chocolate fondue and coffee. Liam mentions he's building a greenhouse for a Christmas gift, bringing amused expressions from the Floridians. Our conversations are merry and light, delegating the problems of the world—flooding, climate change, broken trucks, and little boy hackers—to Tomorrowland. Amber sneaks off and pays for the substantial bill and tip. Afterward, sated with food, we meander through the rose garden, and I understand why reservations are made months in advance and people hotly pant inside their highway-strangling vehicles. Jerry stands on the beach of the Seven Seas Lagoon and gazes reverently at Cinderella Castle. My daughter and I hold hands. A delicate moment together, a small thin square of churned cream in Florida heat. Oh, how I long to freeze this moment, use Tinker Bell's blazing wand of shimmering, iridescent magic to keep this now from melting away.

Paradis

Chapter 8
Orlando is more than Mickey Mouse

Orlando is now the most populous officially recognized city in the State of Florida, and very nearly the most southern. A few newly formed archipelagos south of Winter Haven and several highways are also considered within Florida State's jurisdiction. After breakfast at our hotel on International Drive, we schedule an AutoLyft to drive us to the Apple Store and Jerry to the service center. The ride in daylight exposes the pains of this rapid population growth. Once you leave the Disney sector, the city becomes a swarm of humanity. Giant sanctioned refugee centers dominate every major church, school, YMCA, and city parking garage. Tents scatter the sidewalks and amalgamate together into slums under each overpass. Around almost all corners, lines of humanity stand waiting, presumably for food and water.

The Apple Store we arrive at stands in stark contrast—white, shiny, and besides a bouncer at the door, frozen in the time before the flooding. Once approved for entry, we head straight to the Genius Bar. Our eleven o'clock appointment is with Genius Kobee, a thin, black twenty-something. He wears a tie strobing with multicolor Apple logos, a red Apple iGlass, and a black silk shirt, jeans, and red sneakers.

He leads us to a place along the bar. "Coffee? Water?"

We decline refreshments and sit on tall stools. Amber and me on the customer side and Kobee on the Genius side of the counter. The wall behind him cascades with LED snowflakes. I relate my story. He informs us that he can't run a diagnostic on the Chameleon, but there is a Samsung store two doors down that can. He can, however, help with the iGlass. His quick diagnostic brings bad news immediately. He expresses surprise. "Well, there's definitely something here. My diagnostic is showing what's called hypervisor-based malware. It allows the hacker to eavesdrop on conversations, record keystrokes, and watch as lockboxes containing private key codes are opened; in other words, become a virtual you. It runs unobtrusively beneath the operating system so the computer's cleansing program won't pick it up, and the victim's none the wiser." He gives a horrified shiver. "Nasty, nasty. A twelve-year-old boy, you said? This was some pretty savvy twelve-year-old." He explains this type of malware requires some sort of secondary trigger to be launched, like opening an email, responding in a certain way to a phone call, or connecting to a particular website. He asks if I remember doing any of these things and if I have any other devices linked to my iGlass.

I let Kobee know I had only used my iGlass to email the bank and FaceTime Amber the one time. I ask again about the camera.

"The hacker probably didn't care about your pictures, but you need to go to the Samsung store to be sure," he says. He asks for the kid's name.

Kobee does a metasearch for Richy Kicklighter to see if he'd ever been reported before for hacking. No reports have ever been filed. He suggests I notify my local police department and check with my financial institutions.

Amber has been silent this whole time, but I can see discontent on her face. "Hypervisor-based malware? Seriously?" she eventually says. She wants him to rerun the test. "There must be some mistake," she insists.

Kobee's irritation is apparent. "Ma'am, the Apple diagnostic software doesn't make mistakes." He dismisses her and leans across the counter, speaking to me in a low voice. "The police may be able to check Richy's devices to see if there's any evidence that he's been hacking." He emphasizes that considering the sort of malware, I am most likely not the only victim.

Amber says, almost under her breath, "Why would he do it?" I'm unsure if she's speaking to me, herself, or the Genius.

Kobee ignores her, continuing to explain to me about anonymity software and methods of routing things through multiple VPNs, commenting that most hackers are pretty good at covering their tracks.

I nod, though it's tough to process this hacking confirmation. I wish they served appletinis at the Genius Bar.

Kobee presents a veneered smile that takes up half his face and explains the solution is to wipe my device and install the latest OS30 with built-in protection package. A tap of his red-framed iGlass brings up a 3D feature list of OS30.

Amber acquiesces, commenting that it was time for an upgrade anyway.

"How much?" I ask.

"It's a great value at seven hundred plus tax."

He takes my iGlass and directs us to a plush waiting area surrounded by about nine thousand new Apple products. A tall, gangly man heads over and shakes hands with me and Amber. Kobee introduces us to Sine, one of the Geniuses in Training. "Sine will remove the malware from your iGlass and install the new operating system," Kobee tells me. "Afterward, we will meet back up and go over how to access the tutorials for the new system and complete the warranty info. This new setup has improved two-step ID: facial plus retinal scan."

Kobee turns over my iGlass to Sine, and I watch as he goes to work on his new client, a curvy Mediterranean beauty wearing a tight, faux-snakeskin dress, which is ill-adapted to sitting on the high Genius Bar stools.

Amber sits in the chair next to me. Her expression is one of distraught puzzlement. "Well, this has thrown me," she says softly. Her eyes turn from me, and she looks around the store. "We'll talk later." The comment is an aside. She gets up from the chair and tests out VR gear from a shelf. I study her immersed movements for some minutes before being drawn back to the interplay between the Genius and his client. The

Paradis

woman has one of the more expensive iGlass varieties, a type of wrap-around tortoiseshell frame. She also has a habit of tapping her maroon fingernails on the counter. Kobee flashes his overly bright smile and opens up a series of holograms advertising Apple devices. She finally extends one of her impeccably manicured nails and selects a showy, iridescent, teardrop-shaped wearable. An iBot scoots from the stockroom to drop a small box into Kobee's hand. The Genius looks like he is about to propose.

"Adeline Thorndyke?" Sine is standing over me, informing me my iGlass is as good as new. I leave Amber to her game and Kobee to his sexy Mediterranean client and follow Sine to the Genius Bar so my face and retina can be scanned. A little past noon, Kobee completes the sale, and I digitally sign the warranty agreement.

Amber goes to pick up salads, pretzels, and Cokes from the Café Apple Automat while I stop by the Samsung store. After a short wait, I'm informed that a scan of the Chameleon checks out clear. While I wait for Amber to return, I call the eight hundred number for the Orlando Police Department. The recorded message tells me to report my "computer intrusion" to the Internet Crime Complaint Division of the Security Agency and to the Federal Trade Commission.

Amber brings over the food and sits down. "I still don't buy that a twelve-year-old could have modified your device with that sort of malware. That was some crazy advanced stuff you had on your device," she speaks in a confidential tone. "I also don't think it's a good idea to involve the SA and the FTC in this thing, at least not until we know for sure if it was really Richy." She takes a bite of her salad and looks around carefully. "With Tobias and his family being celebrities or whatever, these agencies will be compelled to do at least a cursory investigation. The scandal news teams will fly in on helicopters, and it isn't like Tobias won't be able to figure out who contacted them."

I push my half-eaten salad away. I am not feeling very hungry. "What about that friend of Liam's who works for the auto industry, the guy that was supposed to have some malware tracking something or other?"

She fiddles with her fork. "We already asked. He signed a non-disclosure agreement with his company. He can't do anything." She sips some Coke while taking in all the cameras in the store. "I have an idea, though, a way we could know for sure if Richy was the hacker, but now's not the time." She looks past me and smiles. "Hey Jerry!" she remarks loudly, signaling the end of our conversation.

Jerry approaches and grabs a chair. "Truck's good as new. They said the computer needed an upgrade. The tires are full. The tank is so full of hydrogen the truck should float; at least that's what the technician said, but I think he meant it as a joke. Did you get your iGlass repaired?"

"Yep, everything's good!" bubbles Amber.

"Great!" he says and asks if it's okay if he picks up something to eat. Amber and I recycle our trash while Jerry gets a hot dog from a vending machine. The truck meets us outside on the curb, and soon, we are rolling away from the Apple Store with Jerry dribbling mustard on the seat of the Ford's newly steam-cleaned upholstery.

Paradis

◆ ◆ ◆

Everything in the credit union is banker-gray; even the air that spills from the air-conditioning ducts possesses a gray dankness. Leaving Jerry in the lobby, Amber and I cross the low-pile carpeting to be seated in heated-acrylic chairs in the clear chamber of Ms. Dorothy Grigio, Customer Accounts Manager. The petite, young woman dresses to match the decor in a gray suit with matching pencil skirt. I tell her my story as she brings up a holographic image of my accounts. Although she can view my money, only I, with my two-factor identification of iris and retinal scans and my personal private key, can unlock my accounts. An additional computer-generated private key is necessary for funds to be transferred to another party whenever I make a purchase. As Ms. Grigio talks, I feign understanding, but my brain is much too exhausted to process more information. Instead, I stare at the walls behind her desk, where a stream of ever-mutating international digital currencies ebb and flow on the acrylic walls. I glean from her explanation, however, that my accounts are still secure, and it is not necessary to have a new unique personal private key generated. I unlock my wallet and practice transferring funds by purchasing Apocalypse Bonanza from the Apple Store for download to Amber's iGlass.

Ms. Grigio suggests I report my suspicions to the FTC and the SA.

I nod, but Amber's comments over lunch have made me indecisive. Ms. Grigio pings the agencies' contact information to my iGlass. We wait for a long ten minutes to see if use of my private key triggers any illicit tampering. I chew my lip. Only my transaction registers. Ms. Grigio mentions again the importance of placing a call to the government agencies, and again, I nod, remaining silent. She instructs me to check frequently for any fraudulent activity. "Be vigilant, and for your protection, call the numbers I messaged you."

In the lobby, we collect Jerry and let him know my account transfers cleared successfully. He wants to get going to make it to Snug Harbor before sundown. We first attribute the traffic backup to rush hour, but we soon understand that in Orlando, all hours are rush hour. Once we reach the Turnpike, we realize that reaching Snug Harbor before sunset will not be possible. Amber and Jerry begin a dedicated search for a motel—even a Bates Motel—somewhere along the route to Snug Harbor. Once we get forty miles outside Orlando, however, the sun deposits itself into a massive fog bank. Our truck, along with seemingly everyone else's vehicle, decides to call it quits for the day and withdraws to a parking lot in a rest area. At least Amber has Apocalypse Bonanza to occupy her after Jerry and I fall asleep in the truck's reclining seats.

We hit the snack machine early, and it rewards us with surprisingly tasty peanut butter crackers. We leave the rest area by seven, and the truck navigates tenuously through an opaque dawn. Once off I-75, the roads deteriorate rapidly. Amber, used to living on what might as well be another planet in the Pacific Northwest, presses her nose to the window like a small child with cataracts. "Surely," she comments, "we've been transported through a wormhole and have landed on a steamy world mega-cratered by a tremendous pummeling of meteors." The fog doesn't lift until one, and only then is she willing to admit that we are actually in a Florida that's returning to the wild. "I had no idea the damage was this vast."

Our journey from Orlando ends around 6 p.m. when the Ford pulls into Jerry's garage in Snug Harbor. We enter the living room, where we see Hilda placing little cotton balls between each of Cici's toes.

Cici sparkles when Amber walks into the room.

Amber gives her a light hug. There is a communion between them that is joyful to observe.

Cici explains to Amber that Hilda offered to paint her nails Christmas red. She plans on getting all dolled up and accompanying us to Joey Pelagro's the following morning. Her goal is to sit on Santa's lap.

Amber winks through her iGlass. "What will you ask him for?"

"I've been thinking on it. After all, I've been a relatively good girl, so I think I'll get my two wishes." Cici hums for a moment before continuing in a more serious tone, "One is for you, young woman, to take off that device of yours and look at the world with your own two eyes." Her tone is now very stern. "Listen with your own two ears. Touch with your own two hands. Life is mundane. Life is dangerous. Life is exhilarating." She throws her hands up. "Amber, appreciate the wonder of it."

Hilda and Jerry snicker slightly. I spot Amber behind the tinted lenses of her iGlass, smiling a little crooked smile. She looks uncomfortable, but I'm glad Cici said out loud what I had been contemplating since seeing Amber in the hotel lobby. With everyone's gaze on her, Amber turns her attention to the paintings on the wall. She asks if these are Cici's paintings and wants to know the names of the wildflowers.

Cici answers, "Of course I know their names. The yellow tickseeds behind me all have names beginning with D. They are Daisy, Dalia, Delilah, David, Dagwood, and so forth." She points at the door. "Went traditional with the poinsettias over by the entrance, named them Jesus, Mary, and Joseph. And the white sabatia over there are all members of the gentian family—a tenacious, scrappy brood." She looks back down at her toes, examining Hilda's progress, her voice becoming reflective. "The flowers remind me to not overlook the wonder right under your foot. Their bloom is small and brief, like life. We have to appreciate the world for the moment we have."

Still wearing her iGlass, Amber stands in contemplation before each of the paintings, the room silent other than the sound of the dogs' tails thumping like the dull tread of time.

At last, Jerry coughs. He inquires as to his mom's second wish.

Cici withdraws slowly from her meditative mood. She has all our attention. Her voice is a whisper. She winks. "No hurricane."

At the word, we inhale air in unison. Even the dogs pause their thumping. My mind fills with visions of caved-in roofs, toppled giant oaks, and lashing waves washing away the remaining roads into the sea. I shiver at the thought.

Cici surveys our worry and chuckles. "Well, at least not until I'm dead and y'all have moved to higher ground."

Paradis

Jerry attempts a smile. "Well Ma, then we needn't worry. That'll be a long time from now."

"Son, I hope you're right!" She admires her manicure and pedicure and pats Hilda's hand. She glows with a wicked grin. "Hilda dear, Santa's going to be all over me with these pretty nails!"

Chapter 9
-ddy's -edgie

I cut the engine and steer my boat alongside a stationary dock at the Paradis marina. Mike and Gary are busily scraping sea creatures off the hulls of their catamaran. After making me proud with having remembered how to properly tie up a boat, Amber records a video to send to Liam: sloppy softness of the mud, fish that weave through the seagrass like shiny needles, a small white crab with stalk-mounted, peppercorn eyes studying us with a worried look.

She hands over her iGlass to Mike. He takes a photo of us on the dock. She is spirited and young; I, windblown and old. I like looking at her without her iGlass, her eyes the same shape and shade of hazel as my own. Full of energy, she prances off, pirouetting across the grassy area of the marina. The wind ruffles her hair, flicking the orange-flecked tips like

Paradis

the embers of a campfire. She turns a cartwheel; she revels in Cici wildflowers.

Gary emerges from under the boat and lifts up his mask. He waves in Amber's direction as we get to chatting. I relate the state of Orlando and our adventures there. Gary, unsurprised by the current state of the world, asks if I'm reporting the kid to the FTC. I let him know I have the numbers but haven't decided if it's the best idea. "We aren't even sure if it was really Richy," I state softly, the uncertainty in my own words obvious. Gary looks exasperated at my response, puts his mask down, raises his scraper, and returns to the barnacles. Given that Mike and Gary are clearly busy and we have plans to see them later, Amber and I start the process of trudging our supplies to Addy's Wedgie. As we collect our belongings, Mike comments that they left a Christmas present at my homestead while I was away in Orlando. "It'll be real obvious," he says with a wink.

The half-mile trail is a sandy slog. I wear my backpack and tug at my loaded supply wagons. Amber struggles with her huge rucksack and a cage of chickens. I learned last night that half her pack consisted of gifts: touristy tees, a pair of Sasquatch shorts, socks from the University of Washington, a Sounders rain poncho, smart Duck Boots that display the temperature and time of any place in the world, two pairs of custom 3D-printed Neo-Tech closed-toed shoes, and a family portrait of Liam, herself, and the two dogs laser-etched into cedar. She also brought a bottle of Columbia Valley Cabernet Sauvignon from her favorite winery in Woodinville. That she still had room for her own things with all the gifts she'd packed was impressive.

As we trudge, my mind is not so much on the trail ahead as it is on last night at the Jefferys'. It was one of those nights when you haven't seen a loved one in a long time, when words hang in the air, and you reach up, grab the words of the other, marinade them in the sauce of your own paradigm, and then serve them back into the air. We were sharing the bed in the Jefferys' spare bedroom. Amber, wearing her iGlass, flopped on top of the comforter. Across her red nightshirt read the words "*réalité virtuelle*" in white letters. I asked her the meaning.

"Words coined by Antonin Artaud, a French playwright and actor. It means to make the subconscious conscious," she answered. "I got the shirt when I went to a lecture on perception philosophy ethics in VR." My daughter's life was so foreign to me. "Basically," she continued, "virtual reality works so well because the subconscious likes to take shortcuts to make sense of what we are looking at." She sat up in the bed, setting her eyes on me through her iGlass, making me wonder if she had been giving attention to something other than me in her augmented view. "I still can't believe your device was hacked!"

I frowned. "Do you think it was Richy?"

She bit her lower lip, which meant she didn't know.

"Didn't you research this place before you came?" An edge to Amber's voice.

"I was in a National Guard Shelter. I needed somewhere to live before I was kicked out." Truth is, I wanted beach sunsets, diverging roads, peace alternating with adventure. I wanted Florida. I wanted wild. I wanted somewhere that reminded me of Mark. I remember at that moment wishing for Mark; he

Paradis

would have known how to deal with this hacking problem. Then, we would have watched sunsets on the beach and pressed shells to each other's ears to listen to the rhythm of the sea.

"So, you spend your life's savings on a patch of sand on a barrier island?" Amber shook her head.

"It wasn't all my savings." She dangled her iGlass from her finger, arm outstretched. I took it and put it on. There were multiple articles about Tobias and the Kicklighter family. Mostly information I'd already seen. I took the thing off, handed it back. "I've seen them, but it's all tabloid stuff! It's one thing to read about something, another to see it happen in front of you." I sighed. "The oddest thing was seeing the others not reacting to Tobias slapping Richy like that. Everyone just kept on like it was normal…"

She set her iGlass on the table, and I wondered what wearing that thing all the time must do to her eyes.

"I just worry about you," she said, gently. "Come back to Issaquah with me."

Well, that was blunt, I thought. When I didn't answer, she flopped back on her pillow. I turned out the light.

She started talking again through the darkness. "I was reading, and it mentions Richy being crazy smart. Like a 150 IQ. I bet he's super frustrated, conflicted. Both hates his dad while craving his acceptance."

"So do you think he hacked my stuff?"

"It's possible. Maybe it's his method of getting money to somehow flee the island and get away from his dad." She sighed. "Richy is just a kid in a tough situation. We shouldn't involve the SA and FTC. At least until we know for sure he hacked it." A pause. "And understand why." I could picture Amber biting her lip, a habit she developed after Mark died. "Which brings me to my idea." Her voice lowered. "Quench has this new technology we just patented. We're actively looking for investors, marketing it as a tool for therapists. With all the mental health issues these days, it should make billions. But it can also just be used to improve graphics—create more immersive games, better digital vacations, and we think let people relive their memories. Super cool stuff." Her voice softened even more. "We have a few experiences showing promising results. One is this roleplay scenario where the player interacts with avatars that transform into whoever's on their mind."

"How does this help us know if he hacked my device?"

"Well, I could download some of the code to Richy's iGlass, make it look like it's just a normal VR game of his and use the software. If he is feeling guilt or remorse for hacking, which I suspect he would be, you would show up as an avatar, proving he was the hacker. I bet he would even start explaining why he hacked you once your avatar appears."

"I'm not sure, is that ethical?"

"Is identity theft?"

"Hmm, hack the hacker?" I paused. "Are you asking my permission?"

"Is it so wrong not to jump to conclusions?"

I found myself reaching for her hand as we lay in that high, four-poster, chenille-covered bed. "You haven't even met Richy."

"And yet I feel I know him. He's just a kid."

"Okay," I relented.

Paradis

Even with the tense conversation, I had fallen asleep that night with a smile on my face, happy to be with Amber.

Amber's giggling brings me back from my recollections. She is pointing at a gopher tortoise crossing the trail and takes photos through her iGlass. I take pictures of the tortoise with its head in its shell and my daughter lying alongside. She returns to her bag to gulp electrolyte water and gripes about the brightness of the sun. The tortoise peeks out cautiously and eventually finds a patch of grass to nibble. Amber searches through her pack in a frenzied state, even sticking her head inside, looking just like a gopher tortoise digging a burrow in the sand. "Where's my sunscreen?" she shouts loudly, dumping everything out. The chickens cluck, the tortoise returns its head to its shell, and I laugh. I find her sunscreen at the bottom of my bag, and we take turns smearing it on ourselves. The tortoise's head reemerges to grab a mouthful of grass, then retreats to watch us from the shade of a palmetto. I stare at Amber with a dollop of white sunscreen on her Washingtonian white nose. She is so young and beautiful. I stand up and brush the sand off my bottom. "We need to get on," I say. We cram her sandy stuff back in her bag, put on our packs, pick up the chickens, and continue tugging along. I think to glance back toward the palmetto bush, and there's no more sign of the tortoise, only some vague clawed footprints in the sand.

"That Joey's place is crazy," she says as we struggle along. "I swear I've played a level in a video game just like it. Christmas decorations, high-tech sentries, the whole thing. Déjà vu. Sent Liam some great pictures of Santa and the sentries." She laughs.

Yesterday, we had all piled into Jerry's truck, and Cici, with her red nails, had her photo op with Santa and shared her wishes. Amber recorded it and took her own turn with Santa. All of us were happy. We cavorted in the aisles and ate pizza. However, the tomfoolery ended when it came time to pay, and the monitor at the exit said I had to go to Customer Service.

"Didn't you think it was weird that their checkout system didn't recognize me?"

"Yeah, but I guess they're just using some old software for their facial recognition." She goes on to explain various ways my new OS and updated facial scans could have confused an older system. "Uncommon, but not impossible."

Embedded in the Customer Service counter, a cheery yet no-nonsense humanoid hologram named Al told me there was "an ambiguity in my facial recognition." Amber retorted that barring me having had my face eaten off by a chimpanzee, my facial recognition should be fine for years. Her statement gave Al momentary pause, but then, it reiterated that if I wanted to make my purchase, I would need to take an updated photo and confirm my identity by clicking a link they would email. In that moment, I had an unaccountable feeling of unease. However, I didn't want to spoil everyone's good mood, so I pushed the feeling aside, smiled at the camera, and wished Al "a blessed day."

"Could someone at Joey's have hacked my device?" I ask.

"Well, have you ever let anyone there use your iGlass?"

"No," I answer.

"Then I don't think it's very likely. Facial recognition and email verifications are common practice everywhere. You're just paranoid now. If Joey was doing malicious stuff, like lifting excess cash from customers, someone would have reported him by now. I looked up his bio, nothing kookier than the average small-town Joe—" She stops suddenly, and I think she's seen a snake on the trail.

I had been looking down, but Amber's sudden pause has forced me to look ahead. Evident even at a distance, the pinewood sign looms as large as a wall of my house. The top of the sign is peaked, and a metal crossbar runs underneath and parallel to the peak. Taken together, they form the letter A. The bottom of the sign forms a W. Under the crossbar of the A, welded with metal gleaned from island debris, are the letters DDY'S. At the bottom half of the sign, attached and extending from the right side of the W, metal letters connect to read EDGIE.

Amber removes her overpowering backpack. She gazes in awe, as do I. She films my Christmas gift from the guys—ADDY'S WEDGIE—and sends it to Liam's iGlass twenty-five hundred miles away.

Mary Burke

Chapter 10
The Sandcastle

When I was a denizen of St. Petersburg, I loved thumbing through stacks of vintage postcards in antique stores on Central Avenue. They spoke to me, these mini-Impressionist paintings of sunsets, bougainvillea, and tropical pink soirees at the Vinoy Resort. I thought this painting effect was intentional. But the truth was less romantic. It was just far cheaper one hundred years ago to print on paper with a high rag content. Nevertheless, the soft edges and pure color saturation in these linen postcards gave me the feeling that I had somehow fallen into the shade of a Tiffany lamp. My favorite place on Paradis inspires similar feelings.

This place is where the path from my house meets the beach, two palms leaning toward one another as if they're sharing gossip. Like Saint Louis's Gateway Arch, these palms

Paradis

mark a gateway to western vistas. I'm sitting cross-legged and sipping cabernet in the floury space beneath them. Above me, the Chameleon hovers, framing Amber within the curving palms as she continues her construction of an elaborate sandcastle gleaned from a half-dozen fantasy novels.

We have been enjoying mother-daughter time, baking bread, and cooking elaborate meals from fresh garden produce. Sometimes she brought Liam into the mix. In the evenings—his afternoons—he floated along with us as a disembodied virtual presence. I can't say how I really felt about his company—his floating along. There was a feeling that it was an invasion of my all-too-brief daughter time. However, there was also this feeling of solidarity, a realization that he had become family. We both love Amber, but in different ways. Somewhere there is a postcard in all this, one where we are together on a bench beneath an arbor of scarlet bougainvillea.

There was practical stuff to endure. Amber taught me the Chameleon's operating manual, schooling me in the various flight techniques and sending me off to practice. She scrutinized the video of the chickee build, threw up her hands, and combed her fingers through her short, orange-tipped hair. "I wish I knew what he was typing. I wish I could view the second day." She lectured me, again, on ways to keep my devices safe from hackers and even added additional security requirements for using my iGlass, which she then had to draw instructional diagrams for, so I could get it to unlock.

Mary Burke

```
[Soft electronic tone]

> Chameleon 3D60 connected to Adeline Thorndyke's iGlass
> 12/23/42, 17:28:12
> Recording Started
```

Beneath the frame of the palm arch, a cat stretches beside an older woman in the cool sand. Together they watch a younger woman thickening walls, dripping mud towers, and gathering sand dollars for windows. Sticks of driftwood forming a door. Her young hands smoothing the walls and shaping the crenellations, the sunlit clouds reflecting pink as Tiffany glass upon her cheeks.

I gaze up at the Chameleon, my wine-haze in the Florida sun causing me to reflect. What does a camera really record? Does the camera subvert memory or enhance it? What was it that Cici said…? Absorb the moment with your own five senses; attend to the greatness of the small? But Cici had her black-and-whites. Is it not all postcard images? Comforting snapshots of what we want to remember?

• • •

In the middle of the night, I cannot sleep. Careful not to wake my daughter, I take my iGlass from the charging stand, turn on its headlamp, and walk down to sit under the palm arch. With the headlamp off, I lie in the sand and breathe violets in the moonlight. Waves beat out slow jazz rhythms. I bring up

Paradis

the recording called Sandcastle Build. My eyes adjust slowly to the brilliance of the 3D60. Gulf hues in as many shades as aviator sunglasses, and beyond the waves that pound the beach, porpoises swirling and shrieking like those bouncing beach children printed on those nostalgic postcards. Oddly, I had missed the porpoises in real time.

I take off my iGlass. Once more, I'm in a world lit by moonlight, the sandcastle an invisible presence. I contemplate Amber building her castle. It is twenty years ago; it is now. She is a child and an adult—a montage, a vintage postcard.

I go back to my iGlass, fiddle with the shading settings until I find something resembling a linen postcard. I rerun the video with the new hyper-bright, watercolor images. My manipulations have achieved a perfect vintage filter. My beautiful daughter builds her fantasy sandcastle. She soothes me, lowers my blood pressure, brings me balance. Oh, for the ideal of vintage postcard reality. Oh, for an actuality of whimsy in a dream.

Mary Burke

Chapter 11
Uncanny Valley

The asphalt sky is paved with clouds, which occasionally split and allow the full moon to spotlight into view. Beneath the thatched roof of the Kicklighter chickee, LED lights blink and toasted marshmallows waft up from the grill.

Sleigh bells jingle-jangle down the path from the house. From under the chickee, five pit bulls emerge. The rest of us gather at the edge of the platform, pausing from our peppermint hot chocolates to watch a ruddy-hued, bespectacled, black-booted Santa figure amble down the path. Tobias-Santa, illuminated as he passes under Solar Tiki torches, pulls a red Radio Flyer wagon containing a big black bag. At "Santa's" shoulder, the tiny red dot of Sue, a popular recording and surveillance camera drone, bobs along like a

Paradis

disembodied Rudolph's nose. A sleigh-bell-jingling Tommy, dressed as Santa's elf, runs ahead toward our group.

Tobias-Santa lumbers into the clearing. "Y'all been good boys and girls?"

"Santa, we wouldn't do anything you wouldn't do!" Gary calls out.

"Well, I brought y'all gifts anyway!"

The dogs part around Tommy to encircle Tobias-Santa.

Tobias kicks at the dogs. "Down ya mangy mutts!" From the wagon, he picks up a cage of five terrified rabbits, unlatches the cage, and empties the rabbits into the midst of the salivating pit bulls. A couple rabbits land directly into the dogs' mouths, and the dogs, in a frenzy of joy, shake and eviscerate their prey. Amber and I retreat to safety behind the guys' backs. The grotesqueness of the Kicklighters seems to increase every time I see them. I wonder if this is some terrible Christmas gift, or if it's how the pit bulls are typically fed. Amber looks horrified, and I worry she will cry. My face is hot, my stomach tight with embarrassment and shame; these are my neighbors. Amber is going to be even more concerned about me living here now. Looking around Mike's arm, I see the surviving rabbits hopping high and haphazardly. They flee into the night, pursued by the less dominant members of the pack. Eenie and his mate trot off with their quarry in their mouths.

Little Tommy steps deftly around the puddle of entrails, doffs his elf hat, and bows low. This is Tobias's cue to reach once again into his pack. Prepared for any sort of horror, I duck back behind Mike, emerging gradually when the gifts that follow are less grisly. Elf Tommy distributes crossbows and quivers filled with bolts for all the kids, and fabrics for MaMa's iFashion pattern maker. Elias receives signed sports memorabilia. Richy is presented with a VR fantasy game, and Mindy a Japanese calligraphy set. Mike and Gary dance around like four-year-olds getting their first bicycle when Tobias-Santa reveals a bottle of forty-year-old Bordeaux. Are Amber and I the only ones mortified by the rabbit thing? I'm still looking for signs of the living ones in the shrubs. Tobias takes out a plastic, twenty-ounce baby bottle from his Santa sack and gives it to Little Elf Tommy, who reads aloud the attached tag. Tommy is now the proud daddy of a baby goat born this very afternoon. He appropriately christens the kid Noel.

Toby Too now trundles into view, riding atop an ATV. He stops in front of the chickee, gets off a blue Kawasaki Tiger, and hands me the starter and a plastic bag, which, I assume, contains the access codes for the warranty and owner's manual. "It's from all of us." Gary waves his arm between the Kicklighters, Mike, and himself. I'm frozen; the bunnies that were circling my thoughts have vanished in a puff of dust.

Amber pulls on my arm, forcing me to stand and carefully step down off the platform. My hands are shaking. I touch the ATV gently, to verify it's real, I suppose. "Thank you," I manage to mouth slowly as I pet it, like an animal I'm attempting to gain trust from. Amber and I circumambulate the Tiger. When we hear mounting applause, we look toward the platform. The applause is not for us but directed toward Tobias. Toby Too and MaMa gift him a heavy-weight fishing pole, reel, and lines. Amber manages to elbow me in the ribs just in time for us to grin for the Sue drone, which is right

Paradis

before Santa slips and, together with his fishing rod and reel, lands heavily in rabbit guts. My brain decides this is all too much, and I start laughing. I laugh until my eyes water and it is hard to breathe.

◆ ◆ ◆

Everyone spends the night at the Kicklighters'. Amber and I share the sewing room, which has been converted into a bedroom with a huge airbed and a lounge chair. Along one wall, fabrics—new ones on top—rest on the shelf next to the iFashion maker that MaMa uses to design her patterns. Next to that is MaMa's well-cared-for Singer treadle sewing machine and a wicker basket filled with sewing supplies, including a pincushion shaped like a tomato. Four of MaMa's quilts hang on the walls: a family tree quilt, one patterned with deer, bears, moose, and buffalo, and two traditional star quilts. Together with paneled walls and hardwood floors, the room feels soft and woodsy.

It is already one in the morning. I stand in my PJs before the room's plate-glass window. Amber is with Richy, playing his new VR game. I try not to think about what she might be up to. Bats flit by in the night. The lights on the chickee produce thin smudges of color. Now and then, sheet lighting above the clouds breaks through the night's viscosity.

My emotions whirl. I have been trying to sleep, but I keep seeing Tobias feeding the rabbits to his vicious dogs and then slipping on the guts in his dingy Santa robe. Instead of sugar plums, visions of dogfights, arrows loosing from backwoodsmen bows, and 911 calls for domestic disturbances dance before my eyes.

I feel vulnerable. As much as I try to deny it and act strong, under the surface looms a sedimentary fear. A deluge of emotion, apprehension, and self-doubt: Am I too weak, too small, too old, too alone? All of them feelings Mark's comfort would have easily dispelled. But Mark is gone. As much as I like to think of him existing here in the trees and the earth, it's a game of pretend. This night has heightened my longing for Mark; revealed in me a Grand Canyon of emotions worn down for years by the river Despair. Life told through layers of sedimentary rock, each telling their own depressing story. Mark killed by the Mountain. My functional senior citizen condo and my sweet St. Petersburg neighborhood swallowed by the waves. My daughter drifting away into a world of technology, reaching out for me. Should I float away with her? Amber wants me to return with her. Instead, I cling hard to this old world. If I were thirty years younger, maybe I would enjoy a career in making VR vintage postcards for the populace. Measuring success in creating moments of virtual happiness. Discovering secrets through the manipulation of digital worlds.

The door opens.

The lights are out in the sewing room, but I can see my daughter in the subdued lighting of the paneled hallway. Her iGlass dangles in her hand. She comes into the room and closes the door.

"I thought you'd be asleep," she says.

I grope for the lamp switch and sit down in the lounge chair.

Paradis

She sets her iGlass on the console table and sits down on the air mattress. Her hands move over the mattress, straightening the covers. Her eyes study the walls. "I hope this place doesn't have cameras," she says and goes on to describe Richy's room, which, along with tech gear, houses a kingsnake, tree frogs, and a lizard terrarium. "Reminded me of your biology classroom except it also opens into a large rec area."

She continues, "His VR space was top of the line. It could be subdivided into three smaller rooms by closing two wall panels. I told Richy I would start the install of his new game while he set up the room." She looks at me. "That's when I installed my custom software, which will modify his game. I told him the additional program was a special expansion, and he could launch both together to unlock content personalized specifically for him. Richy believed me one hundred percent." She bites her lip. "Then we donned haptic garb, and I brought out the Quench MEG headband accessories, one for him, one for me. I told him the headbands were brand new gear, meant to increase immersion." She sighs, sensing I'm not understanding. "The headbands are how the software knows what the player sees, or thinks they see. The software works on the idea that what we *see* is not always what is there. I showed him how to connect it to his iGlass. Mine wasn't actually enabled; multiplayer doesn't work yet."

She's rambling, and I'm still not following. What he really *sees*? I sit silently and stare at her face. Her eyebrows look exactly like Mark's when she's excited.

"Finally, the game starts up, and it's the title screen for his new fantasy game, *V.* Then, my additional software kicks in.

For a split second, I recognize the default ambiguous landscape, but quickly the world is transformed into what Richy wants to see." Her tone shifts, becoming more animated, like she's telling me about some grand vacation she went on. "This tech is so cool, we basically show some blurry shapes, the player thinks they see something, the MEG headband sends what the person thinks they see to the software, and then the software modifies the graphics to look like that. This feedback loop continues until the world feels perfect for the viewer, and the entire process takes only a few milliseconds. *Réalité Virtuelle!*"

"To make the subconscious conscious," I answer, my eyes widening. "So, what world did Richy create?"

"Vines sprouted, thickened, and spiraled around tropical tree trunks. The sky was red. There were cliffs full of yawning caverns. A carpet of algae flooded over an emerald river. Chirping birds gathered into great flocks and fled the scene." Her voice volume is increasing.

"Shh, quiet," I remind her.

"Oops." She covers her mouth and leans forward on the mattress. "Richy's avatar transformed into something akin to a ninja, and he was able to camouflage to match the evolving world with precision so perfect that only the glint of red sky on the blade of his katana gave away his presence. He started slicing through the thickening green vines." She mimics a slicing motion with her arms. "I was only playing as an observer role in his game. I figured I would be invisible, but when I glimpsed a reflection of myself in the river, I discovered that my character was a dragonfly!" She laughs. "A dragonfly! Richy is crazy creative!"

Paradis

She describes flitting upward, tree vines changing to writhing anacondas, shafts of lightning piercing the sky, cliff caves gaping like the maws of Hell. "This was all just a prelude to the antagonist avatar's entrance. As in our standard simulations, the game spawned a blurry humanoid, but quickly the feedback loop between what the player *sees* and what the computer *shows* morphs the ambiguous humanoid figure into someone from the player's life. Actually, it's just going to be whoever he's been thinking about at the moment, real or not. But it wasn't you, like I thought it would be. Instead, a giant Tobias took form. It was one of the most detailed characters I've ever seen the program make! I guess Tobias being a celebrity and all meant there were a lot of references to him in the large visual models our software uses when fine-tuning the graphics."

"Then what?" I whisper, leaning forward.

"They started to battle. Tobias-boss reached into the sky, grabbed a bolt of lightning, and hurled it toward us. I evaded the strike on a drift of wind like a bug evades a windshield." Amber is gesturing energetically. "Ninja-Richy back-flipped between the arcs of lightning with classic Neo-in-*The Matrix* agility and scored hits with a slew of ninja stars thrown toward his nemesis. Tobias-boss plucked them out one by one, his hot blood sizzling like acid as it dissolved the jungle foliage. The environment continued modifying. The water percolated. The atmosphere suffocated." Her description is so much more elaborate than I would have imagined.

"I maneuvered my dampened insect wings and oriented myself to watch the battle. Neo-ninja-Richy was doing awesome, but Tobias-boss rebounded from every hit, hardening and growing until he dominated." She pauses for dramatic effect. "The two struggled; Ninja-Richy's health meter dropped. With camouflage dissolving and energy ebbing, Tobias-boss was able to reach out and grab him by the throat, shaking him like a little boy in a Walmart ninja costume." I notice beads of sweat covering Amber's forehead. "Tobias-boss actually yells, 'You little piece of shit,' just like you described."

She pauses, running her hand across her brow. My heart is racing. I hand her my glass of water from the table. She takes a drink.

"Then, up came Richy's knee. He kicked his father squarely in the groin, and Tobias tumbled backward." She finishes the water and hands me the glass.

"Just when I thought the program could not offer any more surprises, Richy turned toward me, looked directly into my tiny compound eyes, and yelled, 'Why is he here?' Wind flew from his mouth and my dragonfly character was blown way back. The world morphed again. Only the two of them remaining, facing off upon a crystal-like platform in a blank fathomless world. I tried to glide back close to them to watch when—God, it's so hot in this room."

I am literally at the edge of my chair. "And?"

She rolls back her head and laughs nervously. "Oh, Tobias ate me. In a flash of sticky red, out came Tobias's tongue and swallowed me. Game over for me. I was so discombobulated that I had difficulty remembering how to disable the VR mode in my iGlass."

My mind races with questions. "Why was Richy's world so dark? Should a therapist be involved? Did you find out if he hacked my stuff?" I ask, my last question really too loud and a tad too shrill for so late at night.

Adamantly, she answers all three with a single "No."

I'm puzzled.

"There's more." She continues, "I remained in the room after my character's death. Richy's movements became less frantic, and he started talking out loud. Saying something like, 'I don't want to disappoint you.' Clearly, he was talking to his dad. 'I'm sorry I disappoint you.' Then more struggling and flailing from Richy. I crouched against the wall, hoping not to be a victim of stealth-blows and side-kicks." She laughs uneasily. "He grew quite assertive during the fight, kept demanding his dad send him up to Wisconsin. 'I hate it here!' he shouted. There were long pauses, which I assume was the Tobias character replying. Then 'Tommy's seen you hit Mom!' His words were so sudden and loud, they made me jump."

I gasp. "What then?"

"Well, these heart-to-heart conversations interspersed with crying and fighting continued for some time. But then suddenly, in real life, Richy grew quiet, lay down on the floor, and just went to sleep. It was the strangest thing."

"What did you do?"

"I came back here. I assume he just got super tired." She throws up her hands and turns to lie down on the air mattress. "He mentioned you, though. Said you were nice and wished Tobias treated him like you did. So whoever rifled with your device, I'm pretty sure it wasn't Richy."

I turn off the light and move to lie down next to her. "I wonder who hacked me, then."

Amber yawns and shifts in the bed. With a voice heavy with sleepiness, she mumbles, "These days, could be anyone."

The ceiling above is dark. I float in a glossy Gulf, surrounded by silvery fish and schools of stingrays. The sky overhead blue, dotted with white castles of clouds sifted by wind and broken apart. At some point, I hear Amber's breathing change, and only then do I fall asleep.

◆ ◆ ◆

The sun streams powerfully through the window. It's already 11 a.m. I have to call Amber's name several times to get her to wake up.

We repack our overnight bags and head down to the kitchen.

MaMa is sitting at the kitchen island. She wishes us a Merry Christmas and calls us sleepy heads. She expresses how glad she is we came for Christmas Eve. Her words bubble with too much enthusiasm. "Please, please, Addy, come again. I really wanna see more of ya. And Amber, you are a total delight!" She wants to whip us up some eggs and pancakes.

With a strain to my smile, I mumble, "Orange juice and coffee, please."

Amber claims to still be full from last night. She shoots me a look that asks why I am placing a drink order.

MaMa pours coffee and juice for both me and Amber.

"Merry Christmas! Thanks so much for your amazing hospitality," says Amber. "I'm sad to say we need to get back to feed the chickens and let the cat out."

Paradis

Tobias comes in from outside and plods his muddy shoes on the kitchen floor. He stares at Amber and me, and then looks askance at his wife. "Has Richy been down to breakfast?"

MaMa shakes her head.

Tobias twists his mouth.

"He is an amazing gamer," interjects Amber quickly. "You know there's a lot of money to be made in competitions."

Tobias's eyes are red and watery. It seems a little early for him to have hit the booze. "Koont sleep all night," he claims. "Went in dere dis morning, and the boy was sleepin' with all dat VR stuff on. Had to struggle with him to get the gear off, ya know."

MaMa's shaky hand pours a glass of orange juice for Tobias.

"I knew I shouldn't have let ya talk me into gettin' him dat goddamn game!" His words, directed at MaMa, seem strained like a raw nerve.

Too loudly, I repeat, "We ought to get going to check on the cat and release the chickens."

Amber scoots off her stool, grabs her overnight bag, and signals me with raised eyebrows over her iGlass.

MaMa's face falls. "Yous guys really don't need to leave so soon."

"We just can't wait any longer to try out our new Kawasaki!" exclaims Amber, hand on the doorknob.

I pause next to MaMa and promise we'll both be back before Amber leaves.

Once aboard the Kawasaki, I can't help but look back toward the house. Tobias stares through the kitchen window as he gulps down Amber's untouched glass of OJ.

Paradis

Chapter 12
A Keen Eye

[Soft electronic tone]

> *Chameleon 3D60 connected to Adeline Thorndyke's iGlass*
> *12/26/42, 7:20:43*
> *Recording Started*

Sea oats silhouetting against a golden ribbon of clouds at sunrise. A flock of skimmers scattering in disarray. South, an uncombed beach is freckled with shells. A turn inland and the island is mostly palms and pines. The sandy route to a farm, forming a thin parting in the island's greenness. Brilliant white sand marking the island's southern shore. From west to east, the beach curves until it narrows into an ever-thinning peninsula of mangroves protecting an aquamarine cove. Sandbars filled with giant magnolia blossoms. The magnolias hurling themselves into the sky, becoming scores of white pelicans with black-tipped wings. Pirouetting in the air before floating back down, becoming once again magnolia blossoms in a bowl of aquamarine.

◆ ◆ ◆

Mike, Gary, Amber, and I gasp out statements of delight as we take turns flying 3D60-style around the island, all while remaining inside the guys' house at Tierra del Fuego. They invited Amber and me for "the best vegetarian spaghetti this side of Issaquah." Even though they didn't uncork the forty-year-old Bordeaux, we had to agree that their boast was most likely true. According to Amber and seconded by me, only she could make vegetarian spaghetti to rival the meal we just ate. Amber marveled at Tierra del Fuego, wishing for more time to absorb all the artwork. She had the Chameleon take 3D60 video of their place and shared the glamour shots to Mike's and Gary's devices.

It's Amber's second time in the immersive island experience when she notices the aerocar. She pauses to magnify the focus and projects the zoomed-in image for us. "Look!" At first, I don't see it, but then I spot something under green camouflage netting on the Kicklighters' property. "Beneath the netting, it's an aerocar!"

"I want to see." Gary grabs toward the iGlass. After dodging his excited flail, Amber hands it over. Gary puts it on, makes some gestures in the air to increase the contrast and sharpness of the projected image. "Nice! Looks like an Osprey 300? New model, too!" He whistles. "Like I knew those Kicklighters had money, but these cars are out of this world pricey!"

Paradis

Amber retrieves her iGlass from Gary and pulls up a 3D spec sheet for the vehicle, reading the details aloud, "'Osprey hybrid with AI-controlled tilt rotors, five hundred horsepower, cruising speed two hundred miles per hour, distance five hundred miles before recharging.'"

"Good for a quick getaway," deduces Mike.

"Yup," agrees Amber. "They could get to Orlando so quick with that." She rotates her captured images of KickAss Farm, looking for anything else interesting. Somewhat disappointingly, our spying yields no other exciting findings beyond the Osprey car.

Amber shrugs. "I'll make a copy of the flight for everyone's devices." Amber works on her iGlass while Mike goes to the kitchen to make coffee for everyone. I follow Gary out to the porch and sit in the Barbie-pink chair. Gary pulls over the powder-blue chair and places a green table between us. He sits down and inquires if I'd be up for fishing on the south side of the island in a few days.

"Just say when," I answer, and he claps his hands excitedly. He says he'll verify when with Mike.

Amber joins us on the porch and pulls up an orange chair. The Chameleon, in its little bag, hangs around her neck. She pushes her iGlass up on her nose and announces that she's uploaded the video and shared the links with us.

Gary smiles approvingly. "Liam must be missing you," he says.

She taps her iGlass and remarks that Liam's here in the spirit of FaceTime, occupied with building the greenhouse in their backyard.

"How's life on the other coast?" Gary asks.

My daughter takes her iGlass from her face and sets it upon the table. She leans back in her chair, taking a moment to peer at the nature through the mesh of the screened-in porch. She answers pensively, commenting on how crowded it's getting. "Business is rocking; everyone is craving a cheap, virtual escape from the summer fires. Like skiing on mountains that entice and forebode."

I expected proverbial lemonade, a scripted explanation on how hapless people crave technologically-laced, ephemeral joy. But I have misread the depth of her thoughts. She is like a little bottle that I have cared for lovingly and cast out to sea, a bottle that has briefly floated back to me with a new message inside: "Everyone is so full of fear." She stares beyond the screen, her eyes focusing on nothing in particular. "There's a lot of work in creating virtual weddings, vacations, retirement villas. People yearn to explore and to learn, but they're too scared to leave their homes so they explore virtually, learn digitally." My daughter has voiced a truth; exposed the raw wound of current life and the need for someone to apply a salve.

We are silent in our thoughts when Mike comes out with the tray of coffees. He sets it down on the table, carries over a yellow chair, and tentatively asks, "What's wrong?"

"The way of the world," remarks Gary, gesturing emphatically.

Mike grunts and sits.

I choose a cup of coffee and add coconut milk. The smell of coffee, my daughter at my side, the warmth of friends, the sounds that drift through the screen enclosure, insects and birds singing thick, sultry Gershwin melodies. Can Amber capture this moment, make it virtual? Can ephemeral joy be virtually simulated?

"So, what's next on the agenda?" Mike asks.

"We're headed over to the Jefferys' tomorrow afternoon," I answer.

"Then back home for me," finishes Amber.

"Well, we are so glad you came for dinner, Amber!" Gary raises his coffee cup and adds with a chuckle, "Don't get many visitors over here."

◆ ◆ ◆

Amber and I ride down to the Kicklighters' the next morning. Mindy answers the door, and Toby Too rushes down the stairs to greet us.

"I was looking for your parents," I say. "I told MaMa we'd stop by before Amber leaves."

Little Tommy, coming in from outside with a basket of eggs, jostles my arm and answers, "Dere not here. Richy hurt his arm, and dey had to take him to da doctor."

Elias bounds down the stairs, coming to a sudden halt behind his brother. "Don't think it's anything serious," says Toby Too, "but they may be a while. Would y'all like breakfast?"

My daughter's serious glance confirms my reply. "We're good, tell your mom we came by."

As we ride away, I feel disheartened. I hope Tobias didn't hurt Richy.

Amber asks me to keep her posted. She feels things have been left unfinished.

Mary Burke

Afternoon comes quickly, and we are off to the marina. Under a merciless sun, Amber struggles with her rucksack. I'm several steps ahead, speculating nonstop about Richy's injury. "What do you think happened to Richy? Do you think Tobias hurt him? Could it have been related to the game? Tobias seemed really upset about that VR game. Could Tommy have seen Richy fighting with Tobias in the game? Is that possible? You were in the game; could Tommy or someone else have entered the game? What if Tobias knew Richy had been fighting a digital version of himself?" When Amber doesn't answer, I turn around to realize I've been dialoguing with the palmettos. "Amber?"

I spot her about twenty feet behind me, her rucksack abandoned on the trail. She is kneeling down, excavating the sand around a palmetto bush. She stands, scooping grime out of something. Smiling smugly, she returns, displaying the treasure she has found: a giant, impeccable horse conch.

I stare incredulously. I must have passed that shell a hundred times and never noticed it.

"So perfect for Cici!" she announces, uncapping her water bottle and streaming water over it.

I watch as she carefully wraps this prize in a towel, places it in her backpack, and joins up with me. I start thinking about all the secrets the island may hold, and suddenly the problems with Richy and being hacked seem so insignificant. When we get to the marina, we see the Kicklighters' yacht, the *Kickback,* still moored. "Their boat is still here," I ponder out loud.

"Maybe they took the flying car," Amber says.

We head swiftly over the glass-smooth waters of the Sound. Jerry meets us with the pickup, and by three o'clock, we are in

Paradis

the Jefferys' kitchen. Hilda is frying plantains gathered from trees down the street.

We fill our plates from a flavorful pot of greens, adding the fried plantains and slices of my jalapeño bread. In the living room, the two dogs are in their usual places, and Cici snacks on plantains and bread at the tray by her La-Z-Boy. I take the center couch cushion between Jerry and Hilda, and Amber sits in the other chair. She describes her island vacation, playing down the strangeness of our Christmas Eve, highlighting the gift of the ATV, and saying nothing of her exploits in *V*-land with Richy. "I hope no one minds," Amber continues, "but I reserved rooms at the Omni in Orlando for tomorrow. My plane is a redeye, and I'd rather not be the cause of anyone driving home in the dark."

"That sure is nice of you." Jerry smiles in response. "Will be a definite improvement over sleepin' in mah truck at a rest stop."

After we finish eating, Amber brings the shell from her sack to Cici in her La-Z-Boy. Cici puts on her glasses and examines it with great care. She is appreciative of the Florida state shell. "When this beast was alive," she confides to Amber, "it was as orange as the tips of your hair."

Amber kisses her on the cheek. "Could we be pen pals?" she asks.

Cici is excited by this idea of youth reaching out to age, and later in the evening, as we watch the terrible world news, Cici falls asleep in her chair with the skeleton of the mollusk on her lap.

Mary Burke

Chapter 13
An Excursion to Pelican Cove

Winter in Florida is like summer everywhere else. As a child, I felt the insinuation that Florida was a cheap knockoff compared to the other contiguous states. In the fall, teachers stapled colored leaves to classroom bulletin boards, and stores did the same in their display windows, displaying inorganically what we wouldn't experience in our climate. Winter was even worse, with snowmen glued to ice-blue construction paper. And everywhere, snow: plastic snow, machine-made snow. Why the adults just couldn't go with what was out there—rain, lightning, humming air conditioners, avocados, and cups of café con leche—was always beyond me. It is the tenth day of 2043, and as I stroll toward the marina with a fishing pole, a scoop net, and a

Paradis

tackle box, I must confess, all other states should be envious of today's perfect weather.

For the last two weeks, I've been suffering from Amber withdrawal. I've been making too much coffee, talking to her invisible presence, and checking compulsively on the eroding sandcastle. She sent me photos of fireworks augmented with foliage and fish from the New Year's show at the Space Needle. I replied with pitch-black photos taken from the porch. Other than some Kicklighter moxie banging from the south end of the island, New Year's passed here with only the sounds of crickets.

Gary and Mike are already at the marina, untying a confusing number of lines from their boat, when I arrive. I stow my fishing equipment on board and lather up with sunblock. In the communal marina storage shed, I get out the cast net, which Tobias's kids had stored in good condition. A couple casts yield bait fish, which I release into a plastic bucket half-filled with bayou water. By the time I clean the net and double it over a fence to dry, Mike and Gary's catamaran, the *MG-Cat,* is seaworthy.

As the wind catches the mainsail, we set out heading south toward Pelican Cove. I sprawl on the bouncing deck and watch various seabirds soar in the invisible wind currents overhead. The breeze from the Gulf, coupled with the warmth of the sun, feels incredible. This is the first day I have "taken off" since Amber left. Each morning these past couple weeks, I assiduously tended to the garden, which paid off in greens and root vegetables so thick and luscious I could skip Joey Pelagro's for the month of January. The fruits of wild oranges and lemons were baked into breads or bottled and preserved.

Maggie was plucked and simmered into chicken noodle soup. The new girls were named ShawnRee Too, Esmeralda, and Maggie Too. Amber laughed at the names and was happy I used her Esmeralda suggestion. I even had a brief but strange visit to the Kicklighters'. I brought soup and bread for an ailing Richy but never actually saw him. In fact, I didn't even make it very far past the farm gate. MaMa met me just beyond the entrance. "Oh yes, thank you," she said. "What a sweetie you are. And—yes, yes, he's fine. Hurt his arm. Much better now. See ya in around a week over by the guys' place?" And that was that. I handed over the soup and bread and turned the Tiger around. Their little security drone escorted me out the gate.

Back at the Wedgie, I took on a new hobby of palmetto frond weaving like a New Year's resolution. Chopped palmettos were transformed into a basket, a hat, a floor mat, a fan, and a wreath for the door. Palmetto placemats and cup koozies will be party favors for my February cookout, and my new crisp palmetto sandals can rival any squirted out by the best 3D printer. Also, inspired by MaMa's room of quilts, I placed an order for a 1950s Singer Class 99 sewing machine for delivery to Joey Pelagro's warehouse.

I feel a shift in the catamaran as Mike and Gary lower the mainsail and drop anchor. I sit up and see Pelican Cove. Over the mainland, clouds are puffing up like popcorn. Gary checks the weather report using the catamaran's VSAT. Nothing unusual, just the possibility of a late afternoon thunderstorm. We bait and drop our lines, watching the fish skip around our lines for a half hour before we hear a fishing skiff motor

Paradis

moving toward us from the south. Rocking in the waves, the boat stops alongside us.

A wiry, middle-aged man with deep brown skin and a strong brow balances atop a cooler near the bow, and a weathered white woman with long gray dreads tucked under a cap sits at the stern with her hand on the throttle of the outboard motor. The man introduces himself as Miguel; his friend is Fiona. "We heard sheepshead bitin' by the old Snug Harbor pier, we're headed that way."

I ask about Pelican Cove.

At first my question baffles the man, but then comprehension dawns on his face. "Boatswain's Cove?" He jabs a thumb in the direction of the inlet. "Pelican Cove is a better name. You all from Snug Harbor?" His accent is thick, but familiar. Cuban, I postulate.

Gary responds with a long something in Spanish. Both men laugh. I'm embarrassed that after living in Florida for so long I could only make out the words *casa* and *isla*.

Miguel's massive eyebrows rise in surprise. "So you all are from the island? I didn't know anyone was living there."

He continues to let us know they're from right down south, somewhere called Holiday-in-the-Hammock. Once our pleasantries conclude, we wish them good fishing fortunes, and Fiona wishes us God's peace and makes a V with her fingers. She throttles up the outboard, and the two are soon rocking onward in the direction of the dilapidated pier.

After another fishless hour, we reach a decision and motor on to Boatswain's Cove, henceforth designated Pelican Cove (a unanimously better name). We drop anchor again, taking time to marvel at the hundreds of white-feathered, yellow-beaked birds. They have a well-practiced synchrony, their webbed feet line-dancing on the sandbars. In the water, they operate like a fishing fleet with small fish entering into their pouched mouths. They swallow just enough; no trawling, no waste.

We realize we have anchored over a school of drum, and in short order, we are frying three of them in a cast-iron skillet on the boat's small propane stove. We mop our plates with lemon bread. In the early afternoon, we snorkel and discover tiny seahorses with tails clutched around the stalks of shallow seagrasses. By 2:30, we have the lines back in the water and our lips around white wine and Bacardi Gold. We are silly from the sun and drink. The drum have taken their leave, but Gary isn't ready to call it a day.

"Let's sail to the Gulf side and check out the flying car!" Gary's mischievous smile is on full display, and his enthusiasm is infectious. He has us all snickering at this idea. "I've always wanted to be up close with an Osprey, Mike can take my picture!"

"I don't know," I say apprehensively, "it's on Kicklighter property."

"Half the island is Kicklighter property!" Gary scoffs. "They'll never even know we were there."

"We'll be super sneaky," Mike adds, laughing.

Gary, Mike, and the Bacardi are convincing, and I find myself agreeing. "Okay, but we have to be covert, like secret agents."

Everyone laughs, and Gary pulls up the anchor. Mike starts to hoist the mainsail, but then he gasps. "Oh no! I didn't bring

Paradis

my metal detector! We are totally going to walk right over the Paradis buried treasure!"

Once again, we burst into laughter as the boat sails toward the island's southernmost point.

Sedated by rum and sun, I fall asleep on one of the couches inside the cabin. Deep-throated mating calls of alligators ripple the night waters, their eyes shining like headlights. The Eye's rim crusty with a dirty-green infestation of algae, hydrilla, and water lettuce. The plants sway with gators crawling out, ancient as dinosaurs fossilized and mounted in museums. Choking back a cry, I awake and expel a mouthful of soured Bacardi onto the couch. I clean up my mess and look out the window. It's overcast, and the boat rocks in three-to-five-foot waves. I hear Mike's voice. "The dinghy is ready." I have a passing thought to remain on board, but I don't want the guys to think of me as cowardly. Plus, walking on level ground is sounding really nice about now.

We row through the chop and beach the dinghy. Mike locates KickAss Farm with the GPS on his microLens, and we quickly find the road leading inland. At a half-mile down the road, Mike steps off and turns south into a palmetto patch. Gary and I follow. Soon, we spy a clump beneath a tangle of kudzu-green netting. Although it is not far off the road, it would have been easy to miss.

"There are two cars under the netting!" I exclaim, my voice louder than it needs to be. So much for being discreet.

"Man, those Kicklighters must be richer than I thought!" laughs Mike, also apparently forgoing any pretense of stealth.

Gary is closely examining the camouflaged cars when, out of nowhere, the little Kicklighter surveillance drone, Sue, appears hovering behind Mike's right shoulder. I point. He flinches, and we clumsily hightail it through the palmettos and down the road with the camera trailing behind. I expect to encounter the Armadillo kicking up sand on the road. However, when we reach the beach, we're greeted by Eenie and the rest of his pit bull gang. Eenie approaches silently with, I swear, a smirk on his face. His buddies flank him. Eenie's eyes glint dream-gator malicious. He sniffs. I freeze and try to look at him askance, anything so as not to raise his ire.

Gary decides to incite the dogs by waving a branch of driftwood. It would be funny if I wasn't so terrified. With Eenie's attention drawn to Gary, I inch toward the water. The dogs stand directly in the path of the dinghy, so my strategy is to reach the waves and swim for the catamaran. To make matters worse, I notice the clouds are hanging like an apocalyptic wall of Spanish moss. The *MG-Cat* is equipped with steps at the rear, so I think I'll be able to hoist myself aboard using the aluminum ladder we'd used to enter the dinghy.

One of Eenie's minions inches toward Gary, taking care to remain a safe distance from the arc of his swinging driftwood sword. The dog is pure muscle, his teeth bared, and his growl low. I take another tentative step toward the surf. The female behind Eenie sniffs the air. Eenie briefly shifts his gaze my way. I think if he so chooses, he could be at my throat before I could take a breath. But he seems to dismiss me. He turns his head slowly, still smirking—I'm sure of it—and I sense it's the signal to direct the pack fully toward Gary. Has Mike moved closer to Gary? Perhaps he hasn't moved at all.

Paradis

Water is lapping over my sneakers, the wind blowing salted spray. I shuffle sideways, crab-like, never taking my eyes off the dogs. Time seems almost still. Water reaches my knees. I fall into the waves and swim underwater in the direction of the boat. My shoes inhibit my swimming, and I shed them into the water. A gasp for air brings me a mouthful of saltwater. In the rolling surf, my sole purpose becomes to reach the catamaran without drowning. Back under the water. Up again. Fifty more feet to the boat? Saltwater in my eyes and in my throat. Twenty more feet to the stern? The boat seems to recede before me like a bad dream. The waves bounce me like a rubber duck and attempt to drown me like a lead weight. Underwater, my hand brushes the aluminum ladder hanging from one of the steps. In the rock of the waves, it's difficult to catch hold. Thoughts of a shattered jaw and broken teeth pass through my head. No choice but to keep up the effort, and finally, I manage to hoist myself aboard with only a scraped knee. On deck, I grasp the handrail and look out over the water. The mossy wall of clouds now touches the Gulf. The rain forms a wall. Thunder follows lightning. I look toward the beach. No Mike or Gary. No Eenie pack. A flattened dinghy abandoned on the beach. The eye of Sue winks dimly. Is that a cry? "Help!" coming from the green-gray chop. A wave smacks me in the face, nearly knocking me overboard. The wind brings a slanted downpour. I look again toward the beach—nothing now but that wall of gray rain.

A second weak cry is swallowed by wind and rain. "Addy!" In the water by the stern, Mike's head bobs a few feet from the ladder. Beside him, Gary's mouth spits water. Their two little heads are barely discernible between the peaks of the waves.

Mike has a hold on Gary's shirt. He's attempting to gain purchase with his other hand on the bouncing aluminum ladder. There's a life ring attached to the cabin wall. I throw it down to Mike, and he puts it on Gary. Mike manages to grab the bottom rung of the ladder. He gets Gary to the ladder. I reach down to help Gary up to the deck. He's dripping red salt water when I spot the nasty bite wounds on one of his calves. Mike climbs the ladder and crawls on deck just as a white bolt of lightning flashes and Armageddon-announcing thunder rumbles through our bodies. Mike pulls open the door, and we stumble over the threshold. Inside the cabin, I stare down at their feet. The two men are still wearing their shoes.

I help Mike get Gary to a couch in the cabin and lift his leg on a cushion. Mike goes for the first aid kit. I crouch by the armrest of the couch. Gary is understandably frenetic, his eyes are squeezed tight, and he is mumbling a prayer between gasps "...Santa María...ruega...por nosotros pecadores...fuck...en la hora de nuestra muerte...Amén." When he opens his bloodshot eyes, he immediately starts yelling, "Mike, Mike, everyone knows if you run from a dog, it's going to run after you! Mike!" He looks at me, his face one giant frown, and he grabs my hand. "Oh, Addy!" He sighs dramatically. "I was guarding Mike with my sword, and then he trips over the side of the dinghy and into the water." Gary looks away from me in the direction Mike has disappeared to and, in a somewhat louder voice, adds, "Mike is lucky he didn't break his neck. I wonder where the life vests were. Not in the dinghy, that's for sure! Mike! Mike!"

Gary continues his description of the incident, how he threw the driftwood at the closest dog and grabbed an oar. His

Paradis

plan was to push the dinghy off the beach, but then the dogs attacked, and he lost hold of the oar.

"Those dogs gnawed my leg like it was a turkey leg!"

For a moment I ponder this image, but he quickly continues with his story—how he scrambled over the side of the dinghy and into the water. That the dogs did not follow but instead consoled themselves with gnawing on the fabric side of the dinghy. The dinghy did not fare well.

Mike finally reappears with the first aid kit, his appearance equally disheveled and frantic. "If you hadn't suggested trespassing to look at a flying car—um, cars—we wouldn't be in such a pickle!"

Gary winces and squirms as Mike attempts to swab Betadine over his wounds. The rock of the waves, the stuffiness, and their senseless arguing bring back my wooziness. They continue yelling, and when I mention that I thought Gary would need stitches, he turns to me and screams, "It's your daughter's fault! She found the damn cars in the first place!"

My only comeback to this rude remark is in the form of bile washing up at the back of my throat. I release my hands from the couch's armrest and make my way toward the door. I need air. I get one hand on the door handle and the other to my mouth when the puke escapes my hand, refreshing the cabin with the aroma of soured Bacardi and fish.

I push open the door. The storm has evolved into a steady downpour, and the rain washing over me helps with the nausea. I stay there for a moment, holding fast to the door handle, staring into the gray. By the time I go back inside,

Mary Burke

Mike is cleaning my puke. He's brought over a plastic bowl. "Sorry," he says.

I nod miserably. My stomach starts roiling again, and I puke into the bowl. My head throbs. Mike waves his hand through the waft of stink and goes back to cleaning and bandaging Gary. Eventually, he brings over the Betadine and cloths for my scraped knee.

When I ask him when we are leaving, his answer is not to my liking. "We'd better stay anchored through the storm. We've got to get the dinghy back. I think we may be stuck out here till morning."

I moan. I barf. My head throbs.

"Stay hydrated," he advises, patting me on the shoulder and handing me water in a lidded cup.

Gary yells across the cabin, "Do you think those beasts of his have rabies?"

Mike walks over to him. "Nah, those dogs are in peak condition, and now, you have a story complete with battle scars. You'll be okay, Gary. I'll watch over you like a mother hen. Cluck, cluck."

"Oh, fuck you." If those words could be said with gratitude, they were, and Gary gives a sputter of a laugh. "I can just visualize that old coot chugging back a bottle of Hog's Breath while watching the surveillance video. Right now, while we're rolling around in these waves, he's slapping his knee and laughing at us."

"What do you think we should do?" I ask between dry heaves. I sip water, spit it out. Sip some more, force down a swallow.

"I feel like I should sue him over his damn pit bulls."

Paradis

Mike is applying pressure with his hands.

"We were trespassing," I mumble. I examine the yellow sludge in my container. "Should we message Tobias that we're sorry? Tell him we were just curious about the flying cars? Should we let him know my Chameleon was videoing the island and we only accidentally noticed the camouflage netting? We shouldn't have gone." My head aches. I think of my earlier dream, alligators crawling out of the slime. I barf and barf again.

I spend the night with my plastic bowl, and at some point, I fall asleep. When I awake, my bowl is upturned on the floor. The light of dawn is easing through the window. Gary is asleep with his leg still lifted on a couch cushion. I stagger up out of my chair and clean up the vomit from the overturned bowl, which smells bad enough to make my stomach take yet another heave-ho. God, I can't wait to get back home.

I open the door. Outside, the Gulf is calm, the pink sky dotted with white pelicans. Mike is swimming in shining waters with his hand wrapped around a line, towing the deflated dinghy and its oars.

When he is on deck, I help him hoist the thing aboard. The dogs did a job on it. "Are you going to Joey's this month?" he asks.

I tell him no, that my veggie garden is growing gangbusters. He points to the torn dinghy. "Don't think we can patch this, do you?"

I shake my head. "You've got the cookout coming next week. What should we say to the Kicklighters?"

"Addy, what's to say? They got the full livestream off Red Eye Sue. I'm going to see if we can get into the clinic tomorrow to have someone look at Gary's leg."

When we're back inside, Gary is awake with his red and swollen leg.

"You need help getting him to Joey's?" I ask. Truth is, the last thing I want to do tomorrow is go to Joey's, but I thought it neighborly to ask. In the growing light, Gary's leg looks worse.

"I think my mother hen can handle this," Gary says. "It looks worse than it feels, but thanks for asking."

Mike thinks for a moment. "Addy, you know what you could do? Do you mind bringing your boat up to the north end of the island?"

I assure them I will. They offer their ATV for me to ride back home. Mike will pick it up when he returns the skiff.

◆ ◆ ◆

Back on the beach by my homestead, I pause to study the crumbling walls of Amber's sandcastle—transformed from fantasy castle to ruins. At the house, the cat and chickens reproach me with clucks and howls. I feed them, let them run free, clean the coop, and make coffee. I sip the coffee slowly like a tonic, happy to be back on solid ground.

In the evening, I fire up the oven and put in a pan of white bread. My stomach still churns; my head still aches. I feel unease over our drunken tomfoolery—why did we care so much about some damn flying cars? I have to write something to the Kicklighters. While the bread bakes, I turn on the overhead lamp, sit at my table in the front room, and type out a brief email:

"Dear Tobias and MaMa,

Rude of me not to have at least asked. I hope I can regain your trust. I hope you and the children are alright. Give my best to Richy, hope his arm is better. Let me know if I can help.

Postscript: Fishing off Pelican (Boatswain's) Cove was crazy with drum."

The adult version of the note Richy had written. Complete with a vision of Tobias slamming his fist into his palm. I hit send.

After I return from taking my boat to the guys', I check to see if there is any response to my email, but there's nothing. Five minutes later, I check again. I continue my compulsive checking to no reprieve. I didn't tell Gary or Mike that I emailed Tobias. I'm ashamed by how bothered I feel. I'm ashamed by how intimidated Tobias makes me feel, like one of the little marsh rabbits, hiding, haunted by memories of vicious pit bulls. I think it prudent to give a wide berth to the beating bravado of this odd backwoodsman. Apologizing was the best course of action. But it doesn't shake this feeling, this adrenaline. This time, Eenie let this little marsh rabbit go free. I think of Gary's leg and shudder. I imagine injuries of a similar caliber to Richy's arm and shudder again.

Mary Burke

Chapter 14
Virtuosities

Everyone is gathered on the Tierra del Fuego patio or nearby for January's dinner. We lounge bloated in the aftermath of yellowtail with sweet potatoes and orange and lemon scones. Gary rests in his hammock with his wrapped-up leg. The doctor at the clinic prescribed antibiotics. Tobias and MaMa messaged them within a day to wish a speedy recovery. My email remains with no reply. The beach escapade pretends to be forgotten by all. Except Gary's leg.

Richy sits tipped back in a blue chair beneath the porch overhang. He did not partake in the yellowtail or sweet potatoes or any of my delicious scones. Sullen, with his arm in a sling, he doesn't stir at all. Gary, Mike, and I wish him a speedy recovery. His heavy-lidded eyes and slouched posture

Paradis

make me concerned. I feel responsible, like maybe Amber's modifications to his game are somehow to blame.

On my way back from the toilet, I run smack into Tobias's stomach. He reeks of Hog's Breath, hands me a beer, and holds another for himself.

"Addy, I gotta talk to ya real quick," he says.

I twist open the bottle, take a long sip, and walk with him toward the front of the house. My heart is beating fast. Does he want to talk about the dogs? Trespassing? Richy?

"I wanna let ya know we got ya email. Sorry we didn't reply, thought I'd see ya soon enough."

I cough, choking on the beer. Tobias continues, "I respect the person who has the decency to own up to somethin' when dey in the wrong."

I nod, feeling some respite. I stare in Gary's direction. "I understand the dogs were only protecting their property." But after saying the words, I feel ill. That isn't how I feel at all. I hate those dogs. I hate that I can even "trespass" on a deserted island. I hate that I'm so damn scared. I hate that Mark isn't here. My mind races between images of bunnies being devoured, Gary's leg dripping blood onto a boat deck, pit bulls snarling. A body under the ice. I take another gulp of beer.

"Eenie got dat critter sense." Tobias laughs. "Knows to defend his own."

I look down and mutter, "I won't be on your property again without permission. We were just curious about the cars." I feel sick, feeble saying those words.

Tobias's attitude seems light, however. He waves his hand in front of his face as if swatting no-see-ums. "Water under the bridge."

When we reach the rainbow steps, he climbs up a third of the way and plops down on the green step. He motions, and I take a seat beside him.

I'm reluctant to sit down. What else could he want from me?

He finishes his beer and wipes his mouth with the back of his hand. He sets the empty bottle alongside him on the step. "I wanna talk to ya 'bout Richy. Ya bein' a teacher and all, I thought ya might be able to offer some advice."

I'm curious now. "I did notice he seemed rather"—I want to pick my word carefully—"withdrawn." Downright catatonic would have been a more appropriate description.

"Did ya notice if he ate anythin'?"

I shake my head and frown. Can't say that he had.

He harrumphs loudly. "Been dat way since Christmas when I caught him sleepin' with dat goddamn headset on his face. It was like he koont come out of the game." His voice sounds concerned. "Ya know, dat game I bought him for Christmas, the one ya daughter played with him." He sighs. "Nothin' we did could get him to stop playin' the goddamn thing."

He narrows his eyes at the horizon. His words come out with a sharpness now. "Caused an upheaval in the whole family. Not eatin', not drinkin' or sleepin', woont take the thing off. Days passed, and I got real annoyed." He attempts to take a drink from his empty beer bottle, frowns, and places it back on the steps. "Went into his room in the middle of the night, ya know, to try to sneak it off, and Richy just starts fightin' me. Wrigglin' and kickin' at me, ya know. So I'm tryin' to lift it round his ears, and I feel an arc of electricity.

Paradis

The blasted thing shocked me! Goddamn!" I can see his forehead veins bulging. "Finally, got the damn thing off him, and Richy's howlin'." He quiets, then continues, "Geeze, I dunno what happened, must have hurt his arm strugglin' with me." Tobias turns away from me and his arm bumps his beer bottle, which bounces down the colorful steps and rolls a good way down the shell path before coming to a rest.

He leaps from his seat on the green step, fists the air, and blurts, "I've half a mind to sue dat fuckin' game company!" He strains to gain composure, sits back down, takes off his smudged glasses, and resmudges them by spitting on the lenses and rubbing them on his shirt. "His arm's gonna be fine," he mumbles. "MaMa and I flew him to the mainland. The doc said dere weren't no fracture. He relocated dat shoulder quick and easy." He looks for his missing beer, spotting it on the shell path. "But Richy's still not eatin', won't talk to anyone, just lies up in his room all day."

The twittering of birds is all that breaks through the uncomfortable silence that follows.

I'm not really sure what Tobias wants me to say. After an awkwardly long pause, I ask, "What can I do?"

My question only seems to annoy Tobias. He gets up, stomps down two or three steps, then turns around. "Goddamn Addy, I dunno, I was askin' you, with you bein' a teacher n' so."

Geez, I think, *I'm not a psychologist*. "Has he played the game anymore since then?" I probe.

"Nope, won't be playin' games anymore. Burned dat thing."

He turns and stomps back toward the patio.

Burned it. I assume the destruction of his game, in addition to the arm, is the root of Richy's silent treatment. I stand up and half run to catch him. "Tobias, what can I do?" I ask again. Then, to make sure Tobias is aware that helping sad boys wasn't my job as a teacher, I follow up with, "I was a biology teacher, so I'm just not sure how I can help Richy."

Tobias grabs a fresh beer, opens it, takes a sip, and looks me straight in the eyes. "I don't know what to make of ya. One moment I respect ya, old lady dat you are, comin' and livin' here. The next, you sneakin' round takin' pictures of my property, trespassin' with dose fairies, n' so."

I squint my eyes, studying him, making note of our drastic size difference. Is he trying to scare me?

"What can I do?"

He bites down on his whisker-fringed, chapped bottom lip and studies me hard. "For a start, he's not been feedin' his animals. Not like him at all. I want you to talk to him. Ya bein' a biology teacher and all, maybe you can help him wit' dat."

"Okay." I find I'm actually impressed that Tobias gave a suggestion for something I can help with. "I'll check in on the animals, talk to him when I do."

Tobias marches off. Maybe I *can* fix things. Help Richy somehow.

Richy is still seated in the blue chair, tilted back against the orange fence. I pull up a yellow chair and sit next to him.

Gary and Mike stare quizzically in our direction.

"Richy," I begin, "your dad said you haven't been feeding your animals, and that concerns me."

He doesn't respond.

Paradis

"I don't want to infringe upon your vow of silence, but I'm going to ask your dad if I can visit you tomorrow and make certain your animals get fed." I pause. "If they're still alive."

He stirs and, to my surprise, speaks. "My sister's been feeding them."

● ● ●

In the evening, sitting beneath the palms, detoxing from dinner, I could really use a visit from Thoreau. I am living among all this beautiful, wild nature, and yet I have not been able to escape society's dramas. *"An efficient and valuable man does what he can, whether the community pay him for it or not."* Easy for you to say, Thoreau, who—through the generosity of your chum Ralph Waldo—had the luxury of camping out in the woods for two years so you could tout self-reliance. I bet during your camping in the woods, you didn't accidentally cause the psychological torment and injury of a young boy because your tech-ridden, society-generated anxiety convinced you he had hacked your device and made it seem like a good idea for your daughter to create an addictive virtual experience to probe his brain and understand why. I grab a fistful of sand and throw it.

A twilight world is succumbing to darkness around me. In the distance, crickets start their songs. "Mark," I whisper, "are you here?" I search up and down the shore, squinting into the darkness. The flora around me morphs into amorphous blackness. I close my eyes, feel the breeze tickle my skin. I smell the salty air, allow it to fill my lungs. As I exhale, I try to imagine Mark is sitting beside me. Instead, my mind flashes with images of him under an ice bridge, flowing into nature. A sight I never saw, yet I can picture so perfectly. *"All good things are wild and free."*

◆ ◆ ◆

The following day I travel to the Kicklighters'. Mindy greets me at the door. She is wearing overall shorts layered over a tank top. Her light brown hair is pulled back into a high ponytail. Up close, her freckles make her look like a pointillist painting. Tobias, MaMa, and Toby Too are away, but she provides no explanation as to where they are. I explain my visit's purpose—to check in on Richy and his animals. She responds amiably, accompanying me up to Richy's room where she raps on the door. When there is no response, she pushes it open. Richy is curled into a ball on his bed, his feet tucked under his butt, his right arm cradled in his left, his eyes shut. Tinny music spews from the earbuds in his ears. He's wearing pajamas. Mindy shrugs and leaves the room.

Amber's descriptions of the room were understated. Vivariums fill the room. One holds an impressive four-foot kingsnake. Another contains a three-foot indigo. In a third, two slender green snakes intertwine like a caduceus around the twigs of a young bamboo. A gopher tortoise lodges in a sand-filled crate at the foot of his bed. Scribbled on a sticker on the side are a T and a 3. I wonder what it means. The tortoise appears stuck in the corner. I reach inside, pick it up, and reposition it toward the center of the box. I notice it's missing a portion of its front foot. The lettuce inside is brown and slimy. A shelf running the length of the plate-glass window at

Paradis

the northwestern exposure of his room holds a terrarium where brown and green anoles extend their dewlaps while lounging on a hollowed-out branch. I wonder if the anoles can see through the double glass into the piney woods framed by the window. Next to the lizard enclosure is a rattlesnake skin on a board and a row of skulls. Six skulls in total, all arranged as if looking out the window.

I pick up a sea turtle skull and visually compare its cranial shape to the human skull at the end of the row. I look over at Richy. His eyes are still closed, but I know he is awake. "I wasn't aware that you were such a budding naturalist," I say, turning back to the shelf and setting the skull back among the bird, opossum, and raccoon skulls. "I hope you got that human skull online." I force a chipperness into my voice. "You know, when I was a teacher, I had an entire human skeleton hanging in my classroom!" I look back at him to see if my comment has sparked any change to his expression, but nothing—not a twitch of his mouth nor a movement behind his eyelids.

I wander to the other side of his bed where shelving supports a vibrant colony of hermit crabs. They skitter up and down miniature planks in a tank cluttered with glossy shells, glass vials, and miniature Darth Vader and Stormtrooper helmets. The artificial sun of a heat lamp beams down upon them. A colossal terrarium filled with ferns, bromeliads, crickets, and tree frogs rests on a thick shelf positioned above his headboard. The frogs suction themselves against the glass walls. Inside their ecosystem, a misting machine thickens an expanse of slimy algae across the tank. I imagine them screaming small, inaudible tree frog screams. As I take a step backward, my sneakers brush a plastic container of crickets on the shadowed bedroom floor. When I look down, I see other containers filled with palmetto bugs and mice.

"This is quite something!" I announce, attempting to sound enthusiastic to hide my horror at the dirty cages. "Mindy's done a swell job keeping them fed, but from the look of things, everything really needs a cleaning." I wish I could take the whole menagerie—with the possible exception of the gopher tortoise with the missing foot—and dump them outside.

I take a seat at the edge of Richy's bed and attempt conversation. I ask about his music; he remains completely still. I sympathize over how drowsy his pain meds must be making him. I let him know my plan to clean his animal containers and remark with affected excitement about how ancient his animals are. "They've been living here way before the Tocobaga Indians, before the Spaniards, before the swamp and cracker folk!" He stirs not a muscle, continuing his wax figure repose.

I leave the room to go seek Mindy. Together we struggle to haul the frog container outside and transfer the frogs to an enclosed box. After we give the habitat a thorough scouring, we replant the interior with a fresh assortment of tree frog-friendly bromeliads, philodendrons, mother-in-law's tongues, and crotons gathered from the yard.

"How long has he been lying there like that?" I ask Mindy.

"Since Pa tossed his iGlass in the stove and shut down the VR room."

"Why do you think he did that?" I ask Mindy.

Paradis

"He woont stop playin' dat game. Didn't leave his room, refused to take the headset off." She shrugs. "It was gettin' a bit creepy."

"Has he done this before with a new game?" I probe. "I heard he plays games a lot."

"Nothin' like dis." She struggles to keep a plant from tipping over. "Must have been a really good game."

After returning the frogs to their renovated abode, we seek out Elias, who begrudgingly assists us with carrying the replanted environment up the stairs. We carefully reposition it above Richy's bed. Richy is just as we had left him.

I drop new crickets into the terrarium to be gobbled by the frogs. Elias leans over Richy and says loud enough to be heard above the music leaking from the earbuds, "You're a fucking asshole." On his way out, he takes care to slam the bedroom door. I wonder if that is just a standard teenage boy response or some behavior learned from Tobias.

I tell Mindy that if it's okay with her father, I'll return tomorrow to tackle the snake cages. She is clearly relieved by my offer to help.

Before I leave, I find that Tobias is back, loading two deer carcasses into a large outdoor freezer. He reports his plan to sell them outside Joey's tomorrow and asks how things went. I let him know the details and that I'll be by tomorrow.

He nods. "Dat's good, and the snakes will be better off for it." He motions toward the truck. "Ma and I goin' over by the mainland tomorrow, ya do ya best with the boy."

Mary Burke

◆ ◆ ◆

I call Amber when I return home. I decide it's best not to share the pit bull adventure with her; I don't want her to worry even more about me living here. Amber is standing at her kitchen counter, wiping down wild mushrooms. She responds immediately, "Hi Mom, Liam and I are alright. The storm hit north of here, near Everett. Really tragic. Last estimates were around three hundred dead in the tornadoes and mudslides."

Liam rinses rice and leans in for a wave.

I'm taken aback; I have no idea what storm she is talking about. "I didn't know," I say. Washington lies beyond my event horizon.

She scowls and pushes her iGlass up on her nose. "What's this?" she asks. At first, I think she's talking to me.

She picks up an odd-looking fungus.

Liam's back in the picture. "Coral of the northwest." He takes the colossal mushroom to clean and chop. To me, he says, "One of our friends went out foraging."

I mention I'm glad they didn't die in a mudslide and, for a moment, feel validated in my Paradis choice. But this feeling is quickly replaced by guilt and concern; it appears Washington is no safer than Florida.

Amber shrugs and puts on water to boil. "It's the way of things now."

I tell her about my talk with Tobias and my attempted meeting with Richy.

She listens and plucks apart garlic cloves. Liam chops shallots.

"Threw it into the fire, huh?" Amber comments.

Paradis

"Keep trying to talk to Richy," adds Liam. "It's a good thing. Gives him hope and helps him through the pain."

I watch him add the rice and set the pot to simmer.

"Mom, I was going to call you after dinner, but this is a good time."

"I already took the butter out." Liam motions toward a stick of butter.

"I'm looking for the wine. Mom, I emailed Cici, and she emailed back an album of old photos from Snug Harbor. Did you know she'll be ninety-four on February twenty-fourth?" In the background, I can hear bottles clinking. "For her birthday, I'm creating a special VR experience. I've been using her photos and other imagery from 1960s Snug Harbor I've found to train the Quench system. As much as possible, I want her to be able to step back into the past. I hope she won't find it too unsettling."

I'm surprised by her mention of Cici's birthday. I didn't even know it was coming. I hadn't ever thought to ask. Here is my daughter caring for a ninety-three-year-old lady she barely knows. February will be my turn hosting the eating party. Maybe the Jefferys could bring Cici to the island to celebrate?

"I didn't see any VR equipment at their house," I say aloud.

A mounting exuberance rings in her voice. "Can you believe that? I went ahead and droned over a new iGlass, haptic gloves, and a newly released Quench MEG headband to Joey Pelagro's." The last part she announces with an especially large smile. "It was easiest for me to send Cici the full iGlass setup ready with compatible software already downloaded. And with the headband release, I got a huge discount, so it wasn't a big deal." She concentrates on opening a wine bottle while she continues her chipper exposition. "So far I've gotten Main Street working. Well, I think so, anyways. It's using the Quench predictive feedback system, so it's tough for me to test since I wasn't exactly alive in 1962." She pours herself a glass of dark red wine and swirls the contents carefully. "But I think for Cici, it will be crazy realistic, full of details." She pauses to take a sip. "Actually, you should try it! What do you say? Take a stroll down Cici memory lane, circa 1962?"

I'm hesitant; I don't exactly follow how I could possibly relive Cici's life. "Cici memory lane?"

"Yep. It's easy, just think of Snug Harbor when you put on the headset. Oh, and you need to wear the headband. I left one at the house when I visited." She giggles softly. "I'm sending what I've got so far." She moves over to her computer. "Give it a few minutes to download, then go ahead and switch over to the VR extension on your iGlass. I'd really like your opinion."

I bite my lip. I'm not sure this is an appropriate gift for Cici—she isn't exactly the prime audience for today's VR technology. Regardless, I tell her I'll check it out and call back later to give my opinion. Unsure of what else to say, I return the focus back to Richy. "But what about the boy?"

"Too bad Tobias threw away the device," she replies.

Liam's voice materializes in the background. "Food is going to be done in two minutes."

We send dancing hug emojis and sign off our devices. I find myself craving Pacific Northwest mushrooms. Disappointingly, the kitchen shelf yields only a boring can of Joey Pelagro's cream of mushroom soup. After soup and a sandwich, I locate the headband my daughter secretly left next

Paradis

to the Chameleon, plug it into my iGlass, and put both on. I launch the executable labeled "Cici Snug Harbor draft," think about Snug Harbor, 1962, and find myself suddenly transported.

◆ ◆ ◆

Bright sunlight sparkles from the perfect blue sky above. I am sitting on a sidewalk bench on Snug Harbor's Main Street. On a twin bench facing me, a snappily dressed man in a brown suit reads a newspaper. He wears a fedora. The woman next to him—they seem not to be related—wears trousers and a tailored, button-down white shirt. A little girl in a white sailor dress holds shiny white shoes tightly in her hand. People dressed in sixties fashion stroll on the sidewalk. Clearly visible from my spot on the bench, the marquee of the Main Street Cinema advertises *The Innocents*, playing at 7:15 and 9:10 p.m.

I get up from my bench just as a bus pulls up to the curb. An accordion-type door opens, and the bus driver stares down the bus steps at me. It takes me a moment to realize he is waiting for me to board along with the trouser-clad lady, the little girl, and the newspaper man. Sheepishly, I step aside. They climb up the bus steps and drop coins into a metered machine.

The bus pulls away, and I decide to walk down the busy sidewalk. If I was wearing haptic tabs, I'm certain the bright sun would be warming my shoulders. At a newsstand in front of a building adorned with Doric columns, I pause to read the headlines on a copy of the *Snug Harbor Sentinel*: "West Side

Mary Burke

Story Wins Oscar," "President Kennedy and British Prime Minister Macmillan Agree on U.S. Resumption of Nuclear Tests," "World Satellite Ready for Launching."

"May I help you?" The voice comes from a man wearing dark glasses. The newspaper vendor is a blind man. I reach into the pocket of my pedal pushers and try to retrieve a coin purse, but without haptic gloves, I realize it's a lost cause. I inform the blind man I am just looking, feel a little stupid for my remark, and depart quickly down the street.

Many cars are parallel parked up and down the street: a black-and-white Chevy Impala, a baby-blue Thunderbird, a black Galaxy sedan, a yellow-finned Cadillac. At the curb, I gawk at the stoplights posted on street corners, the phone booth, the fire alarm call box, and the mailbox. A man sells bananas from a cart. Only bananas. A banana man. I can't help but hum Harry Belafonte lyrics. The light changes, and I merge with the crowd and cross the intersection.

At the opposite curb, a man is standing before a shiny aluminum cart. Hot dogs rotate on metal tubes. He uses tongs to place the dogs into buns and distributes them one by one to the people waiting in line. I stand in pure delight—a time-traveling tourist—watching people squirt ketchup and mustard and spoon pickle relish on their hot dogs. It is all very Norman Rockwell.

Hinson's Drug Store is the building at the corner. I am drawn to the store's plate-glass window where I notice my reflection. I look both like myself and someone else. Perhaps I'm a young Cici? I'm dressed in a white button-down shirt and tan pedal pushers. Pink rubber flip-flops on my feet and cat-eye glasses frame my face. Through the glass, the green

Paradis

counter is lined with chrome stools. The teenage boy behind the counter is scooping out ice cream delights. I clap my hands and grin like a six-year-old in a sixty-two-year-old body. I am soon inside, sitting on a green, padded stool at the counter.

"Ma'am, may I help you?" asks the boy.

"Banana split, please."

I swivel on my stool to take a look around the store. A girl with pigtails and a boy sporting a crew cut spin a rack of colorful comic books. I see shelves of hair products and a bonnet hair dryer, a rack of Hallmark Cards, a druggist counting pills, and a couple of giggling teens waiting for a photo booth to spit out a strip of black-and-white photos. Tucked into a corner, I spy a curious machine with the sign "TV tube tester." Swiveling back to face the restaurant counter, I watch a waitress scoop vanilla ice cream onto a cone and hand it through a sliding window to a black woman standing outside. I spot another sign: "Blacks Served, Carry Out Only, No Inside Sitting." An unpleasant reminder of the past.

My banana split arrives—three flavors of ice cream topped with pineapple and strawberry chunks, chocolate syrup, whipped cream with nuts, and a cherry on top. I have heard of such a marvel but have never indulged. Did the bananas come from the banana man on the street corner? With my six-year-old yearning in my sixty-two-year-old body, I attempt to lift my spoon to dig into the mixture and, of course, am sorely disappointed. Without haptic sensors, there is no way to spoon anything up; no ice cream to taste.

This realization pulls me from the imaginary world back to the present. I take off the iGlass and find myself back in my chair at my table. I check the time and discover I've been walking around old Main Street Snug Harbor for two full hours. My neck is stiff, and my eyes are tired from the virtual experience. I remove the software from my iGlass, power down the device, and go outside. The sun has fully set, so I sit on the steps in the moonlight, breathing in the night air, reacquainting myself with the here and now.

◆ ◆ ◆

The following day, I FaceTime Amber.

"So, what'd you think?" she asks immediately.

She's so full of young energy, I can't resist smiling. "You teased me with a banana split."

"What? Oh, automated simulation of olfactory nerves and taste buds are still in beta testing. But I sent Cici the oral haptic tabs we are working on. She'll be able to experience textures, temperatures, and some semblance of flavors, all calorie free."

"The past through an iGlass," I muse. "Were the people on the street from her past?"

"Yep, constructed from old high school yearbook photos, news clippings, any public records I could scrape up, and the photos she sent me, of course. For Cici, they should be even more detailed, especially if she remembers them." Amber is so chipper as she talks about the experience. "In theory, she should be able to interact with all the characters, too. The AI should understand anything she says and build the characters' responses based on information Cici provided, her memories of various people, and recordings I've gotten from that time."

Paradis

She pauses, the largest of smiles on her face. "So, Mom, do you think she'll like it?"

I hesitate, unsure of how I feel about my brief excursion into Amber's Snug Harbor virtuosity. It was so real. I cannot fathom what Cici will think. I don't want to diminish my daughter's clear enthusiasm, and I also don't want to admit how long I spent in the experience. I give what I decide is a measured response. "I think Cici will be entertained, and it'll jog old memories. It's looking really good so far. Keep working on it."

Amber's whole body seems to relax. "Well, hopefully I can expand the experience to a larger portion of the city and have it ready for Cici by her birthday." She runs her hand through her hair. "What's your plan for the day?" she asks.

"I'm going to clean Richy's snake cages this afternoon."

"Good luck! I hope he opens up this time. You were always good at helping your students feel at ease."

As if her words didn't tug enough on my heartstrings, she floods FaceTime with heart-hug emojis, and I counter with two hearts dancing together.

Chapter 15
Richy

Shortly after noon, I arrive at KickAss Farm. I find Richy sitting at the kitchen island, wearing yesterday's pajamas and spooning cornflakes with his left hand into his mouth. I am delighted to see him eating and mobile.

Mindy offers me cereal, but considering the time, I opt for only a glass of goat's milk. Once I empty the glass, I say to no one in particular, "I guess we'll clean those snake cages today."

I detect an almost imperceptible nod from Richy, accompanied by the faintest of smiles from Mindy.

"Your parents at Joey's today?" I ask.

"Yup!" replies Mindy.

Barefoot and still in pajamas, Richy follows Mindy and me as we haul the indigo snake vivarium down the stairs and outside to set it down next to a rain barrel. I reach into the

Paradis

cage for the black snake, but I stop short when Richy says, "I'll get him." I'm both shocked and relieved to hear his voice. Richy reaches down and uses his good hand to scoop up the snake. The animal curls around his arm and up his shoulder, where its tongue flicks out as if to kiss the boy's lips. I am sure I see the trace of a smile on Richy's face as he squats down and lets the snake slither away from him. It moves away quickly, but with the uncertainty of freedom, it hesitates atop a bed of pine needles a short distance away.

Richy turns toward his sister and me. His words are barely audible, but we are close enough to hear. "He wants to explore."

Mindy and I stare as Richy wanders over to the snake. He stoops down and runs his good hand along the snake's smooth skin. Once again, he turns to look at us. "His name is Angus."

"I'm glad you're talking today," I say with a burst of hope.

Richy turns away, his attention focused on the snake.

I'm watching him carefully when Mindy gently taps my shoulder. "We should clean da cage," she suggests.

We dive headfirst into sponging out the container, and when I look up next, I notice Richy is gone and my gut tightens. Angus is also missing.

Mindy, however, is unalarmed. "Day's so nice; he's probably gone down by da trail. I'm just glad to see him out of bed. Dad and Mom were really gettin' worried 'bout him."

She convinces me to return to cleaning the vivarium, but I can't keep from looking around; the tightness in my stomach remains. Something feels off. Meanwhile, Mindy talks and talks, her words like a small woodpecker knocking against my skull. As the vivarium's glass dries in the bright sunlight and

Mindy goes inside to get a couple filtered waters, I stroll down the trail and call Richy's name. The thickly-padded pine needles give no trace of his path. Mindy returns, and as we drink water, I express my concern, but again, she remains completely nonchalant, and I allow her to talk me into cleaning out the kingsnake container.

"If he isn't back by da time we finish cleanin', we'll go searchin'," Mindy says between sips of water. "He koont have gone far. It's an island, and he's not even wearin' shoes."

We finish with the kingsnake by three, and Richy has still not returned. We split up to go search for him. I follow the road down to the beach while Mindy enlists Tommy and Elias to help her search the farm. The four of us communicate our lack of progress via iGlasses and various makes of smartbands.

We regroup at 5 p.m. The parents and Toby Too haven't returned yet, and still no sign of Richy. Mindy, Tommy, and Elias look concerned, but I can't tell whether they are more worried about their brother being missing or about what their father's reaction will be when he gets home.

◆ ◆ ◆

Tobias's pleasure about their successful game sales fades quickly when he hears the news of Richy's disappearance. My personal hope of getting back to Addy's Wedgie before nightfall sets along with the sun.

Tobias is less angry than I expected; MaMa is more distraught. We take flashlights, spread out, and partner up. Mindy and I search the house, looking under beds, inside closets, and inside silly places like cupboards and drawers. I

Paradis

even check inside the refrigerator, twice. Toby Too and Tobias set out with Eenie in the truck. A couple hours later, we meet back up in the kitchen. They tell us they shined flashlights up into oak trees and plunged through palmettos while Eenie sniffed the beach. They even checked the compartments of the Ospreys. MaMa says she and the two younger boys searched the farm. They looked in the animal pens, in the garden, up in the branches of fruit trees, and under the chickee. The name Richy echoed in every limestone crevice.

We are still up at a quarter past midnight when Tommy runs into the kitchen. He has spotted Richy dragging himself down the main road. We all run out to meet him. MaMa is weeping. She brings him into the kitchen, holds his hands under the kitchen faucet, and cleans his face with a washcloth. She lifts him up on the island and washes his feet, which are now covered in blisters. Dirty and bedraggled, Richy is without his snake and acting sluggish like a zombie. I pour a glass of water and set it before him. Despair and puzzlement fill me. Where is that life that sparked in him just hours ago? What happened?

Tobias's face is scrunched, his palms clenched, the groove between his eyebrows now a heavy fold. He turns to me. "A lot of goddamn good ya did!" Spittle flies from his mouth.

"It wasn't her fault!" Mindy's small voice rises to defend me.

Richy, the sad boy, continues to sit with his chin to his chest.

I'm exhausted, emptied from the day's experience. "You need to calm down," I say to Tobias. "At least he spoke to me today. Said something like his snake's name was Angus, and it wanted to explore."

MaMa's tearstained face turns to me. "He spoke?"

"Then he wandered off, apparently," adds Tobias, bitterness in his tone.

Mindy once again defends me. "It wasn't Addy's fault. I told her we had to get the cages cleaned."

Tobias stares her down. Tears start from Mindy's eyes, and she runs from the room. With an exhausted grimace, Tobias rubs the back of his neck and glances at Toby Too. "Toby, get the truck for lit'le Addy."

Toby Too responds with a roll of his eyes, but he leaves to get the truck.

We stand in awkward silence. I stare in the direction of the running water, not exactly looking at it, but merely to avoid eye contact with Tobias or MaMa.

"I named him after you," a quiet voice says through the tension. The three of us jump in surprise and turn toward Richy. "My tortoise. Tobias 3—T-3." Richy's speaking. "Remember when we found him with the fishing line around his foot?"

"It was gangrene," Tobias responds, then steps closer and squats to be eye level with Richy on the counter. "We took him to the vet in Snug Harbor, and the limb had to be amputated."

"You wouldn't give up on him, Pa."

Tobias gives a little gasp. Even behind his glasses, it is difficult for him to hide the tears welling in his eyes. Richy notices, and it brings a straightening in his posture.

Paradis

He's talking. I breathe out everything I was holding in so tightly.

Richy relates the story of his day: how he sat on the dunes, how he watched the birds, how he's decided to free his animals. Well, except for T-3, but he thinks the three-footed tortoise will be happier in an outside pen.

Tobias clears his throat. "We'll get started on dat tomorrow." He holds Richy's head and repositions so their foreheads are touching.

Toby Too appears in the kitchen doorway. I sidestep, turn, and attempt a quiet exit, hoping not to interrupt this much-needed bonding moment.

But before I can get out of the room, Tobias turns toward me. "See ya tomorrow, Addy?"

Not *lit'le Addy*, just Addy. I smile and nod. With that small change, I can feel some of my fear toward Tobias melting. Progress.

Toby Too takes me home, and I navigate up the steps of my house by the truck's headlights. Dandelion winds precariously around my feet and demands to be fed. Inside the house, I turn on the light and fill the cat bowl. I pour myself a shot of Bacardi and reflect on the day. I attempt to quiet my brain, unravel the tangle of emotions, search for stillness. I breathe in the night air and listen as the crickets sing their songs, songs indifferent to lost little boys.

◆ ◆ ◆

Hermit crabs skitter down Richy's bound arm to freedom in a patch of mangroves. It's an afternoon where salt twinges the nostrils and a warm, moist breeze kisses the face. I've been reminiscing, like old people do, about my high school students, about camping, about trips with Mark, about St. Pete and Tacoma, about Amber—and hey, what does Richy want to be when he grows up?

"A world builder," he says with a sly grin, "like Amber."

I ponder his response. I think back to when Amber said she wanted to build worlds. Is the world we have no longer worth saving? Why must we build new ones, artificial reproductions? I think of tree frogs in elaborate terrariums and 1960s Snug Harbor. I cast my eyes toward the archways of mangroves where the parade of crabs taste the ground. He's talking, I remind myself; I can't miss this opportunity by becoming introspective. "What happened in the game?" I ask him.

He explains that he knew something was weird from the get-go, how the environment was different from the landscape he had seen in the trailers and in online chats. That he didn't understand how it was possible his father was the boss character, but that fighting with Tobias was fun. "It was like another dimension. I was talking and he was listening." He laughs, but there is a sadness in it. "Like when I told him what I wanted, he responded that he wanted that for me too." Richy looks back into his terrarium, searching for hidden hermit crabs. "I hated being on TV," he continues. "People mocked us, called us stupid country folk. And then we ran away to this stinking barrier island. I hate it here." He slumps his shoulders and turns to me. "Ms. Addy, do you still think I hacked your iGlass?"

A slow exhale from me. "Did you?"

Paradis

A shake of his head. "No. But I know who hacked my VR game"—he grins at me, a sly expression across his face—"and it was totally genius!"

◆ ◆ ◆

Seventeen days have passed since the release of Richy's bedroom menagerie. Since then, Richy's bedroom has received a deep cleaning, and Tobias has been focused on the father-son bonding activity of constructing an overly complicated tortoise pen. When the housewarming day arrives, I join the Kicklighter family in introducing T-3 to his new abode. I have the honor of carrying the critter in an Amazon box from Richy's bedroom down to a ten-by-fifteen-foot enclosure past the barn and against a cinderblock wall near the goat-grazing area. If I were a three-footed tortoise, I would be very content in this nicely landscaped pinewood-edged pen with a roomy house at one end and a burrow surrounded by rocks and asters. Prickly pear, palmettos, and various grasses fill the center. Richy sits in the enclosure next to a flagstone filled with a smorgasbord of Spanish moss, sedge, and plantains. Behind him is the entrance to a partly excavated burrow. Definitely an upgrade from T-3's previous accommodations.

The pine edging is about three feet high with overhangs at the corners to keep T-3 from escaping. I step into the pen and release the new resident, who immediately takes a poop on my shoe and then heads as rapidly as it can in the direction of Richy, or more accurately the flagstone with the food. I clean up my shoe and rest my rear a little distance from Tobias, who balances atop the pine log perimeter downing a Hog's Breath. "Whaddya think?" he asks. He is evidently feeling very smug.

"T-3 has moved into a tortoise mansion," I reply.

Tobias gives the tour, describing how he placed galvanized metal grating under the ground to prevent the tortoise from digging out. Overhead gates can be pulled over and locked into place to keep out the raccoons and the mutts. MaMa intends to place several potted plants along at least one of the sides of the enclosure. I add how I like that the concrete wall will provide shade in the heat of the afternoons.

"He wasn't much help buildin' dis thing," admits Tobias, quietly enough that Richy can't hear, "but we had some talks. He wants to go back to Wuh'scahsin and live with his brother. Dere's some high school up there dat specializes in..." He pauses to sigh loudly before finishing, "*Game development.*"

"That's a positive step," I say. "He's thinking about the future."

Tobias huffs. "Really, Addy? Makin' dem games? We live here. He needs to learn to live off the land."

MaMa redirects the subject, mentioning that day after tomorrow, she and Richy are flying up to Orlando to see the orthopedic; he should be ready to get out of the sling.

I am still watching Richy, who, at least for the moment, seems almost carefree as he sits in the midst of the tortoise garden.

"Well, it's a year before he's ready for high school," I say, "and we all know a lot can happen in a year."

Paradis

• • •

At the week's end, I visit the farm again. Richy is in the T-3 garden, and MaMa is planting greenery in large pots she is setting alongside the enclosure. I've brought peanut butter and marmalade sandwiches and iced tea. After washing up, the three of us sit atop the perimeter and munch and drink. Richy is out of his sling but wearing some sort of collar and cuff thing. The doctors' visits went well, they tell me.

I ask if they're free on the twenty-fourth for Cici's birthday. MaMa laughs. "Finally, we'll be able to enjoy dat chickee Tobias is always braggin' 'bout."

We watch T-3. MaMa takes a swig of tea and reveals they paid a visit to another doctor while in Orlando—a psychologist. "Everyone always sayin' I should leave him, but I don't wanna. I love him."

I'm amazed by her openness toward me. I had hoped early on we could be friends.

"Would he go for counseling?" I ask.

She sighs and gives a shrug, leaving the question unanswered.

Chapter 16
Ninety-four Rose and Fly Perspectives on Tuesday, February Twenty-fourth

I cannot sleep. The night is an oily black-and-white painting. I'm sweating, and from the window in the loft, the moon beckons like a streetlamp. Up and dressed, I head down to the beach. There it is cool enough to drape a towel over my shoulders. I shine my iGlass headlamp beam on the sand dollars, over to the driftwood, and then to the collapsed mound of sand and shells that was, at one time, Amber's carefully crafted sandcastle. I switch off the iGlass, remove it from my face, and fall back upon the sand. I listen to the palm

Paradis

fronds' rustling mixed with the waves. The stars illuminate infinity, and I belong to the landscape of the night.

◆ ◆ ◆

Earlier in the week, I went with the Jefferys to Joey Pelagro's. I waited in the postal line while Hilda shopped and Jerry took Cici to the clinic. Cici had been ailing with back pain and some stubborn abdominal upset.

A congenial, yellow-haired fellow, with sharp features and blue eyes, greeted me at the postal counter. He introduced himself as Gavyn and brought out a wooden case, unsnapped the latch, and revealed my sewing machine—majestic, sleek, and ebony. The word "Singer" scrolled across its arm like a golden tattoo. Gavyn confided that he and his wife make most of their five kids' clothing on such a machine. I signed the release. The friendly postal clerk even shared his contact information, telling me to give him a shout if I got lost in the instruction manual or overly mad at a snagged, jammed, or tangled thread. Together we lovingly placed the machine back into its case and set it on my wagon. I enjoyed its heavy, old-fashioned feel as I pulled my wagon over to Hilda in aisle 26-A.

Hilda informed me Cici had seen a clinician, and they were awaiting imaging and blood test results. Meanwhile, we continued up and down the aisles gathering ingredients for a strawberry cake with pink butter icing for Cici's birthday. The cost of strawberries was a staggering twenty-five dollars a quart, but we decided to split the cost. We even found wax candles in the numbers nine and four. I informed Hilda that

Amber's immersive 1960s Snug Harbor experience was complete, and she'd be attending Cici's party via FaceTime. Hilda agreed to bring over the VR gear when they came over for the party. Travel logistics were discussed on the way to the fabric aisle. The Jefferys would sail over to the island the night before with Mike and Gary and stay at their place. Toby Too would swing by to give Hilda and Cici a ride to the party, and the guys would follow in their ATVs. I was placing a bolt of tropical cotton fabric into my wagon when Hilda got a message from Jerry. We needed to come to the clinic right away.

Since I wasn't a family member, I had to remain in the waiting room while the Jefferys talked with the doctor. An hour and a half of Bible verses scrolled across the waiting room walls.

At last, the Jefferys emerged. I could tell by their faces that we would not be having lunch at Pelagro's Pizza.

Cici had been diagnosed with pancreatic cancer, which had metastasized to her liver. She also had diabetes, a byproduct of the disease. The diabetes drugs and hormone, enzyme, and nutritional supplements were available at Joey's, but they would need to go to Orlando for Cici to receive the nanoparticle-delivered chemo and gene-targeted therapies. The doctor on duty at Pelagro's, Doctor Melaro, gave them medications to treat the diabetes. He provided an IV bag and tubing if Cici should need fluids. Nutritional supplements could be purchased in aisle twenty-two. He wrote a referral for Doctor Angel Rodriquez, an oncologist at Florida Hospital in Orlando. The first available appointment was Friday, March 20.

Paradis

This news sent our emotions into a tailspin. However, Cici demanded we cheer up. "After all," she said, "I have the mother of all birthday parties to attend, and I won't have you all spoiling the mood."

● ● ●

Overhead, the night's oily sheen cedes to powered pastels. Black-and-white gulls cross the sky. When I sit up, I see a great blue heron balancing in the white wash of the shoreline. February twenty-fourth. Ninety-four years ago, Cici came out of the womb. Ninety-four years spun in the centrifuge of self.

● ● ●

I am icing Cici's cake when Toby Too drops off the Kicklighters at eleven and leaves to pick up Hilda and Cici. The kids set out the food on the picnic tables, and Tobias skewers Marla and Karen along with two chickens of their own to roast over the fire pit. MaMa joins me in the kitchen as I'm applying sugar roses to the cake. She takes a spoon and stirs a large pot of collards simmering on the stove.

"We brought a star quilt as a gift for Cici," she says as I center the candles on the cake. She asks if she can check out my new Singer. I set the cake on a shelf and lead her to the front room where the sewing machine is on the table. She sits down, places a swatch of cotton fabric under the foot, and practices zigzag stitches. She is behaving carefully and distant.

I pull up a chair and she gives me pointers on adjusting the thread.

There is a tension in the air, hovering between the casual sentences we share. Suddenly she pauses her stitching, her eyes dart, and her voice quiets to a serious tone. "Yesterday, Tobias found out about the therapist in Orlando. He wasn't happy."

"Oh?" I look around to verify we are alone.

"He interrupted a doc-chat. Richy was talkin' nonsense with the therapist, somethin' bout fightin' a giant Tobias alongside a dragonfly in a video game. Then sayin' he wants to study games at dat school in Wuh'scahsin. Ya know, it's still another year until high school. Anyway, Tobias comes in, wants to know what's goin' on." She pauses. Her hands drop to her lap. Her nails are pink; they look freshly painted. She examines them as she continues, "Well, he saw the therapist and panicked. He removed my iGlass, and when I looked at him, his face was pale, his eyes huge." She takes a deep breath. "Fear. I think he was afraid." She shifts her gaze to look straight at me. "Actually, I'm certain of it, and ya know what, Addy? I felt empowered."

Certainly, she must see how my eyes reflect my sympathy for her. I cannot imagine what it must be like to live with Tobias, with his overpowering physique and brash demeanor. "What did he do?" I ask in a hushed voice.

"Well, he just walked right out of the room. I think he just wanted to be anywhere else at dat very moment, ya know. And only after he left did Richy finish his chat with the therapist and remove his iGlass." She pauses and takes a deep breath. "Oh, Addy, I could see dem gears turning in dat little boy's head. 'I'm goin' to Wuh'scahsin,' he said to me. And when I looked at his face, his expression was so different from

Paradis

Tobias's. Confidence and courage beamed from his precious lil' face."

She sighs. "But then last night, when Tobias and I were alone, it all came to a head. He was so angry, but Addy, dere was a fear underneath it. He left and went to sleep in the sewing room." She trembles slightly as tears brim in her eyes. "I don't wanna lose Tobias. I love him! I love dem all so much! I just want us to heal." With these words, she explodes into tears and collapses into my arms.

I'm flooded by a mixture of emotions. The news of Cici is still fresh in my mind, and now I'm sitting in this room being filled with pride, sympathy, and a whole menagerie of feelings. I gently hug MaMa and rub her back. I picture the shoreline in my mind: waves carrying in fresh sand and taking away the old, over and over, the circle of life.

I hear footsteps on the stairs. *Please*, I think, *please not Tobias*. The door swings open. Mike, Gary, and Jerry blunder into the house, inappropriately loud, chattering wildly about their ride down from Tierra del Fuego on the ATVs.

With one look at us, though, they instantly quiet. Their pose is almost comical. Gary stands holding a cane like Fred Astaire, Mike balances a sealed plastic bowl like a Buddhist offering, and Jerry stands with a black bag dangling from his hand, which so much resembles a bag of Rottweiler poop.

"Something the matter?" Gary dares to ask.

MaMa is still sobbing too hard to answer. I wipe my cheek with the back of my hand. I can't help but laugh a little at the inappropriateness of their timing.

From the bag, Jerry produces a napkin. MaMa takes the napkin and flees into the bathroom.

Their eyes follow her before snapping back to stare at me. Gary speaks first. "What happened?"

But before I can put together some kind of reply, MaMa returns, red-faced but with tears dabbed dry and mascara reapplied. She launches into an apology. "Addy and I had gotten to talkin' 'bout Richy. I'm just upset, so very sorry. Please don't mention dis to Tobias. I don't wanna spoil the party." She sniffs and gives another dab to her eyes with the crumpled napkin.

The guys stand like dying fish, mouths agape.

Jerry manages to mutter, "Okay."

Mike breaks some tension by lifting his offering bowl. He asks if he can use my mini-fridge.

I take it from him and walk into the kitchen as Gary follows. I give the pot of greens a stir, and Gary hovers with raised eyebrows that ask what is *really* going on. I respond with furrowed eyebrows that say to stop being nosy. "Today's Cici's day. Let's just leave it at that."

"The decorators have arrived!" Mike announces as I reenter the front room. "Can we borrow your ladder?"

"Under the house by the chicken coop," I answer.

I return to the kitchen and Gary has vanished. I fiddle with the stove dampers and set the collards aside. Once I hear the screen door close, I return to the front room and watch everyone through the screens. Mike and Jerry are taping turquoise paper to the tops of the two picnic tables in the chickee. MaMa and Gary follow behind to set out communally donated tableware.

I can hear Tobias down in the yard. He is shouting military-style commands to his boys. Richy distributes

Paradis

balloons for Tommy to hang from the rafters. Elias and Mindy tie the palm tree piñata to an oak branch. I watch Richy, his arm struggling a little in its apparatus. Richy knows it was Amber who modified his game, and he still wants to be a world builder like her. Amber, creator of worlds, builder of virtual experiences, harbinger of nightmares, heralder of hopes. I realize my lips have twisted into a grimace—an old lady's grimace, where the lines in the upper lip create miniature canyons leading into some great black abyss. Determined to turn the day around, I relax my jaw, take a deep breath, disconnect the Chameleon from its solar charger, and head outside. May as well go down and commit Cici's number ninety-four to the history books.

I set the Chameleon to hover in the chickee's rafters. Mike asks if my "sewing" table can be brought down to hold food platters. We head back upstairs. He's placing my Singer carefully on the floor when I remember all the palmetto party favors I made: placemats, cup holders, and napkin rings. While we transport the table and palmetto goodies down the stairs, Jerry makes the announcement, "Cici is just five minutes away!"

We hustle, setting out palmetto accessories and letting down the mosquito netting to keep out the flies. We set the dishes of food on the table. I check the Chameleon and am satisfied with the view. The scene could serve as a feature spread for *Better Homes and Gardens: The Off-Grid Scratch and Sniff Edition.* The colorful balloons and crêpe paper streamers perk up the rustic ambiance. A soft breeze ruffles the chickee fronds, and the scent of browning birds wafts up from the spit as the Armadillo roars into the yard. I hope for the best.

● ● ●

[Soft electronic tone]

> *Chameleon 3D60 connected to Adeline Thorndyke's iGlass*
> *02/24/43, 16:01:49*
> *Recording Started*

Rose-petal-pink shift dress, white pearls on a thin chest, rosebud earrings in pierced lobes, transparent plastic combs in gossamer hair. Rose-fairy godmother.
Her son plucks her carefully from the truck and leads her to sit at the head of the table.
The woman across from the hostess is wearing a fitted tee, saving a seat for her husband who tends the browning birds on the spit. Strands of hair slipping from a clip, roots the gray of Spanish moss. Shoulders slumping. Eyes red-rimmed.
A boy takes a place at the kids' table. His little brother chattering at his side. Eyes of hostess and boy meet.
She quickly shifts her gaze toward the food: rotisserie chickens hot with greens, cold bean salads, jalapeño breads, chips and jams and bottles of Sriracha sauce. The aroma entices. The hostess fills her hollow leg.
He is large, toting a Hog's Breath and wearing a tee a size too small bearing the motto for the times: *Your Neighbor*.
"What wisdom can you share?" an artist asks of the Rose.
"Appreciate the moment. Moments make the years."
"True, true," another artist comments, admiring the craftsmanship of the sunny day. "And what a moment we celebrate today!"

Paradis

"Richy'll be fine," says the bedraggled woman jabbing a bean with her fork.
Abuzzing.
The boy eats mechanically.
There is not much conversation, perhaps due to the hunger of the participants or the solemnness of the occasion.
Half the food remaining on the Rose's plate. Thin lipstick imprinting on a napkin.
Time flying.
Your Neighbor is up for a refill. He brings white lightnin' on a clear day.
One artist opts for a beer and brings another for his partner.
FaceTime latecomers: two young faces, pointed birthday party hats on their heads. They dress in tie-dye and sit upon a virtual beach. They toot "Happy Birthday" on kazoos. Two hyper-hounds harmonically howl. The FaceTime woman's hair tips resemble the flames of western forests. Her leg marks time. He's tall as a Ponderosa pine swaying with the beat.
9 and 4 candles flickering.
Tiny fly tracks in the icing.
Everyone belting out the song "Happy Birthday." Reflective. Carefree. Blow-away wishes. Slices of sugar-Rose. Godmother gifts: a star quilt, teas, and a tea steeper.
Icing-feet on the lens. Making tracks. Pink speckles. Flying away.
Drowning in a small clay cup. Her man.
The Rose is in her headset, haptic gloves, headband, and stick-on feedback tabs. A thumbs-up signal. For twenty minutes, walking in a dream-past, giggling, and speaking with invisible entities. Happy.
FaceTime woman clapping her hands under her chin.
The suspended multitude droning.
Reaching for white lightnin'.

Mary Burke

Two artists searching in a basket for the ripest strawberries.
The boy staring straight ahead as if he's made a decision.
Grateful Caretakers of the Rose smiling, lost in their past.
He's wobbling, gone off to pee in the woods.
She takes his cup. Pours in her own dose of lightnin'. Downs it in a single swallow. Returning the cup precisely to its place.
Fairy-Rose with headset off, hair slightly mussed, her voice soft as a petal. "Amber, a miracle indeed, but did you mean for me to commune with ghosts?"
"I want you to remember Snug Harbor when it was, you know, before—"
"I saw Ramona Krause leafing through *Tiger Beat* with Muriel at Hinson's Drug Store. Quite the character." A chuckling Rose nodding to past memories. "In high school, she 'borrowed' the keys to the principal's new blue Comet, parked it down the block from the school. Ha! Ha! She secretly returned the keys to his desk, but old man Carlisle, the principal, fell into a dither and called the police. They found his keys sitting right there in his desk. He never did figure out who did it." The Rose reminiscing. "She was real skillful that way; could steal a boy too, if a girl didn't watch out. I had forgotten about Ramona, but here she was, quite real again."
FaceTime man wrapping his arm around FaceTime woman. Tears pooling in her eyes. Any questions, she tells the Rose, if she only wants to chat, just a click away.
FaceTime couple on an imaginary beach towel, singing, "She's a jolly good fellow." Doggies jumping oddly in the ether before all disappears.
Kids smashing at the palm tree piñata with a cane. The boy doesn't join, he is walking into the woods.
The wilt of the Rose beginning.

Paradis

Family loading gifts into the truck. A general bustling, a gathering, and a cleaning.
She's reaching for the lightnin', drowning in a small clay cup.
The son plucking the Rose delicately, placing her into the front seat.
Bloated flies floating like dirigibles in heavy air.
The hostess reaches up, and the day goes dark.

◆ ◆ ◆

Dandi is getting a good scratch under his chin as MaMa and I sit at the scrubbed picnic table. "I think all went well," I say, half to myself and half to MaMa. "I'll get copies of the recording made for everyone."

Tobias joins us. The fire pit is clean, as are his hands and face. He seems weary or alcohol-sated. We sit and stare, and periodically, we swat at flies.

"Toby Too'll be back shortly," I say, mostly to myself.

Tommy comes up to us. "I can't find Richy."

"Not again," Tobias groans.

I'm ashamed to admit, but my first thought is to check the whereabouts of my iGlass, which has been left nakedly charging up in the loft. While they call for Richy, I slip up to the loft and find my iGlass resting undisturbed. Nothing appears amiss, but I have an impulse to hide it under the mattress. Instead, I take it with me.

When I go back downstairs, everyone is calling for Richy. MaMa, Tobias, and I pause to watch the video from the Chameleon in fast forward. We slow it down to watch when Richy leaves, I assume for a toilet break.

Tobias surveys the lengthening shadows. "Will be dark soon." He furrows his brows.

We hasten our search. Perhaps he went with Toby Too, we speculate, but when the Armadillo returns, we learn that is not the case. Suddenly we hear hollers from Tommy. Richy is down at the beach. We all look at each other and suddenly we are running. The scene we approach is no vintage postcard. Standing under the archway of the two palms, eclipsing the sun, the lumpy ruins of Amber's fantasy castle behind him, Richy holds a gun to his left temple—a small pistol, I presume the one he used to kill the rattlesnake.

Tobias lurches forward like a linebacker, tackling the boy and his healing shoulder. The gun fires. Toby Too is suddenly at the spot. He has the gun and dislodges the clip.

Toby Too is breathing heavily. "It was loaded—fully loaded!"

MaMa takes Richy, holds him like a broken boy. There is no blood. The bullet has gone somewhere, but not into Richy. They are kneeling in the lumpy mass which had been Amber's fantasy castle. MaMa is sobbing, as Richy writhes in pain and holds his shoulder. Tobias is on his knees and vomiting into the sand. The whole family gathers under the palm arch. Behind them, the sun is a glowing orange ball sinking into a navy sea. They form a composition for the likes of a Hieronymus Bosch family portrait.

MaMa's eyes flash angrily at Tobias. "Why did ya rush him?"

"It was the first thing dat came to mah head." There is vomit in his beard.

Tommy is crying high-pitched wails.

Paradis

Toby Too is now also holding Richy. "He couldn't have done it!" he shouts. "Not with his left hand." Even *his* voice, which is usually completely devoid of emotion, is bordering on hysteria. "He needs to go to a hospital. Now!"

Elias stands behind the group. He turns to study the drowning sun and asks if anyone thought to bring a light.

Mindy is the first to move. Together with Elias and Toby Too, they assist Richy to his feet. I fumble for the headlamp on my iGlass. The motion feels unnatural as I realize I have been completely still this entire time. The others light their devices as well. MaMa is trying to calm Tommy. He is now only whimpering. We start the walk back together. The light is feeble but enough to get us back to the homestead.

"What are you going to do?" I ask MaMa.

But it is Tobias who answers. "Take him by Orlando, tonight, to the hospital." His tread is heavy. He reeks of vomit. "Shit." The word is as soft as the final exhale of a dying man.

◆ ◆ ◆

Their taillights disappear into the darkness, and all that is left is my reflection staring back at me from the window. I fix a Bacardi and Coke as I FaceTime Amber. It goes to voicemail, but in a few minutes, she calls back.

I tell her everything. I feel numb as I recite the events. My mind loops receding waves and crumbing sandcastles. She wonders if Richy and Cici will be in the same hospital. She says she'll contact Florida Hospital, email cards, and send flowers. We linger long into the night, taking comfort in each other's voices. Together we cry. "The game was working," she says at some point. And then later, "If only there was more time. There is never enough time." I think about Mark.

Long after our conversation ends, I open the window and stare through the screen, pondering the passage of time. Waiting. Three shooting stars streak the darkness before I make the decision to climb up to the loft. But as I lie in bed, my brain is still busy, refusing to quiet down. Dismal thoughts spin and cascade like those awful flies that entered through the chickee's mosquito netting when we brought in the cake. Images piling one upon the other: Mark falling through the ice, Richy crushing the sandcastle, Tobias and MaMa spinning like Mad Hatters in small clay cups, and Cici floating ghostlike through the streets of old-time Snug Harbor. And behind these images rises the suffocating tide, swallowing the remains of Amber's sandcastle and slinking up the path, up the steps, and into my house, washing over my head until my whole world is swallowed by the sea.

Paradis

Spring

*To every thing there is a season, and a time to every purpose under the heaven:
A time to be born, and a time to die; a time to plant, a time to reap that which is planted;
A time to kill, and a time to heal; a time to break down, and a time to build up;
A time to weep, and a time to laugh; a time to mourn, and a time to dance;*

- Pete Seeger

Mary Burke

Chapter 17
Out like a Lion

I pull my skiff up onto Pineapple Way and wait for Jerry. I'm wearing long sleeves and my hat with the mosquito netting, even though the mosquitoes have buzzed elsewhere. I lift up the netting and drink from my water bottle. I've left my iGlass back at the Wedgie, but from the position of the sun in the puffy-clouded sky, I figure it must be near noon.

Around me, nature is busy cleaning up the neighborhood. Flocks of egrets wade about in the drowned yards and spear tiny fish. Marsh rabbits frolic amongst the tangle of wildflowers. Kudzu is replacing caved-in roofs.

Paradis

● ● ●

I never saw Richy again after the episode on the beach. That night, Tobias, MaMa, and Toby Too flew Richy to the Crisis Center at Florida Hospital in Orlando. After he was stabilized, arrangements were made to fly him to James's place in Wisconsin. MaMa shared James's phone number with me, and I left him this message: "Hello, Mr. Kicklighter. My name is Addy Thorndyke. I live on Paradis Island, and I'm a friend of Richy. I'm thinking about him. Please let him know he can call me if he ever wants to talk. Tell him I care." I half expected not to receive an answer from James, but he FaceTimed soon after. His appearance surprised me. He was Kicklighter, yet not—clean-shaven with short brown hair and large but soft, well-manicured hands—a businessman. He explained that Richy spent a week in the hospital but was out now and had an ongoing appointment with a psychiatrist. "Richy isn't available to talk," he said, "but I'll tell him ya called." I didn't push things with James. Instead, I followed up with an e-card full of teacher-type platitudes: "Remain positive; your whole life is before you." I still haven't received any reply from Richy. However, I figure James must have spoken with his dad because Tobias sent a text suggesting MaMa and I meet up to sew.

When I last FaceTimed with Amber, I asked her, "Do you think Richy will come back to the island?"

"No, Mom. I think he got just what he wanted," she replied.

When I visited MaMa, we sat together overlooking T-3 in his oasis. She told me about FaceTiming with Richy. "He misses everyone, and Tommy woont stop askin' us to visit Wuh'scahsin." Then she looked at me sternly. "James said someone called Child Protective Services."

I told her I didn't call CPS, and it's true; I hadn't. "It's probably just a procedure they have to follow in these situations."

She nodded. "We should get together to sew." Her voice was still, detached, with no emotion. Her eyes examined me with caution.

"Yes, soon," I replied.

◆ ◆ ◆

I scan the street. No sign of Jerry. This isn't like him at all. I decide to abandon the boat and walk to the house, keeping to the middle of the road, wary of reptiles. After a half-mile, I can hear the dogs. Jerry opens the front door as I'm walking up the driveway.

He looks up and down the road in confusion. "How'd you get here?"

Perplexed by his intense reaction, I tell him I walked.

"Walked?"

Gary stands behind him with Hilda and the two, now quieted, dogs. Gary had left the island a couple days ago; he volunteered to stay at the Jefferys' house and care for the dogs while they took Cici to the hospital in Orlando. Gary's moving without his cane these days; no hint to his recent leg injury obvious in his motions.

"Where's your iGlass?!" Gary asks dramatically. I shrug with a small smile. Gary very well knows I prefer traveling without my iGlass and I half expect a laugh from him, but instead his tone is serious. "You're so stubborn, you don't even know what's going on, do you?" My smile fades as curiosity and anxiety coalesce into a queasy feeling.

"Come in. Come in." Jerry waves me inside impatiently.

I must have a very odd look on my face as I watch Jerry and Hilda quickly head back to the couch. Gary occupies the chair where I sat on my first visit. He is perched on the cushion's rim, leaning forward.

"I told you I was going to be here in the morning, and it must be past noon," I say to a room of people whose gazes are fixed on the projected images around the room.

Jerry hushes me. "We're watching the news." He beckons me to sit down, his motion suggesting I am to sit in Cici's La-Z-Boy. No one has looked away from the images since returning to their seats.

I take my place, and the dogs come over to sniff and lick my hands. I see a shotgun leaning against the front door frame. On the northern wall, there's a livestream showing three serious-looking men sitting around a table. Behind them is a map of the United States. The eastern region of the map is black.

"What's happened?" I ask.

"There's a blackout east of the Mississippi," answers Gary.

"...We have with us today Dr. Dharmendra Gavaskar, Professor of Computer Science and Electrical Engineering at Stanford University, and Mr. Reginald Petoskey, Director of FEMA. Gentlemen, welcome to Verizon Net. Dr. Gavaskar, could you explain to our viewers what has brought down the Eastern Grid?"

"Hi Jason, thanks for having me. You know, we've had these types of grid disruptions dating all the way back to 2014, but this outage affects fifteen states and Washington D.C. We're experiencing a cascading collapse of high-voltage transformers and their associated substations. Normally, this flow of electricity is regulated by computers with many system guards to prevent collapses of this scope."

"Could the cause of this outage be some sort of terrorist sabotage?"

"Well, Jason, the cause is as of yet undetermined."

"So, we are looking at malicious intent?"

"With so many devices woven into the Internet of Things, malware is a definite possibility. However, the eastern United States has experienced a migration of millions of people from the coastal cities. In just the past two years, Atlanta has experienced a two-hundred percent population growth, Baton Rouge's population has almost doubled, and Cincinnati and Nashville are up by a third. Even with a third of our power coming from green energy sources, such a growth in population density puts a lot of stress upon the grid."

"That's accurate. For instance, the Texas Grid has been overstressed by coastal flooding and from all the evacuees from Houston into Dallas. If we can have a close-up of the map, our viewers can see how electricity can be siphoned from the other grids. Will this cause rolling blackouts in the other grids?"

"There are growing indications that energy rationing could take place."

"Earlier today, I interviewed Morgan Weisbrod, the Director of the Federal Bureau of Investigation, and she assured us and the American people that the FBI and other

agencies are working diligently to determine the causes of the collapse of the Eastern Grid. Turning now to Mr. Petoskey, what can be done to get the grid up and running again?"

"Jason, it's a pleasure to be on your show this morning. In addition to drawing power from the other grids, the Defense Department is transporting one hundred SNRs—small nuclear reactors—into the urban areas where we still have significant population. This includes the New York City area, Washington D.C., Philadelphia, and Chicago, as well as cities mentioned by Dr. Gavaskar and the cities displayed on your map."

"Yes, I see, thank you."

"These small, safe reactors will be transported to these urban areas to provide electricity to get water treatment plants up and operating. Securing clean water is a primary objective. Hospitals, fire, and police stations will be another priority for emergency power."

"What about sewage?"

"Yes, getting water flowing is a priority."

"So what's your advice for people inside these cities and outside? What about us out in the west or in Texas? What do people need to be doing?"

"FEMA has always stressed the importance of having a disaster plan. At least seventy-two hours of emergency supplies on hand, including things like flashlights, potable water, canned food, and batteries. We recommend having a generator and a hand crank radio. Most importantly, people should not panic. Stay inside your homes, conserve your batteries, stay off your devices.

Mary Burke

"Particularly in rural areas, I know many people already have generators, solar power, satellite dishes, stockpiles of food and water. What I can assure you is that FEMA is working as part of a coordinated government effort. We're working very hard and very swiftly with the military, the National Guard, and the Army Corps of Engineers to open emergency shelters and set up tents. We are focused on bringing relief to those affected by this outage."

"And out here and in Texas, if you haven't prepared, now may be a good time—"

—*to call my daughter*, I think. When I look over at Jerry, he is busy fuming at his smartband. He looks up with a despondent face.

"I've been trying to get through to Cici's doctor all morning," he explains. "His office number is dead. His personal device is offline, and the hospital signal's busy. We don't know if we can still head out there tomorrow. All I can say is thank goodness for your daughter and that VR she made."

I ask if I may borrow his smartband to call said daughter.

Jerry shrugs and hands it over. Luckily, FaceTime with Amber comes up right away. On the tiny screen, Amber stands in her backyard wearing her iGlass, jeans, a woolly cap, and a heavy jacket lettered with "Live like the Mountain is out."

She sounds relieved to hear from me. "I've been trying to reach you all morning!" She can tell I've borrowed Jerry's smartband, and I am scolded yet again for not having my iGlass. She then continues to let me know they are okay and that Liam is learning how to hook up a generator to their

Paradis

power-node. She reports that rolling blackouts and brownouts are expected, nonessential businesses are closing, and the weather has been odd.

Liam squats on their backyard deck unpacking crates. He waves. Amber shifts the focus back to her face. "We're fine so far. As soon as we heard about the Eastern Grid, Liam contacted an associate in Canada, and we scheduled all this stuff to be droned in. Everything arrived right after the, uh, snowstorm." I squint at the tiny wristband screen where Amber displays a panorama of tall pines gleaming in a luminous patina of snow. "Between this snow and the mess with the Eastern Grid, getting inside a store here is insane! We waited two hours to get propane, and then they only let us buy enough for one twenty-pound tank." She moves the camera back to point at Liam who continues to unpack crates. "We got crates full of water and food, and we'll be able to use the portable generator to charge the batteries in the power-node."

"A transfer switch," Liam calls down from the deck. "Tom's coming over to show me how to connect it."

"So, soon you'll be off-grid too." I don't know how well my self-righteous smirk relays through Jerry's tiny device. "Aren't you cold? Shouldn't you be inside?"

I aim the camera of Jerry's smartband at the wall broadcast. The engineer guy is lamenting: *"Rebuilding the grid can take months, and even with all the alternative energy sources, rolling blackouts are expected. 3D printing will be used to reconstruct damaged hardware ranging from very tiny electronic components to huge transmission towers—"*

"—obviously, Mom," Amber cuts in. "Most of our transport vehicles are grid-powered and vulnerable to hacking. It's going to take some time to get resources to the right places." She pauses. "Did you ever get a chance to speak with Richy?"

I tilt the smartband to remind her I have company. She waves at Gary, Hilda, and Jerry. "Okay, later," she says. "Why are you in Cici's chair? Where is she? I was talking with her less than a week ago from that very chair. How is she feeling?"

Jerry leans into frame to answer. "Hello, Amber and Liam, stay warm! Glad you're okay so far. Cici's hanging on; she is literally stuck on that VR game you gave her. We're supposed to leave for Orlando tomorrow to start her cancer treatment, but now this mess happened, and I can't get through to the hospital."

"The hospital will have generators," informs Liam from his place on the deck.

"They aren't answering," repeats Jerry. "Look, I hate to break this off, but I've got to keep trying to get through."

"Wait. Before we sign off, can I at least say hello to Cici?"

Jerry points toward the hall leading to Cici's bedroom.

I walk over and knock softly on the door.

Jerry tells me to just go in. "She can't hear ya with her headphones on."

Inside her bedroom, Cici rests thinly on her bed beneath a sheet. She wears a yellow nightgown. A pale fluid enters her left arm via an IV tube. A second tube coils up under her sheet and drains fluid from her abdomen into a bucket-like container. The darkened iGlass shades her eyes; headphones cover her ears. A mere two weeks ago, she had been a rose—

Paradis

albeit a droopy rose—in the last wilted hours of the bloom before you have to admit it's over. Now, Cici's life flows out through plastic tubing into a bucket on the floor. I can't figure out how a hazardous trip to Orlando to receive cancer treatment in an overcrowded, electricity-deprived hospital is possibly going to help at this point.

Amber inhales softly. "Oh fuck. This is turning into a really shitty day."

Cici's right arm makes flittering gestures and her feet walk on unseen pathways. Her mouth utters unintelligible syllables to long-lost companions. Where is she? A teenager sharing casual secrets with girlfriends? Dancing at homecoming with her high school sweetheart?

I fear to touch her. Will I awake her from her dream? Will she crumble into pieces? I back away.

"Cici," Amber barely whispers. "Her hourglass has nearly spent its sands."

My eyes instantly fill. This awful scene of Cici slipping away makes me want to hug my daughter. "I love you," is all I choke out before I abruptly shut down FaceTime. Amber, Liam, and their snow-coated backyard disappear. I didn't want Amber to see me crying right now, but her virtual absence makes things worse. Only Cici remains, dying in a virtually-condensed past. I wipe my wet cheeks and quietly close the door. I give Jerry back his smartband, and I slump into Cici's chair. All the walls are displaying various advertisements. Jerry returns to his fruitless Orlando hospital calls. Gary messages with Mike. Hilda rattles away in the kitchen, and the dogs thump their tails against the terrazzo floor. On the wall to my left, the FEMA guy returns to grimly expound upon mandatory curfews and martial law.

"Let's ride to Joey Pelagro's," Jerry says. He thinks they may know how Orlando is holding up, and he wants to get supplies and stock up on medicine for Cici anyway.

I remind everyone about my boat still sitting out on the street, and quote Gary, "It could get stolen out there all by its lonesome."

Decisions are made. We first retrieve my boat and leave it in the driveway. Gary loads our wagons, and we pile into the truck. Before we depart, Hilda hands Jerry a small bag through the truck window.

"What's that?" Gary asks.

"Cash and jewelry. With the grid down, Joey's, if it's even open, probably won't be accepting digital withdrawals."

Gary winces.

My heart, stomach, and some other parts of my body sink.

Jerry assures us Joey Pelegro will accept IOUs; he knows where we all live, after all. Certainly, they'll have the grid up and running soon, I think.

A half-mile up the road, the truck comes to a full stop and rolls down the window on its own accord. Jerry curses as he tries to get it going again, but nothing seems to be working. While he's pressing buttons, kicking, and attempting to turn the wheel, a robot bearing the "Eye of God" insignia emerges from a pile of rubbish and rolls over to the open window. It takes our pictures, greets us by name, and asks where we are going.

Jerry explains that we're headed to Joey Pelagro's.

Paradis

The robot lets us know that Joey's is open today until 5 p.m., but payment must be in cash, precious metals, jewelry, or firearms.

Jerry angrily shakes his bag and sarcastically thanks the robot for the information. The robot, unable to decipher Jerry's emotional state, wishes us a blessed day and rolls away. Once the robot is out of view, the truck magically returns to its fully operational self.

Vehicle traffic to Joey's is surprisingly sparse. Most people we encounter are either on foot, toting backpacks and pulling carts, or piled three to a motorcycle. Jerry waves at a man walking with his wife and three children. Neighbors, of a sort, he claims. The truck pulls over, and they speak through the rolled-down window.

The man introduces himself as Ogden. He is burly with a large beard and thick black hair. His wife, introduced as Elaine, appears equally strong, with a serious face and brown hair pulled into a tight bun. They are both loaded like pack mules; their three kids line up behind them. The oldest boy struggles to maneuver a loaded, rusty shopping cart over the chunky asphalt. Ogden holds a shotgun in his arms and lets us know they got the last five-gallon container of water. "Ya'll better hurry; the shelves were emptying fast." He gives Jerry the name and address of a fellow named Miguel who sells fuel if we need any. Before we depart, he pats his firearm. "You'll be asked if you want to sell your gun. 'Sides that, they're only taking precious metal, jewelry, and cash." Jerry nods and thanks him for the info. Ogden and family wish the best to Cici and Hilda, and he tips his cap to me and Gary.

Mary Burke

Once we reach Joey's, the guard at the smiley face checkpoint offers Jerry five hundred dollars for the smartGlock. Jerry declines the offer and hands the gun to the guard to pick up on the way out. "You can change your mind once inside," remarks the guard, "and your account will be credited for five hundred dollars."

The Ford is able to park close to the warehouse. No flea market vendors, beggars, or buskers cluster in the lot; no drones buzz through the warehouse delivery windows. I think I can even hear the ventilators whirling on the roof.

By a quarter past three, Gary and I are pulling our wagons through the aisles while Jerry goes to wait at the clinic. The nearly bare shelves rise around us like columns in an industrial cathedral. The footsteps of the other shoppers echo in the aisles. Thoreau would have termed it "footsteps of quiet desperation." I grab a pack of candles from a shelf. "We should start lighting them," I suggest to Gary, "as votive candles."

Gary bows his head. "Have a blessed day," he whispers in my ear. I try to hold in a snicker, but it escapes anyway.

The lower shelves are basically empty. We locate a ladder and wheel it up and down the aisles. Sometimes it pays to be a sprightly old lady. I climb to a top shelf, which yields two twenty-pound bags of rice and ten restaurant-size cans of pork and beans. Gary heaves the stuff down to our wagons, and, now motivated, we keep wheeling the ladder, searching all the upper shelves. We find four sacks of dog food, fifty cans of cat food, two cans of tomato soup, an open box of spaghetti, chicken gravy; we are not keeping to our lists at all.

As we round the bend of the third aisle, we encounter a guard yelling at a teenage boy who is ten shelves high. The

Paradis

guard demands that he climb down now. The boy is waving packs of MREs. He defiantly flattens himself on the shelf and slithers to the edge. Then, agile as a superhero, the boy vaults up to the eleventh tier, where, with a broad smile, he extends his middle finger to the guard. In response, the guard touches a device on his arm, and a moment later, the boy rolls right over the edge. He hits the concrete floor with a solid crack, unlike the thud I expected. A second steely-faced guard comes up behind us. His gruff voice states, "Move to the next aisle." In our nervousness, we nearly wheel the ladder over our own feet and come close to colliding with a woman and man who pass by us carrying a stretcher.

Gary and I are mute after what we just witnessed. All our past exuberance extinguished; misplaced silliness gone. We act suitably somber for the environment as we continue scavenging alternate aisles. By aisle fifteen, in addition to our previous items, our wagons contain three car batteries, six rolls of duct tape, two boxes of waterproof matches, a duffle bag with a hole in it, a pair of hiking shoes in my size, two bags of socks, four shirts for Gary and Mike, and two small butane stoves.

Jerry is in good spirits when he meets up with us. He totes three boxes of meds containing insulin, enzymes, vitamins, IV fluids, sterile tubing, bandages, iodine, alcohol, and antibiotics. "The clinic contacted Florida Hospital," he says. "The hospital's got generators. Cici's chemo-gene therapy appointment with Dr. Rodriguez is still on for the day after tomorrow!"

Jerry surveys our collection of supplies and scowls. "What the hell you got in there, chicken gravy?"

Gary gestures broadly toward the vacant shelves. "Not much for the taking."

Cautiously, I mention the MREs in aisle three.

When we get to aisle three I keep looking for the tiniest blood smear, but the clean-up crew did a good job. We can't find any MREs either. I climb back down and tell the guys I want to visit the liquor aisle. Jerry grabs two twelve-packs of beer, Gary takes one bottle of grocery store red and one bottle of Florida grapefruit wine, and I pick up two bottles of Bacardi Gold.

We scrounge the aisles until 4:30 when the intercom tells us to go to the checkout. As we wait, we mourn the unopened pizza parlor and watch as workers sift through cash and other valuables. The clinic, the dentist, the barber, and the post depot are already closed. Paper and pencil checkout takes a while; people have forgotten how to total amounts without a computer, and appraising miscellaneous items proves complex. When it's our turn, Jerry lays five hundred and forty-two dollars on the counter. If the grid never comes back up, will I be able to repay him? Will another annuity check ever be credited to my bank account? Do I even have a bank account at all right now?

Outside in the parking lot, we silently load the truck. Jerry retrieves his gun at the checkpoint, and Gary returns it to the glove compartment. The pickup grumbles down the shattered road. In the rearview camera, the conjoined warehouses of Joey Pelagro's retreat into the distance. No one speaks. In my thoughts, the boy falls again from the eleventh tier. Was it some sort of crowd control mechanism on the guard's wrist? Microwave heat? Nerve paralyzing gas? Maybe the boy merely

Paradis

lost his balance. Did Gary record the boy's fall on his Lens? Right now, he isn't wearing it. He is staring out the passenger window. Is his artist's eye creating a sculpture from the black-eyed Susans blooming in a tangle of barbed-wire fencing or the tall purple flower rising from between the ribs of a dead dog? Is he pondering repercussions of the fall at Joey Pelagro's? At my other hip, Jerry stares vacantly ahead.

The Ford stops suddenly at a T-shaped intersection, and I see a sign tilting slightly in the muck. I read the famous Ecclesiastes/Pete Seeger verse scribbled on the sign: "To every thing there is a season and a time for every purpose under heaven, a time to be born and a time to die."

I think the sign influences Jerry's decision because he proclaims, "I've decided to go to Holiday-in-the-Hammock."

"I don't think we'll be back by dark," I caution.

"Sure we will." Jerry taps his smartband and resets the truck's GPS to the Holiday-in-the-Hammock address of the black marketer mentioned by Ogden.

Eight miles from the intersection, the plotted course ends, and we find ourselves in an off-road jumble of fruit trees. By the time we've reached this wild orchard, Gary and I have pretty much convinced ourselves that Miguel of Holiday-in-the-Hammock will be the same Miguel we met on our Pelican Cove fishing excursion. So, we are quite taken aback when Jerry drives the truck through the remains of a broken chain-link fence, and instead of the Miguel we remember, we encounter a robust black man with a short afro, standing with a shotgun in a field of marijuana.

"Damn!" exclaims Jerry.

The guard casually strides up to us and taps Jerry's window with the barrel of his semi-automatic shotgun.

Jerry puts down the window, apologizing for being so lost. "Um, looking for a Miguel; musta made some wrong turns, um..."

"What's your business?" growls the man with the shotgun.

Jerry goes on to explain about our need for fuel, rambling about Ogden's suggestion to come here. His tale is interspersed with numerous ums and nervous gulps. Around his fifth "um," the guard cuts him off. "Head over there." He points with the barrel of his gun toward a cluster of Australian pines about a hundred yards straight ahead.

The path to the pines consists of a pair of tire tracks alongside the tall marijuana plants. We drive past three men and a woman harvesting and loading plants into a school bus. When we reach the pines, we spy through the trees a Cracker-style house with a substantial brick chimney and a tin roof with lines of rust at its joints. The truck slowly winds between the trees, avoiding piles of corroding machine parts, crusty mason jars, sports-team tees, camping utensils, and everything else you'd find in a hoarder's dream.

Jerry pulls the truck up to the termite-eaten steps of the house's porch. Up on the porch, a man sits in a rocking chair. He could be Che Guevara's clone. The man makes a movement. At first, I think he's about to acknowledge us, but it is only to lift a large blunt to his mouth and puff out a sweet spiral of smoke.

We venture out of the truck. Jerry pauses at the rickety bottom step. He is practically holding his hands up. "Is Miguel here?" he sputters.

Paradis

At this moment, the house's duct-taped screen door opens. It's Miguel—the Miguel I remember. I imagine he can hear our little party's visceral sigh of relief.

Jerry steps up to the porch and clears his throat. "Uh—"

But before he can continue, Gary leaps past him with his hand out. "¡Qué bolá Miguel!"

Miguel offers a grand smile and shakes Gary's hand. They speak in Spanish energetically, Gary gesturing toward me, Jerry, and himself frequently. They speak much faster than my decades-old high school Spanish allows me to follow.

I make my way up to the porch, paying special attention to uneven boards and rusty nail heads. Once at the top, Miguel shakes my hand warmly. His smile has deflated all our tensions. "I remember you," he says. "You live on the island. I met you while out fishing with Fiona. I'm Miguel Fernandez, and this is Augustine." Miguel points toward the man now known as Augustine, who examines us with a narrow stare and a long drag from his blunt.

Gary explains that Joey Pelagro's was out of fuel and that we need propane, hydrogen, and kerosene. Jerry adds that his friend Ogden Young recommended coming here.

Miguel Fernandez says if we have cash, ammo, or some trade he is interested in, we can do business. Jerry informs him about his cash and the stuff in the truck bed. Miguel nods, and we follow him to the yard behind the house where two young women in peasant dresses are taking laundry from lines strung between kumquat and carambola trees. The women chat merrily and share hellos.

"Lots of customers today?" I probe.

Mary Burke

Miguel offers no reply. Silently, we continue toward a narrow pathway. We duck under the low branches of scrub oaks and walk up to a concrete shed with a corrugated-metal roof held down with more concrete blocks. When Miguel unlocks it, we see fuel tanks stacked one upon the other. We decide on two twenty-gallon tanks of butane and three gallons of kerosene. Miguel says he has a solar-powered hydrogen fueling station out by the pines not far from where Jerry parked his FC Ford. We expect astronomical prices, but Miguel simply wants to look at what we got from Joey's. Jerry summons the truck on his smartband, and Miguel calls over the women who had been collecting laundry. He introduces them as Leona and Water. As the three of them sort through our Joey's purchases, Fiona, who we had seen with Miguel on the fishing outing, appears. She strolls toward us from thick foliage with a line of fish in one hand and a toddler on her other hip. Her skirt is long and hippie-style. She whips her long dreads so they gather over one shoulder. She is braless; her boobs dangle beneath a T-shirt sporting the words "I'd rather be fishing."

"I remember you two; you live on the island, right?" She smiles at Gary and me and then continues to tell us Leona is her fraternal twin sister and the baby is Water's two-year-old daughter, Lilly.

I ask if they are selling the stuff in their shed. She says they are, so I ask about seeds for summer squashes, melons, and beans. "Oh, and any chicken feed, water, or vinegar for sale?"

Fiona asks if I'd hold Lilly. I take the girl and follow Fiona into the house. She sets the fish down on a long stainless-steel counter, opens a drawer, and hands me neatly labeled baggies

Paradis

filled with seeds. "I can't remember the last time we've had chicken feed," she remarks. "The chickens seem happy enough with all the garden scraps and insects lurking about in the ground." She smiles warmly. "Consider the seeds a gift."

I give Lilly back to her and stuff the baggies into my pockets. We go back outside. She rummages through a shed for an extra water filter, but she comes out shaking her head. I thank her for the seeds, and she gestures to the sun, which has dipped low enough to undercoat the clouds in pink. "Are you all gonna try getting back to Paradis tonight?" she inquires.

I shrug. I'm not even confident we will make it back to Jerry's house before nightfall, but I know he will want to get back to his wife and sick mother. Gary spies me and waves me over to join in on the negotiations with Miguel. The trade seems reasonable enough. We reach a unanimous agreement: one bag of rice, three cans of the pork and beans, the car batteries, the duct tape, the duffle bag, a portable stove, the chicken gravy, and the waterproof matches.

With the goods exchanged, Jerry is eager to leave immediately to get back to Hilda and Cici. The men quickly load the propane and kerosene onto the truck bed and then Jerry drives the truck around to the fueling station to get hydrogen. While he fuels, the school bus we saw earlier bounces in from the field.

The three people in the weedy school bus appear to be in their early twenties. The driver introduces himself as Jesus. The other two step off the bus and introduce themselves as Marcus and Selina. They are surprised we aren't staying. Jesus indicates that the bus is stacked full of party favors. In synchrony, Gary and I raise our eyebrows and cock our heads toward the school bus. However, Jerry is a spoil-sport and nixes any such idea. Once it's clear there will be no convincing him into staying, Fiona gathers the entire group into a circle. We join hands, and she leads a prayer for our safe journey home to Snug Harbor. "Heavenly Father, bless these travelers. Keep them safe on their immediate journey and all quests that follow. Let the wind direct them toward joy, the Earth shape a calm path, and the sky provide the light needed to find their way home."

The three of us get into the truck and wait while Fiona goes off to gather up a plate of homemade brownies for our journey home. By the time we are riding through the marijuana patch and waving goodbye to the guard, it is already twilight.

Jerry insists the Ford's GPS will get us home safely. Gary reaches for the brownie tin and offers me a square. He takes a bite, and a large smile fills his face. "Just as I guessed!" Brownie bits cake his teeth as he speaks. "Careful now, pot brownies can be pretty potent." I take a bite of my brownie.

We are four miles along the jungle-rotted road when the yellow warning light on the dash displays and the truck stops abruptly.

Jerry throws his hands into the air. "What now!"

The blinking yellow light on the dash indicates that the truck's sonar is registering a large, oblong object in the road directly in front of the truck. I take another bite of the very good THC-laced brownie and peer out the windshield at the shadowed landscape. I wonder if we are even on the right road; I don't recall a downed tree or anything else that could block the road on our way here.

Paradis

Jerry grabs a flashlight from the glove compartment, opens the door, and gets out of the truck. But almost immediately, he has leapt back into the truck.

"An alligator! It's just lying there!" he says, sounding exasperated.

I lick the pot chocolate from my fingers, my college days resurrected. Gary laughs and passes the tin to Jerry.

"Oh, what the hell?" says Jerry. He bites into one of the sticky squares.

We go easy on the brownies, waiting a half hour before sampling any more squares. The alligator eventually goes on his way, and we are off again. But the journey gets bogged down again another half-mile down the road. The GPS stops making any sense as it displays some roundabout route to Snug Harbor. Then suddenly, the Ecclesiastes sign pops into view directly ahead. Jerry jumps out of the truck with the flashlight as Gary nibbles another brownie. I begin feeling a tad lightheaded, and the men standing about in the road arguing about the malfunctioning GPS strikes me as wonderfully funny. Oh, and how beautiful is the stream of stars! I get out of the truck and hold Gary by the arm. "Remember the night when you and Mike had me over for dinner at Tierra del Fuego and we danced on the stars?"

Gary's response is to take me in his arms, and in front of the Ecclesiastes sign, we dance. As boldly as a rock star, I belt out the lyrics to Pete Seeger's "Turn! Turn! Turn!" Accompanied by moonlight thin as the treble string on a guitar, with stars pulsing in percussion, there is a time for every purpose under Heaven.

Jerry taps Gary on his shoulder, and it isn't to break into dance with me. "Snug Harbor's to the left," he proclaims. "The rebooted GPS concurs."

Gary and I dance our way back into the front seat, and the truck ambles on down the cracked and torn road. Walking would have been faster, except for the fact that we would have ended up as gator-date-night meat. The truck's headlights pick up the shine of gator eyes everywhere.

"They sure are proliferating," remarks Jerry.

I stare at the dash. "Does your truck's bar have anything to eat?"

This strikes Gary as funny. "What'd you have, Addy, one brownie?" He rolls down the window to better hear the gator songs.

"All I have is drinks," answers Jerry. "You want another Arnold Palmer?"

The truck's bar produces an Arnold Palmer. I hadn't really ordered one, per se, but I guess the truck complied with Jerry's suggestion. After a couple sips, my light-headedness turns to full-on nausea. I can't tell if it's from the brownie or from the stop-and-go ride. I slowly sip the drink and wish for a swift return to Jerry's place—ideally a teleportation device. I certainly don't want to be upchucking again in someone's vehicle. The truck continues its stopping for alligators to cross the road, and Gary, who has had a ridiculous number of brownies with seemingly little effect, is describing in detail his special relationship with Old Joe in The Eye. "Mike and I, we just love Old Joe. He's our protector from those wacky Kicklighters. You know what he is? He's our mascot! Old Joe is the official mascot of Tierra del Fuego!"

Paradis

During one of the numerous stops for herds of alligators to trek across wherever we are, Jerry decides to turn on the inside lights. He looks at me oddly. "Good God, Addy, you look positively green!"

Gary chortles loudly. "It must be the marijuana!"

Perfectly on cue, I spill the remainder of my drink onto his lap and barf all over the dashboard.

We attempt some clean-up and drive even more slowly. Gary opens the windows. I'm crying and apologizing. Gary actually eats another brownie as he stares out the open window until Jerry tires of swatting mosquitoes and insists Gary close it.

Finally, after midnight, we pull into Jerry's garage. An anxious Hilda greets us; curious dogs lick and sniff. Hilda hugs Jerry tightly, and I stumble out from the truck. Immediately, I make my way to the bathroom, where I splash cold water on my face and sit down on the toilet seat. I feel very sleepy, but slightly better. I return to the garage, where I clean the truck's seat with Hilda's help while the men unload the supplies. Jerry relates our adventure, and Hilda reports that Cici is the same—still plugged in. We leave the truck's doors open to air out and go inside the house. We lug suitcases into the kitchen, and alongside them, we stack the collection of Cici's medical supplies.

Jerry emphasizes that they have a long day ahead tomorrow. "We'd better catch some sleep. You and Gary can divvy up supplies in the morning." He yawns loudly and leaves to prepare for bed. Hilda makes a bed for me on the couch, and at quarter past one, I fall into dreamless sleep.

Mary Burke

I awake to two dogs licking my hands and to Jerry frying hoecakes in the kitchen. They smell amazing, and my stomach grumbles loudly. After I finish in the bathroom, I join everyone except Cici in the living room at their usual places. I sit on the center couch cushion between Jerry and Hilda. When I grab the last hoecake from the serving plate, Hilda gets up to fry a couple more for me and a couple for Cici. Jerry sighs and rubs his forehead. He describes his sleepless night. "All I could think about was yesterday. All I could worry about was today." He takes his plate to the sink. Gary swallows his final bite, collects his plate, and lines up the suitcases and the bags of medication in the garage. I pluck my two hoecakes off the griddle, shove them in my mouth, and follow Hilda into Cici's bedroom. I help Hilda with Cici while Gary and Jerry transport my boat to the water's edge.

Cici puts up a fuss as we disconnect her tubes and shut down her virtual reality. She manages two bites from a hoecake before adamantly refusing to go to Orlando. We have removed her from her other time and place, and she is angry at our interference. Jerry comes in to reason with his mom, but only when we are able to contact Amber via FaceTime does Cici calm down enough to let us help her to the truck. Amber keeps giving her FaceTime hugs. Once we get her strapped into the front seat of the truck between Jerry and Hilda, Gary and I have a chance to give our own hugs. Cici gives kisses to Amber and we shut down FaceTime. We say our goodbyes, recline her seat, and reconnect her to the virtual reality of her personal fiction.

Once the truck pulls out from the driveway, Gary goes in to leash the dogs. A soft breeze sweeps away mosquitoes. I pull

Paradis

my wagon behind me while Gary pauses periodically to let the dogs sniff and lunge. A mama gator guards her eggs in the long grasses of a choked drainage ditch.

As we walk, Gary and I rehash the strange events of the previous day, and I let him know he has my permission to eat the rest of the brownies. Once at my boat, while we switch off between holding the dogs and loading the skiff, I tell him the full story of Richy and his gun the night of Cici's birthday.

He is clearly shocked. "What the hell?"

"I didn't know if it was my place to tell. I thought MaMa would tell you, or you'd go over there and see Richy wasn't there."

"We knew you were going there to play with the tortoise, or sew, or something—" His voice trails off. He asks if I want help from Mike once I'm back at the marina. I tell him I'll be fine. He asks me to call him when I arrive home.

"I assume you're going to tell Mike about Richy?" I comment.

"Of course. But damn, Addy. We came here to get away from drama; feels like it followed us here. Should have known better. Trouble just keeps following you until you're dead, and then it goes on without you."

We hug tightly. He mentions Richy is probably better off in Wisconsin. "He'll be happier there."

I find it difficult to leave Gary, but eventually I get into my boat, and he pushes me off into the canal-street.

"I'll go over there to check on MaMa and the kids," he calls. "I promise not to say anything about what you told me." He smiles and waves.

I give a final wave back, grasp the oars, and head toward the park.

Out on the water, whitecaps unfurl. The cumulous clouds billow. Gulls and pelicans ride the thermals. At the marina, I tie my skiff to the dock, unload my supplies, and heave my wagon down the sandy road. I am happy to arrive at my front door. Dandi's busy pricking at the screen and scolding me. I explain that I have fifty cans of food for him, but as soon as I open the door, he scoots down the stairs and pauses only for a brief lick behind the shoulders before plunging into the woods.

I message Gary that I've safely arrived, then put away supplies, let the chickens out, and hoe the garden. A little later, I'm at my table, flexing and pointing my feet in my new shoes. Leftover rosemary bread softened with a shot of Bacardi serves as my dinner. The cluck of the chickens, the birds nesting for the night, and the chorus of the crickets bring unabridged contentment. Later I finally notice the blue flashing light on my iGlass. It reports multiple missed calls yesterday from Gary, Jerry, and Amber. There is also a new message from Amber—she wants to talk about Richy, but I am too tired.

♦ ♦ ♦

A fractal of blue divides behind my eyelids—I'm dreaming of laser light illuminating a thousand bobbing heads. The drummer's sticks tap in wild percussion. How odd that Tropical Heat Wave, the calypso-fusion-rap band enjoyed by Amber and Liam, should be performing on the island. The

Paradis

optical effects certainly impress—blue neon breakdancing across the top of tall slash pines, small bushes crowd-surfing over the heads of spectators. The calypso steel drum and dull strum of a bass guitar produce a mesmerizing counterpoint. A fog machine puffs out a damp mist. So curious is this fascinating spectacle—this Earth-vibrating shockwave that resonates through my bones, that pounds in mad rhythm on the solar shingles, and that causes the hairs on my forearm to stand ready for defense.

A huge bang—thunder! I blink open my eyes; I realize I have fallen asleep in my chair. At the perimeter of my yard, the top of a pine sparks green and yellow, its smoke wafting with invisible presence. Stiffly, I'm out of my chair and walking over to peer out the screen. The wind wets my face; the screen billows like a sail. The news had said nothing about a storm; the eastern blackout filled the headlines. Florida has essentially been dismissed as collateral damage of climate change.

I get the windows shut. The water of Snug Harbor Sound *had* been rough. I should have guessed a storm was blowing in from the Gulf. Now, the house sways like a rap rocker on stilts, and I'm sort of dancing, humming Tropical Heat Wave's "Gangsta Vibe," and none-too-gracefully stubbing my toe at the kitchen threshold. I find a candle, light the wick, and set it on the table. My first impulse is to call Amber, then Gary, Mike, even the Kicklighters, but the iGlass—well, I'm not surprised to find the communication function is dead. The satellite dish must be either full of water or off its stand completely.

I remember the chickens and the cat. I'd forgotten to unlock the cat door. I take the candle and find the flashlight

Mary Burke

on a kitchen shelf and unlatch the cat door. I open the back door and shine the flashlight into the rain. I can't get concert music out of my head. With a tight grasp on the handrail, I venture down a couple of steps. The flashlight gives only feeble illumination to a spotlight of moshing pines. The rain is a torrent. The steps sway; the pine bark smokes. The railing must have lost a nail, because it becomes loose, and down I come on the slick steps. Miraculously, I don't fall the ten or more feet to the ground. The flashlight, though, pitches right into the pit of night. I've slipped several steps, bruising my tailbone and banging the back of my head. At this point, any remnants of concert change into the reality of storm, and I determine the flashlight, the chickens, and the cat will need to fend for themselves until things clear. I crawl back inside, remove my soaking clothes, towel myself dry, and wrap up in a blanket. A couple Advil later with a cold cloth on the back of my head, I'm back at the table with the house still swaying, the storm blasting fireworks in a grand finale.

Many hours later, the day emerges like developing film. A soft drizzle and a ribbon of smoke from the pine create a white-mist smudge on a canvas of gray sky. The wild concert of storm moved onward to its next venue, leaving the landscape littered in its wake.

There is nothing to do but make cowboy coffee. Afterward, I very slowly proceed down the front stairs and release the damp chickens to scratch around under the house. They cluck with the glee of freedom. The night concert has brought lots of tiny bugs and worms to the surface. I let the chickens know they'd better get used to this insect diet because Joey Pelagro's is out of commercial chicken feed.

Paradis

By midday, patches of blue appear in the sky. The chickee fared remarkably—all fronds accounted for. I painfully pile up the smaller fallen branches and call for Dandelion. A little later, with a can of Campbell's tomato soup in my belly, I find the tweezers and get two splinters out of my right hand and pour Betadine over my palms. I hobble out to the garden, call again for Mr. Dandelion, and spend some time searching under debris and palmettos. Pain shoots down my right leg, and the fear of cracked vertebrae convinces me to return inside where I swallow more Advil, lie down, and press a cold cloth over my head.

The afternoon sky shines completely blue. The steamy puddles evaporate. With some strength returned, I head out and pull the ladder from the shed. Going up on roofs is not something I savor, and I have avoided doing so since my arrival in Paradis. But I figure it's a deed that needs to be done. Once I get up, I discover the dish full of water. I tilt it, watching the water run out, and then attempt to set it like before. Thankfully, the rest of the roof looks okay. However, when I get back inside, my iGlass is still not working. I pour myself a shot of rum, open the windows, and trade around a wet cloth on my emerging bruises.

When the shadows lengthen, I rouse myself to corral the chickens and then continue, limping ever so slightly, down to the beach. I call and call for Dandi. I'm not sure how I feel about being incommunicado. It is very isolating. Will I be okay? I wonder how Gary and Mike fared. Did the Jefferys' house flood? Did the Kicklighters' flying cars fly away? Did the storm have a name? I decide to name it Dandelion, but only if he returns.

Mary Burke

Back at the house, I keep searching. I find dead mice, two opossums sleeping in a tree, and a snake staring at me from a rafter in the chickee. What if Dandi had tried to return during the storm and couldn't get in because I had forgotten to unlock the cat door? I'm exhausted, sad, and despite the Advil, my head is still throbbing.

The sun drops. The shadows turn to blue. At night, the Milky Way sparkles bright as a crown in the sky, but Dandelion doesn't return.

Paradis

Chapter 18
Another Problem

The following day, Mike visits on his ATV. It is mid-morning, the air is clear and wonderful, and the sight of Mike brings uncontained glee. I greet him on the stairs with a cup of water, which he gulps gratefully. My storm story (delivered with some exuberance) brings a wry smile to his face. "I know a guy who can get you a good price on a slightly used cane," he jests.

I inquire if Gary has talked with him recently.

"Well, if you're asking if he told me about Richy trying to kill himself or all the rest of you all..." He trails off. "Gary called right after you left, but I haven't been able to get in touch with him since."

"Is he angry with me? Have you spoken with the Kicklighters?" He shakes his head no.

"I'm just worried about Gary now." He rubs his head. "No signal from the Jefferys' house, and I'm not sure when they're supposed to be back to relieve him of his dog-watching duties."

He asks if he can borrow my skiff. "Gary has the dinghy, and I need something to get into Snug Harbor to check on him."

I decide to strike a deal. "Are you up for some ladder climbing?" He laughs congenially, and soon, he is up on the roof and down again. He explains that the low noise converter in my satellite receiver suffered storm damage, but he has a spare at home. He'll get it if I let him camp at my place overnight. I happily welcome his company. If he can fix my satellite and help me look for Dandi, he can spend a hundred nights. After a second glass of water, Mike's on his ATV and calling to me that he'll be back in a jiffy with the converter.

"Keep an eye peeled for Dandi!" I yell after him.

Around four, Mike returns and gets the satellite working. I immediately FaceTime Amber.

"Big storm?" No news reports had mentioned it. She laments my injury and again expresses her concern about me being "all alone out there."

I point the camera to Mike. She smiles and waves. "Well, thankfully Mike is there! Hi Mike, where's Gary?"

Mike reports about Gary's disconnected state.

I continue, letting Amber know about Dandi's disappearance. This only increases her concern about my off-grid life, so I decide it best to switch topics from my problems to those of the rest of the world.

Paradis

She informs about the rolling brownouts, how the government is siphoning power to the East. "The generator is juicing our power-node, so we are fine, but my favorite coffee shop is temporarily closed. It's so hard to make coffee at home." She scowls. "And the weather is super weird. It snowed again. I fear the apple blossoms are going to fall."

I share the latest Richy news. She listens intently. "I'm going to do some homework," she replies. I ask what she means and she says not to worry. "Detective work with the grid being down won't be easy anyways."

"Isn't it best not to get too involved?"

"Oh, we're way past that," she responds, echoing my thoughts exactly.

We continue to talk about the Kicklighters for some time, Mike joining in with us. It serves as a helpful distraction from the storm and the power outages. We chat like talk show hosts, dissecting the characters of Richy and Tobias, the game they play: a game of love and control, of power and submission, of caring and wanting to be cared for. "We're already involved, Mom. Already involved." Eventually, she signs off with a screen filled with animations of luck, love, and quick healing.

Mike leans back in his chair. "We moved here to escape the problems of the world. I'm not sure that's possible."

Gary had said the same thing. I offer Mike some Bacardi, and he happily accepts.

After another unsuccessful search for Dandi, we end the evening with a dinner of stir-fried vegetables over rice. Mike lays down his sleeping bag in my front room and is solidly snoring by nine o'clock. I attempt to sew in sync with his snores but after a while give up and go outside and sit on the steps. I worry. I worry about myself, Amber, Cici, Richy, Gary, Dandi, and a hundred other things. Every rustling creature makes me hope for the cat, but at last, the bugs win out, and I retreat up to the loft.

In the morning, Mike leaves for the marina after coffee. I scan the yard for Dandi, call for him, limp around the garden, supervise the chickens, and do my best to slice up brush for kindling. By noon, I'm back upstairs. My iGlass is blinking with a message from Mike, sent from Ogden's house: *The Jefferys' satellite dish had blown off the roof; Gary and the dogs are okay.* I am about to attempt a call back when MaMa FaceTimes. She apologizes profusely for not reaching out sooner and asks if I am okay after the storm. She doesn't pause for an answer.

"A portion of the barn roof blew off, and the door got off its hinge. We're still roundin' up dem goats dat got out. Trees are down just everywhere. Tobias is so exhausted, repairin' and trimmin'." She barely pauses to breathe. "If you see smoke, it's just da kids makin' bonfires with the debris. So don't ya worry. Toby Too managed to get by the marina, koont take the truck with dem trees down everywhere, and ya know, portions of the beach washed away! Ended up usin' the pontoon and found the *Kickback* right off its moorin'! Its hull all scuffed up from hittin' against the dock. I have no idea where we gonna find paint!" I'm staring out the window scanning for Dandi, understanding right away it is no use trying to get a word in. "Oh, I should have had Toby Too check on you, so sorry. And did ya hear dat terrible news 'bout Joey Pelagro—"

Paradis

A boy falling from the eleventh tier. My attention is back on MaMa's words. She finally manages to pause for a breath, so I take the opportunity to mention that I heard his store had to close. "Apparently, he ran out of everything—"

Her harried expression changes to dumbfounded. Her words come slowly: "...Ya don't know."

"Know what?"

MaMa takes a deep breath and then starts explaining. "Joey Pelagro transferred millions of dollars out of customer accounts right after the grid went down. Oh, thank God our eggs were in multiple baskets—"

MaMa continues, or so I assume, but she may as well have been talking static. My brain froze on the words "transferred millions of dollars out of accounts." How can there be another problem?

"—so I don't think we'll be ready to do our picnic dis month, ya know."

I stare blankly. "I got to go." At least I think that's what I said. I must have been ghost white when I disconnected.

I call Amber, who is unavailable. I feel faint; literally, the room is spinning. I run to the sink and heave, but nothing comes up. I splash water on my face. I attempt to get coffee out of the kettle, but failing to do this basic, everyday task, I settle on a glass of water. Then, upon seeing the Bacardi bottle, I abandon my water for a cold rum and Coke. I'm sitting down on the front steps when I remember that I didn't even ask her about Richy.

I sip from the cloying wonder of civilization and study nature's handiwork: scrubbed tree branches, toppled air plants, jays scolding a black-and-white hawk that bursts from

Mary Burke

an oak's upper limbs to fly the pure blue of the sky. The sweet coolness of my drink does nothing to assuage the thoughts that collide in my head like erratic billiard balls. The deluge of recent events is just too much for my brain to grasp—there is an overflow of human-made drama for a barrier island. Cici's illness. Richy with the gun. The grid collapse. And now, my money may be all gone, financial security obliterated.

Money—peculiar little scribbles preceded by dollar signs—erased from my electronic ledger. It all makes perfect sense; of course, it was Joey Pelagro who hacked my iGlass. If it's all gone, what does that mean for me? Will I have to move into my daughter's basement? How would I even get there?

I envision myself drinking homemade lattes in city parks, surrounded by wandering mad-as-hatter Richys, fighting world problems in fictional apocalyptic virtual scenarios. Amber doing her homework about imaginary escapades. White apple blossoms falling into white snow. The orange tips of Amber's hair jumping and dancing among the tops of pines. Billowing smoke turning the scene a haze of gray—the familiar hue of a concrete-laden city.

I can manage without rum and coffee. But what about this beautiful wild? Now that I have it, I don't know if I could just give it away. Reenter civilization? Return? Re-join the grid? The hustle of modern life? Theoretically, I can survive here as long as dry land remains. But could I do without communication? I gnaw my lip and think of Amber. In my musings, I picture Liam holding her in their perfect home, complete with perfect happy dogs. Then the image shifts—Mark, his arms holding me. He turns to lift Amber—she's a child again—and he twirls her in a perfect circle. She laughs,

Paradis

and they hold each other. The wind shifts the pines, sunlight kisses my right shoulder, and I pretend this warmth is Mark's presence beside me on the steps—his age forever frozen.

My gaze drops to my hands holding the cold beverage. The wrinkles are so deep, the veins so clear. I rub my new rough calluses, their marks adding to the story of life these hands tell. I draw a deep breath and shift my focus solely to the untamed beauty that surrounds me. I allow it to embrace me, fill my mind and senses. Its fullness replaces my concerns about money; its vastness makes the stresses of civilization feel insignificant and small.

A dark thought crosses my mind, inducing a chuckle, and so I lift my glass. Saluting my yard with the liquid mahogany dregs, I proclaim, "To Paradis, Florida, the military will probably use you as a bombing range!" I down the final swallow of my drink and listen for a response, but only my voice echoes back from the wilderness.

Inside, my iGlass summons; the spell of the wild is broken. Amber is calling. Civilization beckons, and I sigh and answer the call. Time to tell her the news about Joey.

"Have you checked your accounts?" Amber's voice pierces through, a reminder of the concrete world beyond the wild.

I haven't, and I really don't want to. I want to pretend money doesn't exist at all.

Amber hums to herself, looking up something on her computer. "Okay, I'll get to the bottom of this, even if I have to go to the bank in person, whenever it opens," she promises, her eyes filled with concern. But I can only shrug; I'm numbed by the excessive drama and the Bacardi. I only want to end the phone call and return to my reflections about the wild that is Paradis.

Amber, however, changes the topic, moving on to her true purpose of calling. "The reason I called was to let you know about some info I gathered on Richy."

I'm almost afraid of what she's going to say.

"His therapist is a Dr. Isaiah Moody, and he's worked before with Quench on Imaginative Realm Role-playing Therapy..."

Amber continues talking, elaborating on this virtual counseling, but my focus is elsewhere, my mind racing through the pines like the wind.

♦ ♦ ♦

The following day, Mike arrives a little past one and helps me clear my yard and chop brush for kindling. He informs me that Snug Harbor is a mess. "The Jefferys' satellite was completely off the roof, but Gary and the dogs are okay." He pauses before continuing, a look of concern in his eyes. "However, I found Old Joe lethargic on the banks of The Eye, so I tested the salinity: two hundred milligrams of salt per liter, which means saltwater intrusion, probably been happening for a while." He sighs. "I'm worried about our drinking water supply. Anything over four hundred and fifty milligrams per liter is in the red zone for plants."

This depressing discourse creates an excellent segue for sharing MaMa's bad news about Joey's and my latest news from Amber. Amber called about an hour earlier to tell me she was at my bank. My account had been emptied by three

Paradis

hundred fifty thousand dollars, and truthfully, it could have been much worse. She put me through to the bank, and I changed my private key.

Mike's face drops. "Gary's going to flip. We have a third of our income in a Florida bank, the rest overseas." He anxiously fiddles with his microLens. "After what happened in Dubai, we don't trust any single currency. We own gold, real estate, multiple digital currencies—"

He gets their online account up. "Hmm, looks secure, but with all these bogus websites, who knows the truth!"

He attempts calling their bank. The Orlando bank greets him with a recording about the brownout operating hours: odd-numbered weekdays, 10 a.m. to 3 p.m., followed by information on how to check the website. He tries calling Gary, but no answer. Then he tries calling Jerry's smartband, but he is informed that Jerry isn't receiving messages right now. He even tries Tobias, but only receives a FaceTime image scowling at us with the tag: "I've gone fishin'."

I ask if Mike will spend another night. I don't want to be alone, and based on his quick acceptance, I take it he doesn't either. Before sunset, we make a useless walkabout calling for Dandi. Dinner consists of spaghetti with a sauce of tomato soup, onions, and garlic. We burn brush and offer discourse on loneliness.

"Old Joe could probably swim across the sound to the mainland," I surmise.

"It's a long way for a gator to swim in saltwater."

"True, but he may have to."

"It may be hard for him to be with other gators after being on the island alone for so long."

I agree. We watch in silence as the brush fire's smoke arises to shield the moon.

● ● ●

I keep up with Cici's treatment through Jerry's FaceTimes. Sometimes, Amber and I FaceTime him together. Jerry will pan over to Cici, and Hilda will wave from Cici's bedside. From these virtual visits, it appears that Cici's treatment consists of monitors that record and tubes that drip, suck, and drain. It strikes me as if her cancer and the hospital machinery are competing to see which can devour her first. She wears her iGlass with headphones, and all throughout, she smiles. Cici's mind is home in Snug Harbor. What she experiences, only she knows, but her feet walk under the covers, her hands gesture, and she laughs and speaks with lost friends and acquaintances.

At the hospital, Cici's cancer receives an official name: pancreatic ductal adenocarcinoma. Typified by genetic aberrations galore, PDAC is the second leading cause of death by cancer. The hospital administers personalized gene-targeted cancer therapy coupled with nanoparticle-programmed immunotherapy. But just two weeks after Cici's hospital admission, the health insurance company informs the Jefferys that Cici is stable enough to be moved to a care facility. When I was younger, it was called hospice.

Hilda's FaceTime comes just two weeks later. Jerry is too distraught to talk; his mother passed in the early hours of the morning. My tongue sticks in my mouth, my thoughts conflicted. Cici has passed. Gone away. Passed? Such an odd word for died. When I taught school, students all wanted to

Paradis

pass. Each semester, several came to me begging me to let them pass. These were the students who had done little but breathe during class. "Miss, can you give some extra credit, please, miss? I have to pass in order to continue." So, Cici had continued. Not a bad thing to happen. With or without the extra credit, all of us continue.

The hospital will perform the cremation because the funeral homes still don't have power. Hilda says they will bring the ashes back to Snug Harbor. They'll hold a memorial service and spread Cici's ashes on Main Street. She has more calls to make and asks if I could tell Amber. I tell her I didn't mind at all. She also asks if I can bring my Chameleon to record the ceremony. "We so loved rewatching Cici's birthday, such a beautiful memory."

"Of course, I'll bring the camera," I answer.

As Hilda's face fades from the screen of my iGlass, I smile bleakly. Cici's remains may be consigned to the present day, but her soul has passed to the springtime streets of the golden Main Street days.

Mary Burke

Chapter 19
A Main Street Memorial

The scuffed and still unpainted Kickback *churns across Snug* Harbor Sound. The pontoon boat tows behind. Tobias is on the bridge. The others on devices: MaMa studies a quilting pattern, the kids play games. Mike chats with Gary, and I check the Chameleon's charge. Outside, it's a vulture buffet of open-mouthed fish gasping their final breaths atop sun-polished water. There has been no rain since the storm, and the overheated water blooms with an influx of red tide. It is the day of Cici's memorial service.

A few days ago, Jerry shared some major news. After Cici's service, he and Hilda will be abandoning the house to move to an off-grid community in an undisclosed region of the Panhandle. His friend Jimmy and his family live there currently. Though Jerry didn't say so, I suspect this move may

Paradis

also be a means to escape creditors. The Jefferys had all their savings stolen by Joey Pelagro, and Cici's medical bills are now unpayable. I can't imagine a better plan than hiding in the woods.

Tobias drops anchor offshore, and we carefully balance ourselves in the pontoon boat. I'm decked out in my mosquito ensemble, a rag about my mouth for red tide precaution, and my backpack on my back. MaMa, however, admonishes me for my lack of eye protection. To mitigate her concern, I put on my iGlass, which I brought so Amber and Liam could attend the service virtually. Even still, a spray of caustic water splashes into a corner of my eye, and by the time we reach the Jefferys' house, it is burning intensely. For the next twenty minutes, I'm in the bathroom running "drinking water" in my eye and lying on Cici's bed with a cold cloth over it.

Despite the closed windows, whiffs of decay permeate the house. Hilda gives me an anti-inflammatory, and I improve enough to join everyone else. Jimmy has come alone, his family remaining in the undisclosed region of the Panhandle. I recognize Ogden, his wife, and his kids, and make some chitchat. Then, I visit with Gavyn, the kind postal clerk at Joey's who helped me with the sewing machine. He introduces me to his wife, Nayma, a tall, gorgeous woman, with a golden complexion, and their five equally gorgeous children. I find them a curious brood; while the rest of us weep ourselves red-cheeked, Gavyn, his wife, and their boisterous progeny radiate hope that vibrates from them like some sort of precious golden aura.

"The red tide will pass, and money doesn't buy happiness," he affirms. "Every place has its problems. The West is ablaze, the Plains a dust bowl, the Northeast invaded with vector-borne diseases. Where would you rather be, where the deer come and nibble from the pines or in some half-darkened city wearing a gas mask?" He gestures toward the Kicklighter kids, busy with their various devices. "Look at these kids over here, with their minds buried in fake realities. How will they learn to appreciate the wild art of survival?"

He had me at the word "pass." To everything, there is a season, I ponder. Turn, turn, turn—Richy and Tobias, Cici and Snug Harbor.

Jerry interrupts my contemplation to announce it is time to go.

Seven trucks are parked along the street. Outside in the stench, my muck boots suck their way to the Jefferys' truck. Mike assists me into Jerry's Ford (my bruises are still on the mend) and then scrapes a barnacle-encrusted crab off the passenger-side tire. He climbs into the truck bed. Gary, Jerry, Hilda, and I are scrunched into the front seat. Cici, in a white biodegradable box, balances on Hilda's knees.

For the first time, I find myself in downtown Snug Harbor—the real version. As the truck takes us slowly along Main Street, the Doric columns of the bank, the remaining original benches, and the theater with its empty marquee give me a peculiar sense of déjà vu. Here looms the boarded-up windows of Hinson's where I had watched the soda jerk scoop out ice cream. Here hangs a blind traffic light across the intersection of Main Street and Harbor Way. Here unfurls the dried-up husk of small-town Florida—a mummified carcass without a banana man, without well-dressed citizens, without newsstands and kids perusing comic books. I realize the decay

Paradis

started decades ago. We are merely last-chapter characters in the denouement of the town's story.

A parking spot has been reserved for us in front of the town park. The downtown streets are dry, the wind thankfully blowing the dead fish odor in some other direction. A band shelter, cascading with yellow jasmine blossoms, stands at the center of the park, and about twenty people gather under a large oak tree. Someone has beaten the weeds back and has even prepared a garden plot to the front right of the band shelter. Containers of wildflowers line the perimeter along with shovels, buckets of water, and other planting supplies. I pluck the Chameleon from my backpack and position it to film the proceedings. I join Mike and Gary and the rest of the crowd beneath the shade of a large oak. Jerry and Hilda, holding Cici in the box, go up to sit on folding chairs on the band shelter.

♦ ♦ ♦

Memories of Mark's service are heavy in my thoughts— memories replaying as both blurry and sharp. I remember my nerves were shattered on that day, but my recollections of the days leading up to the service are splintered fragments. Some days seem to be missing entirely, others crisp and clear in their pain. The National Park Service had paid for his funeral costs. Mark's ranger friends and coworkers had organized a "Celebration of Life" ceremony that followed the family-only cremation service. This "Celebration of Life" took place in a conference center at the base of Rainier, a collection of log buildings hidden among acres of massive Douglas firs.

Mary Burke

Uniformed rangers solemnly lined up beneath a half-mast flag and watched Amber and me with empathetic eyes as we emerged from the procession.

Together, we entered the largest of the cabins. The space inside was antagonistically high-tech; bulky screens reported that the service would start soon and displayed how many digital attendees were in the waiting room. A sound man was testing microphones, speakers, and monitors. Rows of chairs faced an overwhelming screen that played a slideshow of Mark's life: drone footage of him scaling mountains, stills of him on a beach enjoying beers with college buddies, a video of me and him, young, kissing, pushing the camera away. Following it, a video of him holding baby Amber, his eyes so full of emotion. The song in the background: Red Hot Chili Peppers's "Don't Forget Me."

◆ ◆ ◆

Jerry stands to deliver Cici's eulogy. Amber joins via FaceTime. Above me the Chameleon hovers.

```
[Soft electronic tone]

> Chameleon 3D60 connected to Adeline Thorndyke's iGlass
> 05/02/43, 15:28:02
> Recording Started


Endings. Farewells. Transformation. The fragility of a
Rose.
A man standing at the edge of a band stage. Yellow
jasmine framing his nervousness. Long face, shiny with
sweat, glittery with stubble. Looking down at a paper in
```

Paradis

his trembling hands. A minute of silence passing. Balling the paper up, cramming it into his pocket. His heavy eyes observing a crowd standing in the shade of a grandfather oak. A clearing of his throat, a mumbling of umms. He starts his speech:
"I wrote down stuff to say to y'all about my ma, about her ninety-four years, about how time passes."
Ephemeral. Pausing, glancing to a woman with a box on her lap.
"Cecilia Mae Smith-Jeffery is in that box." Gesturing with a still shaking hand. "She belongs to this place. Snug Harbor. Even when it recedes to the sea, she'll still belong."
Struggling down his cheek, a tear.
"I came back to Snug Harbor fourteen years ago. I was already sort of retired, and I dunno, but I was the handy one around the house. So, um, I came back to help Ma. Let's face it, y'all know it. Cici Jeffery was one cantankerous, free-willed woman. You know how she could be until you'd just throw up your hands and give in. For all her hundred and ten pounds, Ma could tackle any problem with the strength of a linebacker, and she loved wildflowers. So it's fittin' she's stayin' here, part of the wildflowers she loved."
Soft coughing. A fabric square emerging, dabbing sweat on his forehead.
"I'm not gonna talk much more. I'm not a speech giver, so I'm just gonna tell the pie story."
The crowd rustling. "Huzzah!" rising from a scattering of voices.
A brief smile crossing the son's lips. A bittersweet memory stirs. The fabric square returning to its pocket.
"Ma made the best pies. When I was twelve, old man Hinson says to my ma, 'Cici, why not enter one of those pies of yours in the county fair? You know there's a hundred-dollar prize just for baking a pie.' So, my ma asks me

what pie she should make, and I, making fun, say she should make her diabetes pie."

A chuckle spreads under the oak. Leaves quivering with a snicker.

"Well, she does and wins. This automatically qualifies you for the state fair, and dadgummit, she gets the blue ribbon over in Tampa and two hundred fifty more bucks! Well, y'all know the rest of the story. For the next ten years, she had me baking pies and selling them out of the house, up at the church, and over at that coffee shop used to be here on Main. She'd show up at my football practice and embarrass the holy heck outta me. She'd tell the coach that before I had my brains knocked out, I had to get home and bake pie."

Pausing and exhaling. The memory releasing into the ether. His shoulders dropping along with the corners of his lips. Sadness and release.

"Well, that's all. Um, preacher here's gonna say a few words."

Leaving his yellow-flower frame. Taking his seat and ever so gently resting his hand on the remains of the Rose.

A man in cream-colored vestments talking of passing through doors. Heaven. God. Jesus. Death.

Oak leaves trembling with stories of life's vibrancy. Pies and wildflowers. Shared adventures. A halcyon picture of small-town life. Grade-school tales. Applause for strength and resourcefulness.

A FaceTime attendee sharing her own memories:

"My name is Amber Camellia Thorndyke. I only met Cici in person last December, but we've spent a lot of time FaceTiming. Cici Jeffery allowed me to enter another world. Her world. She showed me her story. I want to say thank you, Cici. Now, I know about Snug Harbor, and I know about diabetes pie. I know wildflowers are not weeds. Thank you, Cici. I hope I never lose touch with what you taught me about valuing the moment."

Paradis

∴

Mark's service was officiated by his ranger friend, Francis. It was very nature-oriented, with Muir quotes galore, focusing on rebirth, renewal, decay required for life, and transformation. It was well done and spiritually very Mark. The eulogy was read by Mark's brothers, dad, and a close family friend. Stories were shared by all, including digital attendees, which comprised of Florida friends and buddies who had moved all over the globe. On that day, I didn't speak. Then, words were too hard. But since then, I've written Mark a million eulogies.

∴

At the end of Cici's service, we each take turns planting wildflowers in the garden. I plant a golden aster. Soon, the garden is an explosion of little blooms of life, whose names, as a biology teacher, I should have cared to learn. Jerry and Hilda spade Cici's ashes into the garden. The preacher posts the marker: *In Memory of Cecilia "Cici" Mae Smith-Jeffery 1949-2043. We Love You, Cici.*

Paradis

Summer

Briny is the bubbling broth
That breeds beneath the boughs.
Rounded mouths pop the larvae fruit
That bobs within the slough.

Summer stokes the steaming sky
That heats this cauldron hot.
Mangroves bead with crabs that crust
The walls of life's soup pot.

Sniper keen an ibis waits
Eyes sharp and black as oil.
A darted bill retrieves its feast
From out the thriving broil.

- Adeline Thorndyke

Mary Burke

Chapter 20
An Uneasy Occurrence with Old Joe

It is Sunday, June twenty-first, the first day of summer and my sixty-third birthday. Perhaps it is the hallmark of having survived 'til sixty-three, or perhaps my coffee is way too strong, but whatever the reason, I feel extra alive today. Not just any old alive, but a good, solid alive. The red tide has drifted off and taken with it the stench of rotting fish. Left in its place is the salty smell of wave-tossed coconuts.

My iGlass is summoning. Amber. It's 5 a.m. in Issaquah.

Her cheerful voice sounds strained. "Happy birthday, Mom! Was up late working on a project with peeps in Thailand, so before getting off for a snooze, thought I'd wish

Paradis

you a happy b-day." She yawns slightly. "I knew you'd be up, so, what's your plan?"

"A kickass birthday party."

She makes the correct assumption that it's the Kicklighters throwing the party. "Hopefully, MaMa will hide the white lightnin'."

I dissolve a smirking emoji over my face, which relaxes both of us with a brief chuckle.

We chat for a little about pleasant everyday things. She sends pictures of her backyard veggie garden and the greenhouse blooming with peppers and tomatoes. Then we move on to the world, discussing the grid outage and continued rolling blackouts, money theft, and hacking. She is thankful for their generator. I tell her about Gary and Mike's unusual Disney trip.

"They reported an open park, not a rolling blackout in sight. Unlike the rest of Orlando, which was apparently a ghost town. Since Disney attendance was down and the park had generators galore, they actually had a turkey dinner at Cinderella Castle." I send her their photos.

"They look genuinely happy," she says, examining the photo. But then her face turns sad and her eyes shift. She shows me a collection of vibrant sculptures of what looks to be Cici's wildflower paintings. "I miss her." She frowns. "I've been using my 3D printer to build these pieces from the photos of her paintings. You think I could send some to the Jefferys?"

I sigh. "I have no clue where exactly they've relocated."

"Maybe they'll message you." Her voice is barely audible.

Liam comes into view behind her. "You're not in bed yet?" His voice sounds sleepily annoyed. His waving hand takes up the full screen. "Hey, Mom, happy birthday!"

"Well, I guess I better go catch those Z's." Is it resignation or exhaustion in her voice? "I love you, Mom." I can see she is about to fade, but then she suddenly sharpens with alertness. "Almost forgot! Richy's therapist, Dr. Moody, has agreed to contract with Quench again, but we're still working out some details. But we'll talk about that another day. Just enjoy your day today, okay? Today should be all about you."

I smile and nod as a Happy Birthday cake ignites and hearts dance. The cloud of smoke above the candles lingers like a Cheshire cat smile, fleeting, and I long for Mr. Dandi.

◆ ◆ ◆

I arrive conspicuously early at the Kicklighters', dismount my ATV, and step over the sleeping dogs. Eenie's favorite is nursing her puppies in the coolness under the chickee. Tobias is wire-brushing the grill. I greet him with my pan of rosemary cornbread.

"Sorry I'm early, but I was trying to time the tide."

"And obviously ya did, so you're right timely. Sun's shinin'."

He's in a good mood, and I am smothered in a giant, sweaty hug and freed with a "Happy birthday!"

Following Tobias's instruction, I take the cornbread up to MaMa in the kitchen. I haven't seen her since the funeral, and I am wondering what type of MaMa I will find. Mindy is helping her peel potatoes, and I startle the two of them. MaMa

Paradis

makes a futile movement to cover a sheet cake on the kitchen island.

"Guess I'm way early," I say, offering MaMa the bread.

She exchanges my bread for her potato peeler.

"Chocolate's my favorite," I smile, and her face relaxes. She also appears to be in a good mood. I decide I won't be the one to bring up Richy today and start peeling potatoes at her side.

MaMa tells Mindy to go ahead and prepare the marinade. I notice a large vat of congealed animal fat on the stove. On the counter, I see a huge pile of chopped meat. I haven't seen a wild pig on the island. Definitely isn't shark. Bottle-nosed dolphin? I have a sinking thought, which is confirmed by Tobias when he and Toby Too bluster into the kitchen. Observing me staring at the meat, Tobias informs me, "It's dat old gator from The Eye. Saltwater gettin' into dat pond, ya know, so Toby and I put the poor thing out of his misery."

Oh no. Old Joe.

"Ever eat gator, Addy?" asks MaMa.

"Actually, I have, once, many years ago." But my words are flat, my thoughts full of Mike and Gary. They loved Old Joe.

"Tastes just like chicken, don't it?" blurts Tobias. He and Toby Too gather up the meat to take down to the grill. On his way out, he turns and says, "Almost forgot, Mike and Gary messaged dat they can't get through on the beach; had to turn around. Said to go ahead and start eatin' without dem. But dere be by later."

◆ ◆ ◆

The food is served. I'm sitting at the picnic table, staring at my plate. Old Joe served with a side of fries. Should I eat Old Joe? Deliver a eulogy? At least I could say some kind words, like "thank you Old Joe for not eating me."

Meanwhile, across from me, squirting Sriracha with merciless ferocity, is Tobias.

"Geeze, lit'le Addy, eat up!" I watch as he aggressively forks Old Joe into his mouth.

My throat tightens. My stomach pinches. I don't even want my bottle of Hog's Breath. I can hear the raucous Kicklighter children serving themselves at the other table.

Tobias and MaMa toast me, Tobias with his beer and MaMa with a suspicious-smelling lemonade. As the two of them dig in, I try my best to take a bite of the Tierra del Fuego mascot, the Lord of The Eye. I never actually met the chap, and I'm sure he would have eaten me if given the chance. I cut a bite, examine Old Joe on my fork, gather him on my tongue, and roll him round in a bolus. The Kicklighters have thrown this luncheon for my birthday. *Your Neighbor*. I only have to get the first bite down.

I cough, sort of, some odd sucking sound. My pants are wet. I have knocked over my beer. *Well, at least I haven't peed myself*, I think.

I wheeze, and my windpipe seizes tight on this morsel of Old Joe. A panicked instinct makes me stand up, and I lean forward on the table.

Tobias, with gator in his beard, asks, "You okey?"

The kids quiet down and stare. Everything blurs.

Is Old Joe trying to have the last laugh? On my birthday! What a silly way to die! Is it hands to throat? Is that the signal?

Paradis

A hard slap across my back is followed by MaMa's voice. "Oh my God, she's chokin'!"

My vision is grainy, like an ancient black-and-white TV screen. I'm watching some flashback from college. Albert the Alligator, University of Florida mascot, running onto the field. Around The Swamp, the stadium crowd roars, and I am tackled!

Forceful, repeated compressions. Another squeeze; I am heaved up over the table and out spits a slimy chunk of Joe into the fry bowl. I'm coughing like the dickens, my throat as raw as gator meat. Blood roils in my temples, ribs throbbing.

Then, just as suddenly, my vision clears. MaMa's standing at my side. Tobias is at the head of the table looking stunned; he just saved my life.

Needless to say, my day of Old Joe eating is over. I recover enough to be led up to the couch in the cabana where MaMa offers me water. My ribs hurt, but she says since the pain was not sharp, I am probably just bruised from the impact. I agree to change into one of MaMa's pants and am shook up enough I even agree to spend the night. I consider not risking eating ever again, except, maybe later, to enjoy just a tiny slice of chocolate birthday cake.

Having missed all the excitement, Mike and Gary roll in around three. By the time they walk into the cabana, Tobias had already shared my near-death experience. They offer broad grins and a giant bottle of Bacardi Gold.

"Glad we don't have to drink this in your memory," jokes Gary.

I don't find it very funny.

He sets the Bacardi on the rattan side table.

"Well, happy number sixty-three."

MaMa comes in and asks if I want anything. She then suggests the guys wash up and we can all eat back here in the cabana. "Tobias is throwin' more meat on the grill."

I want to inform them who the meat belongs to, but before I can think of the right words, the guys are off to wash up. I stare at what they have left near me, a container of salad and a flyer with a download code for a video about a mermaid-manatee sculpture they constructed from refuse washed ashore. I'm not interested in either. I force down a sip of water.

They return in good spirits, talking some more about their Disney escapade, and how crazy empty the park was. I listen, well, sort of, but mostly I remain in my daze.

Tobias enters with two heaping plates of Old Joe balanced in each hand with sides of cold fries. The bottle of Sriracha snuggles under his armpit, and a bag full of Hog's Breath bottles jiggles over his shoulder. He hands the plates, the sauce, and a couple beers to the guys. Somewhat unsteady and reeking of what is unmistakably white lightnin', he asks if I am up for another try.

I shake my head.

MaMa pulls up a chair and attempts to lighten the mood by showing me photos of a new quilt she's designing, but I'm too distracted to pay her any attention. Instead, I watch apprehensively as Mike swallows his first bite of Old Joe. It is eaten without incident.

Gary, however, doesn't take a bite. Instead, he screws up his face and turns the meat over with his fork. "What kind of meat is this anyway?"

Paradis

Tobias takes a swig from a flask he's produced from his jean's pocket. He belches forth, "It's dat old gator from The Eye." He extends his flask to the guys.

Mike Henderson and Gary Hernández seem to blur together like some freak show conjoined twin. They share the same horrified expression.

"¡Dios mío! ¿Mataste a Old Joe?" Gary yelps incredulously.

Mike has stopped eating. In fact, his plate is on the floor.

MaMa gapes at Mike's overturned plate.

Tobias looks confused. "Huh?"

"What the fuck!" Gary rises with vengeance from his rattan chair. "You killed Old Joe! Why? Why would you do such a thing?"

Thoroughly confused and considerably drunk, Tobias stands with his flask in hand. "Ya'll named dat gator? He was gonna die. Saltwater was likkin' into dat pond, I put the damn thing out of his misery."

"That was our gator!" expels Mike.

Tobias laughs. "What?!"

"The Eye is ours. We have a contract!" Gary is flailing his arms wildly at this point, looking unsure about what to do with them. "You had no right! We should sue you!"

"What ya keppin' a ten-foot gator as a pet for? I'd like to see the judge's face on dat one." Tobias is in total guffaw mode now. He lifts the flask to his lips and drains it in one long gulp.

Mike turns his focus to me with hurt in his eyes. "Addy, did you know? Why didn't you stop me? How could you just watch and let me eat him?" He is standing at his chair with his palms out as if beseeching me. Gary is already heading for the door.

"Actually, dat gator was a she," interjects MaMa. The guys stare at her with such force that she immediately thinks better of making more comments.

Before they barge out the door, Gary sets accusatory eyes on me. "That's why you choked, isn't it? You were eating him—ah, her—and you knew!"

Words escape me. I have cabana claustrophobia. I feel dizzy and want to go home. I want to escape to a breath of island where I can run free. I want Mark. I start to mouth out the words "I'm sorry," but the guys are already out the door.

I end up not spending the night at the Kicklighters'. A surly Toby Too takes me home, the tub of chocolate cake balanced on my knees.

Before I left, MaMa gave me the news. "We're leavin'." She sounded sad. "Dis is not how we'd planned to tell you, but ya might as well know." Her face had turned long and drawn, filled with defeat. "We've got to get out of here. Even with the desalination process, we can't keep up with the water demands to keep things runnin', ya know…" Her sentences burned like hot wax in my ears. "…Tobias and James have hired a barge; it'll take portions of the house, our furniture, whatever we can take, up to the Panhandle. From dere, it'll be transported to Wuh'scahsin." Conflicted feelings surged through me. "It was a hard decision. Tobias tried to sell the land back, but the state woont take it, not even for a dollar." My relationship with the Kicklighters is complicated, but they are a lifeline. Power generators, desalination plant, hunting tools, off-grid skills,

Paradis

large house, large boat, flying cars. I had kind of just assumed that come end of times, I could join their evacuation party.

A thought crossed my mind. "Is it Richy?"

The edge of a smile appeared on her face. "Richy's doin' better, and I can't wait to see him."

I reached out and hugged her.

And so was the first day of my sixty-fourth year.

Mary Burke

Chapter 21
The Calm Before

My boots squish imprints in the mud as I crouch at the roots of a two-hundred-year-old oak, finding myself inspired by its fungus. I orate verses to the Chameleon as it hovers at my shoulder. It listens carefully, 3D scanning and live editing the fungus that inspires my words. I find my inner poet while observing purple dune flowers and prickly pears. I hold deep dialogues with the Chameleon as we travel together over gaillardias in the scrubland, searching for the subject matter of more poems.

This is not to say that the Chameleon is my only partner in this creative endeavor. I share video compositions of mangrove tunnels interlaced with my words with Mike and Gary. *Cruising / Mangrove turnpikes / Weaving the trees / while Twittering birds have no iGlass needs. Calusa and Timucua /*

Paradis

Threaded these groves / Weaving barnacle-beaded basketry. They reply with their own art, a video displaying a basket woven from electrical wires, wooden crabs hiding inside. Our relationship has been mending through art.

My techie daughter also works on these pieces with me. She polishes my compositions into holographic wall projections and incorporates Cici's wildflowers whenever possible.

During one of these art sessions with Amber, she informs me about Richy's therapist. "Dr. Moody has secured his contract with Quench." She has even been in touch with Richy. "We are working together, exploring new virtual landscapes." Her voice sounds proud. "Richy sent me such a touching e-card. He considers himself a protégé of mine and he was accepted to the gaming high school! He was so excited, passed the entrance exam, and is going to start this fall, a full year early."

"My daughter has a protégé," I muse cheerfully.

"Yep! I told him to take things to the next level. A little gaming joke there. Ha!"

"Good to hear Richy's future-oriented."

I wonder if she knows the Kicklighters are returning to Wisconsin, but of course, she knows. She even knows why. "Apparently, it's a condition of the Department of Children and Family's investigation. Tobias must live separate from them until he complies with counseling and parenting classes. AA may be in his future as well." She is clearly way more up-to-date than I am. "Richy has expressed anxiety about his father returning. The plan is to have the two of them enroll in a case study collaboration between Quench and Wisconsin Psychiatrics. There's still a lot of details to work out—"

"I hope it works," I answer.

Profoundly, she replies, "Hope is love, Mom. And I love you."

When we disconnect, I feel a surge of hope. Hope—like oxygen surging in my veins. Like life itself, flowing forward. Before my invigorated hope fades to mundanity, I message Mike and Gary:

Through the tangle / Kayaking / An old woman. She glides / Effortless conduction / Frictionless / A spirit of hope.

Can I visit soon?

As if they were waiting for me to write, a reply from Gary comes almost immediately. The next day, I'm over at their home for a meal of swamp rabbit, sweet potatoes, and mango bread muffins.

Together we take a walk down to The Eye. In the knothole of a cypress, a coconut resides as naturally as an eyeball in its socket. It is their artistic memorial to Old Joe. On the side of the coconut that faces The Eye, the figure of an alligator circles snout to tail. With scales of delicate coquina, Old Joe watches over the dark pool like The Eye of God.

This unseen force of hope is bolstered more after a visit to Snug Harbor. Gavyn, of the hope-beaming family, filled the power gap left after the exit of Joey Pelagro. He acts as a sort of town mayor, and although a self-appointed autocrat, he is competent and benevolent with his power. Gavyn has persuaded numerous denizens of Snug Harbor to his cause of improving the town. Together they have reclaimed and transformed the warehouses of Joey Pelagro. On weekdays, it becomes a schoolhouse, a town hall, and a combo police-fire station. There is even an indoor basketball court. A non-

Paradis

denominational church has services on Sunday mornings at ten. Even Gary, Mike, and I were enlisted by Gavyn. His charismatic, optimistic speeches describing a utopian vision for the town are convincing and energizing. Hopeful.

Every other Saturday, I travel with Mike and Gary on their catamaran to the Snug Harbor Community Market. After a morning of bartering, we spend our afternoon contributing to the common cause. I volunteer my biology teacher skills, teaching a series of lessons about dinosaurs. Folks seem to come from all over for these Saturday events. Parents attend with their kids; teens come with their grandparents. Once, we all created dioramas using plastic dinosaurs donated by Miguel of Holiday-in-the-Hammock. Meanwhile, Mike and Gary teach classes on building artwork from recyclables. Sometimes we attend the very popular Cannabis Cooking with Fiona class. We also occasionally join the volunteers who care for Cici's garden. It feels good to be part of this nascent attempt at building community. It is the halcyon days of summer. It is the calm before the storm.

The Kicklighters do not normally attend these market days, but on the first Saturday in August, they are there selling goats, chickens, and miscellaneous household items. I greet Tobias and Toby Too at their table. They have already divvied up supplies for me and the guys, including several new hens and a rooster for me.

I notice MaMa and Mindy at a second table and go over to join them. They are selling quilts, clothing, and small appliances. MaMa says if I give them a hand, they will give me a lift back to the marina in the afternoon.

"Everything's got to go, Great Recession prices," she confides in me as a customer hands her a five-dollar bill for a coffee pot. "Take only cash, jewelry, silver; God knows we got to get rid of this stuff. The movin' barge is supposed to arrive by the weekend."

"We never had our sewing date," I comment, but she seems not to hear.

In front of me, a thin, oily-haired woman places a rusty toolbox full of rusty tools atop one of MaMa's beautiful quilts.

"You need to pay in cash or jewelry," I tell her.

"I can give you twenty-five in cash and the tools."

"Forty dollars," I bargain.

She considers. "Fifteen dollars and the ring." She shows me a lovely silver ring with a chip of red coral.

I catch MaMa's eye. She is dickering with an old man rattling a can of change.

"Twenty-five dollars and the ring."

"Twenty dollars and the ring."

MaMa shifts her eyes in my direction. "Take it," she says.

By the end of the day, the Kicklighters have sold all the animals and almost all the household supplies. MaMa folds the four quilts she had not sold to take back on the boat. Tobias tells the kids to put the remaining items alongside the donation bin. We help ourselves to cups of coffee from an old-fashioned, battery-powered drip coffee pot, and Tobias counts out the day's profits on a rust-flecked ironwork table.

Paradis

"So, the barge arrives Saturday?" My question sounds like a confirmation.

"Supposed to," answers MaMa. She is staring at a wedding photo in an open heart-shaped locket that she has taken in trade. "Toby Too and Elias are flyin' the cars up to Wuh'scahsin right afterward."

Tobias sifts through the pile of booty gleaned from their trade. He fingers a long necklace of red coral and gives it to me. "A small token, Addy," he says. His teeth glint yellow behind the fringe of mustache hairs.

MaMa helps me with the clasp. I thank them.

Tobias is leaning down to pick up a ring that has fallen through the ironwork. He wants to know if I want their composting toilet. He retrieves the ring and examines it. "Looks like a 2016 Denver Broncos Super Bowl ring."

I answer that one composting toilet is quite enough for me to clean. He hands me the ring. I hand it back. "Faux," I tell him. "It's got to be."

"But still, I do think it's the most interestin' take of the day." He tries the ring on for size and raises his fist. "See, made for me. Ya know, Addy, I used to play football in high school."

I suggest he should propose to MaMa all over again. I take a sip of the coffee and find it surprisingly fresh and hot.

Tobias is looking at MaMa. "Maybe dat's what I need to do. Propose all over."

"Startin' over is hard," reflects MaMa. "I can't wait to hug my sons." She takes her iGlass from her bag and hands it to me.

I look through her iGlass to see a very bright-eyed boy sitting on a pony inside a stable.

"James and his wife just adopted him from upstate New York," she informs me. "I can't wait to take him into my arms too."

I hand her back her iGlass and offer my congratulations.

"Richy is back at dat shrink," says Tobias. His eyes drift downward to study the inside of his cup as if to read the future in the coffee grounds. "I've agreed to try da counselin' thing again."

MaMa turns to me. "Do you know when you're goin' back to Seattle to live with your daughter?" She gestures at the motley menagerie of humanity lingering at the dilapidated tables. Two old men fight over a book from the donation bin; an old lady with an almost fully duct-taped walker coughs up her lungs as she sifts through a trash can.

Of course, moving in with my daughter rings logical, especially to everyone that isn't me. But MaMa's words send a fracture through the hope that had been filling me. I want the life I have on Paradis, a life that lies somewhere outside the noise and chaos of the modern world. Would I really give this all up for the comforts moving to Washington would allow?

I guess my silence lingers long enough. Tobias gets up to take his cup to the bin—our signal to leave. "The kids will be waitin' on the *Kickback*."

MaMa sits across from me with her empty cup. There is a twinge in my gut. Loss. Sadness. Emptiness. A stifled realization: I will miss these people. *My Neighbors.* The Kicklighters. People I have, on multiple occasions, found so very annoying. But also, at times, helpful. What will it be like here without them? Have I learned enough to be off-grid without them? Maybe MaMa is right. So much is gone from

Paradis

here. Cici, the Jefferys, and now the Kicklighters. I glance over at Tobias; did I misjudge him? "I think it's the right thing to return to Wisconsin," I say. "It will be good for the family to be all together again." I look at MaMa and force a smile. "Richy's going to be okay."

She leans in to me. "You should send him a text if ya want. Richy really liked ya." She takes my hand in hers and squeezes it gently. "And we'll all keep in touch, I'm sure." Her smile is reassuring, but I know those words are hollow.

I smile at her, and then remember suddenly, "How are you moving Eenie and his pack up to Wisconsin?"

Tobias harrumphs. "We ain't, damn dogs ran off yesterday mornin', haven't seen dem since." He laughs heartily. "Ya better keep dem fairies safe, Addy. Them dogs got a taste for them now!"

I clench my jaw, and any sadness I feel dissolves with this reminder of what kind of person Tobias really is.

◆ ◆ ◆

A week later at the marina, I see the Kicklighters off in their scuffed-up *Kickback*. Toby Too and Elias have already left in the Ospreys. Mike and Gary don't show. As the water churns, Tobias, MaMa, Mindy, and little Tommy wave from the deck. I wave in return and watch until the boat rounds the curve on its way to the wide turquoise waters of the Gulf.

Later that day, I sail with Mike and Gary on the *MG-Cat* to the Kicklighters' beachfront to nose around the farm. Although we know the dogs are lurking somewhere, we decide to explore nonetheless. Luckily, we encounter no Red Eye Sue and no dogs. Instead, we find the roof still holding its satellite dishes and the door to the house unlocked. Not much remains. MaMa's sewing room has been emptied of quilts.

"You can fit a lot on a barge," Gary yells from another room.

We search through kitchen cabinets. Not a Hog's Breath to be found.

"They'll still have to pay property taxes," says Mike.

This strikes us as funny, and we all burst out laughing.

Outside in the Kicklighter garden, the summer vegetables grow robustly. I spot T-3 wandering in his tortoise mansion. I wonder if Richy knows he won't be joining him in Wisconsin. I'm sure a tortoise, even one missing a foot, would prefer Florida's climate to Wisconsin's. Unsure how he will survive on his own, I decide to adopt him as a new companion. The guys agree to help me build a new pen. We take the flagstone from the pen, dismantle the overhangs and the overhead gates, and haul them to the boat. When we return, we head to where the honeycombed graphene desalination membrane glistens with a thin film of water vapor. It is still connected to the solar panels. We determine this is the most necessary device for us to figure out how to disassemble and transport to one of our properties.

On our way back, we stop to fish off Pelican Cove and fry snook on the boat's grill. Thunderclouds are assembling, so Mike grabs his microLens to link with the catamaran's VSAT.

He spends an unusually long time silently checking things in his Lens. His lips grow firm. After a while, he removes his Lens and gathers a fork of grilled fish.

Gary and I look at him expectantly.

Paradis

"Harihara may be coming," he says with his mouth full of fish.

"Who?" Gary and I respond in unison.

"Take a look."

Gary puts down his fork and puts on Mike's Lens. "Where the hell did that come from?"

"Off the coast of the Yucatan," answers Mike.

Gary hands the Lens to me. Satellite images show a Category Three hurricane coming our way across the Gulf of Mexico.

Chapter 22
Hari Came

Numb to sunburn and humidity, I sit under the arched palms. I contemplate the ocean, the sunlight reflecting aggressively from its surface. Water flows through me, filling over half my body. It shapes the Earth, building its shorelines and canyons. The story of civilization can be told by waterways. A dance of control told with dikes and dams, and drownings and floods. Gulf of Mexico, do you know about leveled sandcastles? Did you see the twisted embrace of a family in pain? Are you nurturing Hari, providing her strength with your unusually warm waters?

A check of my iGlass reveals scant info about a hurricane charted to wipe over "uninhabited" Florida barrier islands. In stark contrast, Snug Harbor's social media is pulsing frantically with comments from the locals. A message from

Paradis

Reverend Adams says the warehouse church will be open for anyone who needs a place to ride out the storm. Mayor Gavyn encourages me to travel with his family to Mount Dora, an "off-grid sewing community." I think the "hurricane revel" invite, hosted by Miguel's marijuana farm, sounds the most interesting. My mind generates sardonic images of corrugated metal sheets blowing around like guillotines beheading baked stoners. Truly an interesting way to go, but rum is my drug of choice for the apocalypse.

In the afternoon, Mike and Gary arrive. We work on building T-3 a pen from metal and leftover lumber they've brought from Tierra del Fuego. We work for some time in quiet, tension over Hari hanging in the humidity. Finally, Mike breaks the silence.

"We're going to evacuate the island."

This is not unexpected. I ask where they plan to go.

"Not sure yet," Gary answers. "During last year's raining and flooding catastrophes, we took the *MG-Cat* to the Keys. It turned out to be a wonderful vacation." He laughs lightly. "When we returned, the island and everything we left on it was just fine." He pauses and stares off into space. "The rest of the state did not fare as well." He shakes his head and returns to adjusting a metal pen wall.

"Come with us, Addy." Mike puts his lumber down and looks directly at me, his eyes pleading. "Think of it like a little vacation, a way to take your mind off the storm here."

"How would we know where to evacuate to? Hurricanes are difficult to predict."

"Oh, we got the VSAT. It's never steered us wrong in the past."

I chew my lip and let them know I'm considering my options. However, in my mind, I'm questioning how much they've thought through this boating trip. The rain last year was one thing, but what about hurricane-strength winds?

♦ ♦ ♦

The following day, I join Mike and Gary on the marina pier as they complete their packing and prepping of the *MG-Cat*. Their decision feels wrong to me. Being alone on the island will be difficult, but how can they even consider the risk of riding the waves of a hurricane? My stomach churns just thinking about it. Mike's voice interrupts my thoughts.

"We wish you'd reconsider," he says.

"I wish *you two* would reconsider." My throat is tight on the words. "I'm just concerned about you two being out on a boat during a hurricane."

Mike smiles toward the *MG-Cat*. "We've sailed this girl everywhere; she'll take good care of us. And we aren't going to be anywhere near the hurricane anyways."

"But hurricanes are unpredictable!" I'm exhausted by Hari, and she hasn't even arrived. "We don't even know for sure if Hari will hit the island."

Gary looks at me fervently. "Hari is already a Cat Four. It will cover the island; it could break new passes." He is frantically digging through supplies on the boat and running back and forth from the cabin. His face is red and sweaty, his movement erratic with panicked energy. He pauses en route to the cabin, throws his hands in the air, and turns to face me. "Surely you aren't planning to stay on the island!"

Paradis

My thoughts whirl. Hari, Hari, go away-ee? I have no plan. I'm locked by indecision. Maybe I should leave with them. I really don't want them to leave, and *I* really don't want to leave. I definitely don't want Hari. It could still change paths, weaken, stall. Am I just in denial? Is this that same feeling that kept me believing Mark could be alive? Is this a mistake?

"Ideally, I would just ride things out with my chickens and T-3. But I have plenty of options. I can join Gavyn's evacuation party, or hunker down at the Kicklighter house, twenty-foot piers and all."

Mike urges me to reconsider. "We have two weeks of supplies. Brought our rifle in case of trouble. The VSAT shows a high-pressure area over the northern Gulf, so that's where we're headed." He adjusts some lines and looks toward the horizon. "Might sail over to Texas or check out who's still left in Mississippi or Louisiana."

I shake my head side to side. "Hari could stall or be dissipated by shearing winds. Most likely it will change course."

Gary emerges from the boat's cabin and comments sarcastically, "Oh, aren't you the budding meteorologist." He stands next to Mike, holds his hand, and sighs loudly. Together they block the sun, the backlit Gary and Mike silhouette once more pleads, "Come with us Addy! We'll have a great time, get in a lot of fishing and be safe."

I am too choked up to speak. I grab Mike and Gary by the shoulders and hug them both.

When I release, Gary takes my hands in his. "Whatever you do," he says, squeezing, "don't stay on the island. Go inland to Mount Dora or stay with other people in the warehouse." He squeezes even tighter for a moment and then releases. "Be with people."

I can't even reply; my eyes well with tears.

"Well..." Mike looks toward the boat. "I think it's ready to go. We're going to worry about you, a lot."

"We took the 3D60 video your daughter made of Tierra del Fuego." Gary pauses and looks like he's going to cry. "So we can remember our stuff—"

"In case it all goes underwater," finishes Mike.

"When are you leaving?" I ask.

"Early tomorrow morning," Mike answers.

"We got the art put away best we could, inside and under the house."

The lump in my throat swells, and oddly, I begin to think about marshmallows. "We should have a campfire," I blurt out. "I have some Bacardi that I need help finishing."

Ideas of evening escapades lighten the mood.

Gary gives me a wink and moves to jump off the boat. "Oh, save that Bacardi. We have just the thing for the occasion."

We spend the night in campfire camaraderie, digesting pole beans, summer squash, cornbread, a plucked and roasted Myla, and glasses of an ultra-fantastic forty-year-old Bordeaux. "Santé!" We keep an eye on weather channels. Over the water, the moon is barely there—a pendant dissecting the necklace of the Milky Way.

After dinner, we lie with our backs on the pier and marvel at the overpowering sky. So many stars. A secret held from

Paradis

civilization. Here, air pollution is pushed away, car alarms replaced by crickets, light population yielding to an infinite sky awash with stars. A soft wind rustling the pines indicates Mark's company. A true paradise.

I am certain Gary is smiling up at the sky as he muses, "We'll see you in a couple of weeks with a thick bottle of Louisiana rum, and we'll go dancing on the stars back at Tierra del Fuego."

⬥ ⬥ ⬥

The morning Mike and Gary leave is deceptively beautiful, and after their departure, I sit on the dock weighing my prospects and taking deep breaths of the wonderfully clear air. My gut says to remain on the island. Maybe I'm just being stubborn, or I am in the grips of denial as I face another possible loss, but the decision feels right. I smile toward the turquoise waters. I belong to this place. If it is my karma to drown, it will happen at Addy's Wedgie in a house full of chickens. At last, I arise and move my fishing skiff over to the floating dock. I double up the mooring lines, protect them with chafing tubes, and cover the boat. I lean my kayak against the storage shed and think about ways to transport it to the homestead.

I return to Addy's Wedgie kayak-less, drop in some cactus pads and herbs for T-3, and let out the chickens to peck for insects in the yard. I eat an omelet with onions and place a call to Amber. "Mom, can I call later? So crazy busy!" She must know nothing of the storm. I don't say anything. After all, everything could end up fine, and if she knew ahead of time, she would, for sure, demand that I leave the island. The call ends. I do a quick search of the news: thousands dead in a Philippine tidal wave, a massive fish kill off the Great Barrier Reef, a revolution in Brazil, and a human interest story about ozone depletion causing blindness on the Himalayan plateau. No mention of Hari. Snug Harbor social media shows people battening hatches. NOAA gives coordinates; Hari is twenty-five degrees north, eighty-five degrees west. I ride the ATV back to the marina, tie my boat cover to the back of the ATV, slide my kayak atop the cover, tie it, and drive slowly along the trail. I get the kayak into my yard just in time to put the chickens and myself to bed.

◆ ◆ ◆

Thursday, August twentieth dawns breezy and blue. I have already returned from another trip to the marina where I put the dirty cover back on my fishing skiff and double-checked the lines. Back at the Wedgie, I upend the picnic tables and pull the benches under the house. I look around. The tree branches dance empty of birds and squirrels.

    I try to reach Amber, but her signal is dead. Snug Harbor media is all abuzz. I imagine people aglow in their devices, satellite dishes perked like ears into the wind. The very last news I receive before signal is lost is from the wheelchair-bound Muriel in the warehouse: *Good news: the Pritcher has a feed from NOAA. Hari is fifty miles northwest of Tampa Bay, and the high to the north is dissolving.*

    I heat soup and hunker down. My house is full of chickens. I am only able to keep a couple at a time in a small cage. The others cluck and peck at one another as they flap nervously in the house rafters. Dandi Too, my new rooster, crows gently yet assertively, protecting his hens and keeping the order. T-3 is asleep in an old box.

In the late afternoon the storm comes: clouds churning like a river turned upside down, rain beating against the aluminum roof like a drummer beating his steelpan. The chickens are shedding fans of feathers as they flit from rafters to floor and back again. I could have sought refuge in the sturdier Kicklighter house. I could have Snug-Harbored with people at the warehouse. Huracán is throwing his shoulder against the front door. Will the house lift from its stilts and fly away like Dorothy's?

I'm anxious and scared. All my energy is focused on remaining calm. I position the table in front of the La Nordica, and I crouch beneath it with the Chameleon and iGlass at my feet. I clutch the family photo of Amber, Mark, and me next to my heart. I dare not even look out the front windows. Instead, I squeeze my eyes shut and imagine the day we took the family photo, Amber's blue dress with the taco stain. A time when everything was perfect, and Mark, Amber, and I were safe and together, and our biggest worry was a stain on a dress.

A pine limb hits the kitchen window. The chickens and I jump up in unison. The loud noise has interrupted me from my safe memory. I crawl out from under the table to peek outside. Setting the photograph on a chair, I take the Chameleon to the window and film trees whipping violently and rain angling from the northwest. I point the lens to view the depth of the muddy water flowing in rivulets and gathering into little ponds. I had tied my kayak to one of the stilts under the house just in case.

After some time, the storm's intensity plateaus. I place the Chameleon back on the chair and climb up to the loft, but the view from the loft's windows is so harrowing that I throw my bedding over the ladder, climb down, and make myself a bed under the table.

◆ ◆ ◆

Dark as a pint of Guinness, the Gulf foams white. Mount Rainier rises against the churning horizon. Mark is on the deck of the *MG-Cat*, Mike and Gary in silhouette against the open cabin door. Gary spotlights Mark in the beam of his headlamp. "Mark, get below!" A wave breaks over the deck. Gary and Mike keep a tenuous hold on the door, but when the wave passes, the light illuminates an empty deck. Mark washes overboard into the high bleak snow of surf. Mount Rainier glistening in the bleakness, the catamaran balanced on a wave sixty feet high, freeze-framed like a woodblock print by Katsushika Hokusai. The waves wash the deck again, and the deluge snuffs out the thin beam of light.

My eyes flutter open, and my mind adjusts to consciousness. Dandi Too is crowing. T-3 munches green beans. A white beam of light is streaming through the window. I sit up and inhale deeply. Hari had caressed Paradis with only her tendrils.

Paradis

Chapter 23
Waning

Dandi Too brushes by me when I open the rear door. His harem of hens whisk between my legs, hesitating only briefly at the soaked bottom step before flapping up to the lower limbs of a tree. I study them, contemplating the parallel of partially-plucked chickens tucked like Halloween decorations into the branches of partially-plucked trees. My eyes follow the tree trunks down to their roots where ankle-deep water puddles on the ground. There is time enough to explore later. I return inside, sweep up chicken droppings and feathers, and make coffee and two eggs, which I find in my bed up in the loft.

Two calm days of coffees and eggs follow. I repair damage to the hinge on the porch door. I mend two torn screens with duct tape. T-3 has returned to his new pen. The rain barrels sit full; the chickee still looks immaculate, every palm in its correct place. I wander about in my muck boots, bail water from the kayak, and grin at the chickens as they banquet on insects.

When the mud condenses into firm enough ground, I prop the ladder against the house and climb up on the roof. Signal hadn't returned to my iGlass. On inspection, the satellite mast appears intact, but the reflector plate is missing. I can't see it on the roof or in the muck, but I finally spot it, far overhead, wedged high in naked branches. Back inside, I pick up the iGlass. The battery warning blinks red next to a No Signal symbol. I scroll to my last call. Amber. My throat tightens. Delicately, I place the iGlass on the shelf next to the horseshoe crab. Together they sit like a museum display, relics from different times.

The stench of the dead and the drowned begins on the third day. The first birds back are the vultures. They gather in black, wake the corpses, and feast at buffets.

I tie a scarf around my nose, put on my hat with mosquito netting, attach my kayak to my ATV, and drag it back to the marina. My fishing skiff is none the worse for wear. I uncover it and secure it to the stationary dock. I think it casts a lonely vibe without the *MG-Cat* and the *Kickback*. "Come back guys," I whisper. "We'll eat Louisiana crawfish and sail to the mainland to barter for supplies."

By the end of the week, I can no longer restrain my curiosity, so I kayak over to Snug Harbor. Only the pilings of the pier remain. Some of its planks have drifted into the park where water sweeps the playground swings. Was the water higher, or had the supports sunk lower into the ground?

Paradis

Leafless oaks, gray as the sarsen stones of Stonehenge, encircle the picnic shelters. Do they lift their dead branches in prayer?

Tree limbs, toppled trees, and muck have reshaped the landscape, but I am able to paddle almost all the way to the Jefferys' home. The front window is broken, presumably from the storm. I struggle with the garage door and miraculously find I am able to open it. I drag the kayak into the garage and find the door to the house unlocked. In the living room, the gold-brocade drapes are open, and a brick rests on the terrazzo beneath the broken plate-glass window. A light beam shines through the window, spotlighting Cici's chair, which is the sole remaining piece of furniture in the room. I remove my mosquito hat, brush glass off her chair, and sit down. In the sunlight, the shards of glass shimmer on the green and orange flecks of the terrazzo like the fibrillating heart of nostalgia in cardiac arrest.

The walls are bare. Had the Jefferys taken Cici's paintings? Or had the brick throwers? I haven't been in the house since they left. I decide to take a peek in the guest bedroom. The room has been emptied completely. Only wires dangle from the ceiling. I wander from empty room to empty room and make the mistake of opening the refrigerator, which reeks with black mold. Back in the living room, I gather up my gear. A good solid house, hurricane-proof, I think, and wander back outside. I keep a wary eye peeled for snakes as I cross a yard sprouting with wildflowers. When I'm at the road, I pause for one last gaze at the Jefferys' house. Now, it is just another empty sepulcher.

After a long hike, I finally approach Joey Pelagro's. Squawking gulls circle plumes of smoke. Someone's cooking to the accompaniment of contemporary band music. The rhythm sounds eerily upbeat considering the sentiments being spewed by the vocalist: "Living in the land of the lost, we follow the sun. Fellow travelers, we are one..." I follow the music across the parking lot.

At the main warehouse, one tattered banner still hangs: *Work Together 🙂 Your Neighbor*. I walk under it to where the door stands ajar. I start to go inside just as Augustine, the Che Guevara clone, rounds the corner and calls to me, "You don't wanna go inside there. Roof's part collapsed." As he moves closer, the sweet scent of weed encircles him like a lenticular cloud.

Together we peek through the open door. The large warehouse roof is open in places. Only a couple weeks ago, I joined the Kicklighters in selling goats and quilts there. We had paused to drink coffee, and now, the tables and chairs are buried under fallen plaster and roof girders and shattered solar panels.

"What happened?" I ask.

"Roof collapsed. We're thinkin' too much weight unevenly distributed on the roof, hard to know for sure." He pauses to draw a couple joints from the pocket of his military-style jacket. He offers one to me, but I decline. He lights his own and continues, "See all them ducts?" He points with the joint. "I used to do HVAC maintenance, and I've never seen a system like this. Looks like Joey retrofitted this place with some crazy setup. Probably added too much stress to the roof. And when the storm came, well..."

"Was anyone hurt?" I ask.

Paradis

He takes a giant puff from the joint, and on the exhale answers, "Four dead." He starts walking and beckons me to follow him.

We go around to the parking lot on the eastern side of the warehouse. Clumps of people, shaded under tarps, sit upon chairs gathered from Joey's. I see around a dozen tents and an assortment of vehicles ranging from motorcycles to swamp buggies. Bits of trash scatter the asphalt, and above it all, the fateful lyrics spout from the speakers of the solar-powered drone.

The group from Miguel's farm sits around a table beneath a tarp that is tied to some wobbly poles. They take hits from a bong. Two-year-old Lilly naps on Water's lap.

A woman with gray dreads pinned up under a floppy hat smiles at me. I recognize her as Fiona. "Addy! So happy to see you're safe. Come over. We'll pull up a chair." She leaps up and hugs me tightly. Smoke billows from the swirls of her diaphanous peasant dress. Her voice is vivacious. "You've arrived at just the right time. Miguel and the boys are roasting up skinny Mary." She points toward a thin pig spitted over a brazier of glowing coals.

Miguel, surrounded by his own small group of men and women, bastes the pig.

I turn around looking for Augustine, but he has disappeared. I sit down in the folding chair brought over for me.

I tell Fiona my tale of Hari and the chickens, but I sense she feigns listening. She is undoubtedly high. The bong passes her way. She motions at the bong. I mention Bacardi. She shrugs, moves the bong toward herself, and lights the bowl. As she inhales, I glance around. All the Miguel clan is sequestered under a pale cloud. The smell quite overpowers the roasting pig.

Fiona notes my inspection and raises an eyebrow. "Makes a great spice," she affirms. She gestures once more toward the bong.

I shake my head. "Does anyone know where the Hari-cane went?"

"The mayor." She raises her voice. "Miguel, what's the mayor's name?"

Miguel doesn't seem to hear.

"Gavyn?" I venture.

"Yeah, I think so. He's got a hand crank radio." She points in the direction of the tent neighborhood.

"Fiona, you mind if I go check it out?"

"Do what you need to, Addy, but all that matters is that God took Hari away from here."

I nod, get up, and refold the chair.

While walking toward the tents, a squadron of children, flying by in a robust game of Capture the Flag or Crack the Whip or some such game from the nineteenth century, almost mows me down. Oblivious to little old ladies crossing their path, they roar across the parking lot. An unidentified boy waves. "Hi ya, Ms. Addy!"

I escape unscathed and wander toward a group of ladies shaded under a canopy. They sit on chairs or cross-legged on mats as they crochet or tie rugs. I associate their smiles with the vaguely familiar faces from Snug Harbor social media.

"Nayma." I remember her from Cici's funeral. "Gavyn's wife, right?"

Paradis

The woman, who is tying a rag rug, looks up.

"I thought you were going to Mount Dora?" I ask.

"We came back for Muriel," Nayma replies.

Directly alongside Nayma is an elderly lady in a wheelchair, Muriel. She is stitching a lacy table runner that could have been a museum piece.

She pauses to relate her story of Hari. "The water gushed in like Niagara, right over the heads of several neighbors. So tragic, a husband and wife—barely pregnant—a large beam fell on their heads. Crushed their skulls, Addy!" She sighs deeply. "Two others died too. Praise God! He led me to make the decision to evacuate to Joey's. When I got home, there was my own trailer tipped right over into the mud." She shakes her head and gazes down at the crinkly skin that wraps the bones of her fingers like thin gauze. "I thinks that Ms. Cici left at about the right time. I'll be heading out to Mount Dora now."

I share my story of island survival with the chickens.

Nayma comments, "Well, at least you had those guys nearby."

"They sailed north," I say.

"Oh?" She tips her head in the direction of Gavyn. He and another man sit at a nearby table. "They've got NOAA on the band."

I thank her and go over to the table. Gavyn, wearing headphones, is listening intently to a radio. I recognize the second man as Ogden. He sits across from Gavyn. Ogden, also plugged-in with headphones, records plot marks on a map of Florida and the Gulf.

Gavyn looks up suddenly and removes his headphones.

"Addy? You were so quiet! Couldn't hear you with the headphones, plus this forsaken music." He chuckles and points in the general direction of the hovering drone.

Ogden takes a break from his map plotting to give me an uncertain look. I wonder if he remembers me.

"Nayma said you may have some info on the whereabouts of Hari. Is it still a hurricane?"

Ogden tilts the map toward me. "It's a Cat One now; went in near Biloxi."

Gavyn stares at me with sympathetic eyes and tentatively inquires, "So, you made it okay on the island?"

"Just me and my chickens."

"It turned out to be a good thing you stayed put." He gestures toward the warehouse. "Not sure what we should do." He looks tired, but a glimmer of hope still exists in his eyes. "Maybe we could build something totally new here." He shrugs and wipes sweat from his face with a lacy handkerchief he pulls from his pocket.

Ogden taps his dull pencil point on the map grid. "So, you were alone there?"

There is a pause. The two men exchange glances. Gavyn picks up a legal pad and starts to leaf through it. He pauses and stares compassionately at me.

"Addy, you should sit down." He gestures toward a chair. "Please."

I give them an inquisitive expression and take a seat in one of the folding chairs.

"Your friend Mike, was his full name Michael Henderson?" Gavyn asks. "I thought the name was familiar—regular at Joey's, taught some art classes at the market, and he

Paradis

was at Cici's funeral." He wipes at his face again with the handkerchief.

I feel my heart rate quicken.

"Well, this station's been listing the dead—"

Ogden breaks in, "Coast Guard found a boat; they're trying to find next of kin."

Why are they telling me about a boat? At all times the Gulf is full of boats. I can feel blood rushing to my head, my ears ringing.

"Boat capsized about a hundred fifty miles south of New Orleans. Michael Henderson. Do you know his next of kin?"

I still don't understand the question. Finally, the correct synapses fire, and in the next second, my whole body is shaking, and I'm crying. I manage to conjure words to sputter, "Gary, wait, Gerardo? What about Gary?"

"Says they only found the one body," Ogden answers, avoiding eye contact.

Gavyn unplugs himself and takes me in a hug to try to calm my forceful sobs. "Stay with us today. You shouldn't be alone on the island."

When I regain some composure, I turn toward the sewing circle. The ladies stare with stunned faces. A woman walks over and gives me the most beautiful cloth handkerchief with little green palm trees stitched at the lacy corners.

Gavyn continues in a reassuring voice, "A group of us stayed up at Mount Dora until the storm passed. We're heading there tonight—higher ground, you know? And there's a whole community there, all ages, and everyone's into sewing and living off-the-grid. Addy, come with us." He holds my hands and stares at me with his hopeful eyes.

In the background of my sobs, the children are laughing. And the drone cranks out its strange folk lyrics: "We're living in the land of the lost, sentinels to the wave tossed."

◆ ◆ ◆

I stay only one night with Gavyn, Nayma, and their brood. I am uncomfortable and consumed with grief, and there's little privacy.

In the evening, Gavyn and Nayma have community representatives over after dinner. Even Mount Dora remains without signal, so I'm amazed at how the group coordinated this meeting. I don't want to impose, so I hide out in another room, but still, I can overhear snippets of Snug Harbor's future through the wall. "There wasn't much town to be mayor of anymore... Will people even stay... The warehouse is in bad shape... My big concern is sewerage... Nasty diseases... Salt infiltration..."

After their meeting, Gavyn and Nayma still beam hope as they cheerfully offer me leftover pastries. They are a curiosity. Perhaps I only heard the negative parts of the conversation?

I ask if they will pass along a message to Amber if signal returns. *I'm ok and I love you.* They wholeheartedly promise they will.

The next morning, Gavyn drives me to the Jefferys' old house to pick up my kayak. I'm eager to return home. And who knows? Perhaps the Kicklighters will return. Or Gary— Gary will come back, surely.

"You are always welcome in Mount Dora," Gavyn says as he hands me a detailed hand-drawn map showing routes to the

Paradis

various pockets of civilization that still exist. A physical map—one that is hand-drawn. Such an odd thing to hold in my hands. I'm struck by memories of hiking with Mark, who habitually scribbled and doodled on his trail maps. My throat tightens.

● ● ●

Two grief-filled days stream by. Feelings of pain and confusion sit in my chest with a familiar pang. On the third day, Gavyn meets me at the docks in Paradis with two boats and five men. They help haul tanks of butane, water purification tablets, tools, and canned and packaged foods to Addy's Wedgie. Their charity and kindness overwhelm me. I offer them fizzy electrolyte water, and they compliment my space. "Nice little pocket of paradise you have here." I ask about the satellite dish, but they all shake their heads. "Sorry, we know nothing about them." I don't say anything more; their aid already feels like too much. They say no to coffee, so I walk with them back to the marina and wave goodbye.

There is a certain stillness when I return. The visitors have spurred me from my dissociated state. I can feel the earth squishing under my boots, the breeze pulling on my sleeve and tousling my hair to life, the coolness on my arms from the layer of sweat that has formed. I don't think I've really felt, in a physical sense, anything the last two days.

It is through this awakening that an idea takes form. I search around the leftover pieces I saved after the building of T-3's new home until I find what I want: a small paint can, Night Sky Blue. I also find a fat, thick-bristled brush and a screwdriver for opening the paint can lid. I throw it all in my backpack and quickly head to the marina.

The Gulf is smooth, but below my kayak is the scattered reflection of myself, an accurate representation of my shattered state. As I paddle faster, however, my mind starts to calm, and I begin to focus on the rhythm of my movements. There is something new in my arms and my core. A change in them that has only developed during my time on Paradis. They are strong. I can feel my skin slide over lean, corded muscles with each repetitive flex and stretch, and I can paddle with effortless ease. By the time I reach the Snug Harbor pier, even my watery reflection appears more whole.

I navigate my kayak to the first of the biblical signs. *"Be strong and courageous for the Lord your God goes with you." (Deuteronomy 31:5).* With my kayak nuzzled right against the post, I open the paint can and mix the contents with my brush. Largely covering the words as best I can, I paint jagged lines that generally resemble an oak. Below it, I scrawl, *"I went to the woods because I wished to live deliberately." – Thoreau.* With this small action, a certain tension releases. I breathe deeply and smile at my work. *Much better*, I think. I paddle toward the next fearful omen. *"The wages of sin is death but the gift of God is eternal life in Christ Jesus our Lord." (Romans 6:23).* For this one, I cover the words with my own poem, a personal favorite. "*An old woman / She glides / Effortless conduction / Frictionless / A spirit of hope.*" – *Thorndyke.*

The next sign becomes some loosely painted wildflowers. I write what I remember from Cici's wise words: *"The wildflower bloom is small and brief like life. Appreciate the world for the moments we have." – Cici Smith-Jeffery.* I move toward the next post; on this one, I paint a cute ball of a sleeping cat. *"Sleep in peace, my little Lion."* On another, I paint a stick figure family, the Kicklighters. Tobias has his beard, Richy his glasses. They smile and hold hands; it's the future I hope for them.

At the next signpost, my breath catches in my throat. *"You shall love your neighbor as yourself." (Matthew 22:39).* My eyes gloss over and the emotions prove too large for my constricted throat. My eyes flood, and there in the silent pier, I let the pain free. I wail and I sob and I heave. It is a wild cry, a releasing cry, a freeing cry. When I start to calm, I take a huge breath, and on the exhale I actually feel physically lighter. I grab the brush and paint stars over an ocean. I paint the waves with a thick impasto. At the top, I carefully write Thoreau's famous words, *"All good things are wild and free."* Between the waves, I inscribe, *"For Mike and Gary, dancing forever on the stars."*

Chapter 24
Becoming

Becoming. Blending. Belonging. The flower becomes the fruit. The parent becomes the child. We intertwine. We meld. The cremated soul belongs to the wind. Physical essence folds into the earth. We absorb into the environment we deserve.

At dawn, a bald eagle pierces the golden waters to hook a silver mackerel. She flies on a path I cannot trace. To a nest? It's not the eaglet season. To a mate? I wonder. Does she belong to the sky or to the lofty pines?

Like the palm in my yard with the parasitic vine, I adapt. I fish. I tend my vegetables. I bushwhack palmettos. I cut a rattlesnake's head off with a machete. I am Ms. Robinson, of the Crusoe variety. I still reminisce about evenings capped off with a glass of rum and coke and crave orange rind muffins and key lime pie. But I've discovered how to tap palm trees for

Paradis

sap, making wine and sugar. Once I've saved enough acorns, I will grind flour and attempt to bake something sweet.

My bean plants grow positively berserk, crawling their way through the garden enclosure and coiling all the way around the rear stair railing. A small green snake blends amongst them. T-3 mines his way under the steel wall of his prison to escape to the confines of nature. He is building a condominium for lizards, toads, and moles. Due to his damaged foot, it is methodical excavation, but no redlining here; he truly possesses that "critter sense" and offers a room to all who sign the lease. And Dandi Too does his part, siring the cutest offspring. My eyes watch them over my watered-down coffee. Chickens are not so dumb. While Dandi guards, the girls teach the chicks to scratch for the insects and earthworms brought to the surface by the rains. I cannot bring myself to eat their eggs today, so after coffee, I go down to the beach and find a turtle nest to raid. I poach fifteen eggs and pop several into my mouth. They taste terrible; it is a waste of an endangered species. Perhaps I prepared them wrong as I have no Native Floridian cookbook.

I think frequently about the early Floridians. They understood belonging. They breakfasted upon whelks and clams and strung the shells into wind chimes and necklaces. If I listen carefully, I can hear them blowing the conch, their footprints just beneath the sand. I have always envied them, elegant and strong, burning and carving pines into canoes, engineering a grid of canals, piling oyster shells into giant middens, making coontie, weaving moss skirts, and treading not on the whiteness of the beach morning glory. These days, our similarities grow stronger.

Some days, however, when the rain falls heavily, I become Key Western. Sitting inside, sewing flower-camouflage frocks, wishing for spring breakers bearing piña colada coconuts to drop by to liven the day. Sometimes, I envision Henry David Thoreau penning prose under the chickee fronds. When the wind rustles, I listen for Dandelion leaping from the palmettos and into my arms. I stare down the beach, waiting for the mirage of Mike and Gary bouncing in on their ATV, finally arriving with that Louisiana rum. I expect a young Amber to be running behind a startled chicken, and an older Amber to bound in from out of nowhere to excitedly inform me of the latest happenings in her virtual worlds. On occasion, my thoughts turn to Richy. Is Amber his mentor? Is he her protégé? Are they forging a future I will never know? I envision the son walking with the father, two crippled souls wanting to heal. Sometimes I look at the family photo, but instead of myself and Mark, I see Amber and Liam with some other little girl I don't know. Mostly though, there is Mark. I see him everywhere, in the shadows, the clouds, the blue of the sky, the boundless stars. He talks to me through the frogs and the crickets and holds me with sunlight, kisses me with the salty Gulf breeze. Together we become, blend, and belong to nature.

◆ ◆ ◆

When I decide the time is ripe, I put on my backpack and hop on the ATV. Two miles north from the palm archway, the beach ends abruptly in a tangle of mangroves. I abandon the ATV and take the same old familiar route, except now The

Paradis

Eye ferments in the sun, cataract dull and lifeless. I pause to remember Old Joe at his memorial before continuing. The red fairy points the way.

The trail is overgrown, distinguishable only by the red markings on the trees. At the orange lettering of Tierra del Fuego, I take the shell path to the rainbow steps. The Saint Francis's cords still hang at the four corners of the eaves. With a firm push, I break the door's sticky seal. The house smells musty. The recycled heron dominates the front room. I prop it against the open door to let in some fresh air. Then I make a beeline for the kitchen, open the window, and explore the cabinets. There is the bounty from our last trip to Joey's: a bottle of grapefruit wine, a can of tomato soup, and a can of pork and beans. A lone can opener rattles in a drawer. Next to the stove stands a ten-gallon container of water, two-thirds full, and, alongside it, a fully stacked box of firewood with a box of waterproof matches. I light the stove.

I had stopped by here shortly after Hari hoping for iGlass signal, but there was nothing. The satellite dish lay askew. I returned home without future exploration. It was too soon, and I still had some small hope that Gary could return. But now I'm inside, the stove slowly warming. I combine the tomato soup and beans into one pot and set it on the stove to boil. In the room where I had slept that first night, I thumb through Zora Neale Huston's *Their Eyes Were Watching God*, Marjorie K. Rawlings's *The Yearling*, and Ernest Hemingway's *To Have and Have Not*. I want to fill twelve knapsacks with Florida classics. Remarkable how the thoughts of the missing can be held in the hand, read by the eyes, reflected upon by the brain. I pick up a slender children's novel, *Because of Winn-Dixie* by Kate DiCamillo. I read it in the kitchen while stirring the soup du jour and sipping at the wine. Outside the window, the sky darkens with lightning, and the scent of rain wafts through the window. I shut the window within a couple of inches and wander into the front room and move the heron so I can shut the door. Back in the kitchen, I ladle hot soup into a bowl, slowly savor the soup and wine at the Spanish table, and watch as the storm blows through. On my second glass of the grapefruit wine, I finish the slender children's volume. The novel causes reflection on the company of new friends and old.

I sense a transformation in the works. The freshness brought by the rain coupled with the scent of the soup replaces the mustiness with a homey scent. Outside, the sentinel trees embrace the house with a warm kinship. Crickets and frogs resuscitate in sonorous volume, and certainly, in the encroaching dark, a slice of Milky Way must reflect on the shell path below. No loneliness in Tierra del Fuego tonight. The house feels once again like a home, overflowing with memories of the artists who had engineered it. I give Mark a tour of the place, and he loves how environmentally wild it is. I light the wick on the kitchen lamp and travel down the rainbow steps to walk the path of the Milky Way. Illuminated in my pinprick of light, I see a universe of time: Pleistocene animals, Indians, European conquerors, Florida Crackers, developers. Nature crushes time in excavator claws. I place down the lamp, and Gary, Mike, Mark, and I dance together under the stars.

Paradis

• • •

A few weeks after Hari, I also attempted a visit to the KickAss Farm. I wanted to know if the graphene desalination device and satellite dishes were still functioning. But after only two miles of journeying, I encountered a wall of mangroves and could hear the waters of the sound rushing into the Gulf. When I pushed through the trees, I could see Hari had sliced the southern portion of the island from the larger northern part. Ibises flitted back and forth across the narrow divide, mocking me. I gave them a good startle with my curses, but when I turned around, I stumbled in the mangroves. Covered in cuts and scrapes, an elbow swelling like a large orange, I abandoned the excursion and returned home.

Today, I decide to make a second attempt. It's high tide, so with gear and fishing tackle loaded into my skiff, my boat cuts smoothly through the new passage and into the Gulf. I figure I'll return later to see if the outgoing tide might wash a couple fish onto my fishhook. I beach my skiff near where the guys and I had set off in search of flying cars. I toss a couple of water bottles and the collapsible machete into my wagon and put on my backpack and trusty mosquito-netting hat. The way is a little confusing, with its monotony of palmettos stuck through with cabbage palms that line the entire path from the beach. Time and nature are taking back the old path, but I think I'm approaching the turnoff for the flying cars. It's there when my peripheral vision catches the flash of two lean animal bodies running through the palmettos. About fifty feet ahead, two dogs step onto the trail. Two of Eenie's grown pups, I presume, lean and straggly, with burr-studded fur. The brown-and-white one grins a full cage of teeth. The second dog, black as shadow, sniffs the air and begins barking. Remembering Gary's experience, I back down the trail, keeping my wagon as a barrier between us. Horrible visages of dogs tearing away my neck bring up my blood pressure. Surely, Shadow's barking and Brownie's snarling are the "come and get lunch" signal for Eenie and his hungry minions. On an impulse, I launch my water bottle in their direction. Perhaps they will follow it like a fat stick.

Brownie-white takes the bait, but Shadow is not fooled.

"Go play fetch, you mangy beast!" I shout as I toss a second water bottle toward him. It lands far short, and he runs at me. My impulse is an adrenaline-driven fight response. I don't even remember unfolding the machete, but when he leaps, it is extended fully, and I raise it and hack blindly. With a horrible howl, he falls. Through the sweat seeping into my eyes, there is Shadow writhing on the ground with the blade of the machete in his ribs. His tongue lolls out between his teeth. Ugly, shallow, whining gasps spew from his mouth. With both my arms, I wrench the machete free and bring it down again. My entire body trembles with the unforgettable whack of the blade slicing into the meat of his flank. His body stills. Blood flows down the path; my hands drip red. There is a shrill yelling, and I realize it is coming from my own vocal cords.

When I look up, Brownie stands on the trail looking at me. The machete is slick, and I hold it in my right hand. I yell, growl, and hiss; I flail and thrash the machete madly. Brownie takes a step back, not dropping eye contact, and then turns and runs. I stand silently for a moment, drop my hand to the

Paradis

side, scan the palmettos. Then I too slowly take a step backwards, pause, scan again, and turn and run. I run all the way to the boat, my backpack thudding on my back, the machete still in my right hand. I throw the machete into the boat, followed by my backpack. I scan the beach, my heart pounding full throttle. Not a dog in sight. I wade into the surf and cool my heatstroke-hot body by splashing water over my head.

A safe distance offshore, I cut the engine, snap open the lid on a can of pineapples, dissolve an electrolyte tablet into the juice, and gulp its contents. I wash the blade in the water. I've lost my mood for fishing and want only to reach the safety of the marina.

As I troll along the newly carved miniature bluffs of the inlet, the sun blinks in and out of the clouds and casts angular shadows on the wedges of compacted sand. I coast the boat to where clear waters swirl along the eroded bank. I'm still shaking from the encounter with the dogs.

Something gleams like the beam of a miniature lighthouse. I dig in my pack for the fillet knife and wade up to the bank. The glistening object lifts easily, and I wash it in the surf. I stare at my hand in disbelief. A coin—a gold coin. Someone long ago celebrated Gasparilla at the beach? I turn it a few times, feel its weight, observe how it flickers with the sunlight. Beneath the curly-headed profile of Philippus V shines the date 1745, astoundingly pristine. Tails display the word Hispania minted above a coat of arms. I pocket the coin and start to dig. Silver Pillar coins minted with the old and new worlds of Spain and Mexico cascade into my hands: two pillars and a crown on one side of the coin and lions and castles in a coat of arms and Phillip's name on the reverse. Other gold coins have a T-cross at the center. Out from the packed ledge of sand, I pull a rope of gold chain strung with seven gold rings. My mind conjures a vision of Mike combing the beach with his metal detector. He had it right, just the wrong place. I count out seventy-two coins and the chain with the seven rings. It is beginning to rain, and I set out the pineapple can to catch the water. I take off my shirt, unclasp my black bra, and tie it to the nearest mangrove branch to mark the spot. In my hands, gold and silver coins from the shores of Paradis. I strip off the remainder of my clothing, toss them on the beach, and run into the ocean. I frolic and splash among the waves in the rain. I laugh, and laugh, and laugh.

Paradis

Entropy

...
*And both that morning equally lay
In leaves no step had trodden black.
Oh, I kept the first for another day!
Yet knowing how way leads on to way,
I doubted if I should ever come back.*

*I shall be telling this with a sigh
Somewhere ages and ages hence:
Two roads diverged in a wood, and I—
I took the one less travelled by,
And that has made all the difference.*

-Robert Frost

Mary Burke

Epilogue

Amber's house message board pings: a skyLyft Aerocar rental is available at Paine Field Airport for pickup tomorrow. *Finally,* she thinks, booking the rental immediately. It has been months since she's heard from her mom, and between the transformer hack and the fires, it's been basically impossible to get in or out of Seattle.

Early the following morning, Amber dons her N95, braves the crammed light rail to Everett, and is off the skyLyft pad by 7 a.m. The rental flies in a sky subdivided into sunny blue above and chiffon yellow below. Yellowstone remains closed due to the fires, but the skyLyft's cameras show the Rocky Mountains smoke-free today. The GPS guides her smoothly onto a landing pad at the skyLyft Denver servicing center

Paradis

where she grabs food, FaceTimes Liam, and responds to work messages.

Amber is flying again by two. During the next ten hours, Amber tries to keep busy with work, but as Washington fades into the west and Florida grows closer, she finds it harder to concentrate. She naps over the disappearing wetlands of the Mississippi Delta and above the eroding coastal cities of the Florida Panhandle. She wakes during the automated landing to see a partially lit Orlando, looming below like some bioluminescent octopus. By 1 a.m. she is fast asleep in her generator-powered room at the Garden Hilton.

◆ ◆ ◆

The next morning, Amber flies through a soft watercolor sky. On the skyLyft's cameras, she sees the caved-in warehouses of Joey Pelagro's, then a decrepit Main Street. Spanish moss rustles like tumbleweeds, spiders drape webs between the Doric columns of the bank, and palmetto bugs spill from the cracked shell of old Hinson's Drug Store.

Ah, to switch to VR mode, to clutch some idealized Cici-youth to her chest, to hear the click of stiletto heels on the sidewalk, to feel the rumble of old Studebakers waiting for the traffic light to change, to see Cici in cat-eyed sunglasses, standing with her gaggle of girlfriends and giggling in harmony as she checked out boys beneath the movie marquee. She sheds bittersweet tears, then tries to compose herself; she doesn't know what she'll find on Paradis.

Leaving Main Street, she flies over the streets of drowned neighborhoods. At the Jefferys' house, a giant gator yawns in the driveway. The picture window is shattered. Tall reeds grow high in the yard. The palm trees have become frondless poles. Amber thinks she sees a fish jump in the street. Waves lap at Snug Harbor Park. The fallen pier has almost succumbed to the waves. Amber wipes her weeping nose on her sleeve as the autonomous car flies westward over the sound.

Her heart is pounding as she approaches the marina. She sees Mom's boat tied at the dock and the sandy trail still wide and dry. She misses Addy's Wedgie completely and has to circle back. She sees it then—Mom's little white house, on stilts. She switches to hover mode and scans with the cameras. Startled chickens run to and fro. The screen door of the porch opens, and a wild-haired, disheveled old woman in red, hibiscus-printed shorts and a patched, plum-colored T-shirt bounds down the steps. Her precious mom waves and shouts. Amber's heart leaps with joy, and involuntarily, she beams a message. She sees the satellite dish has toppled from its mast. She gropes in a side compartment where she has prepared a couple of notes. She ties one to a water bottle and tosses it out the window. Both papers hold the same message: "Mom, I love you! Take the skiff to pick me up at the Kicklighter beach where I'll park the car on the charging pad." Hopefully, the charging station will still be working, although she certainly has enough power to make several trips back and forth to Orlando. The first note lands at the foot of a giant pine. Her mom retrieves the message and reads it. For some reason, her mom starts dancing furiously and shouting. Amber is amazed at how her mom resembles the chickens that dart in and out from under the house. But she shrugs and flies on.

Paradis

The island quickly congeals to thick, tropical wilderness as the flying car continues toward the Kicklighter landing pad. There exists an inlet below where there should be none. She checks the GPS and for a moment is puzzled; it occurs to her that the hurricane must have divided the island. Is that what her mom was trying to tell her with that wild flailing?

The KickAss Farm becomes visible, and Amber directs the flying car in a couple slow spins above the property. The pine-sheltered Kicklighter home appears none the worse for hurricane winds. Christmas Eve memories filter like a phantasm through her memory: Richy and his weird zoo, a boy trapped in fear of his father, a Tobias-Santa on his pit-bull-driven sleigh. And as if conjured from her thoughts, the cameras pick up six leaping and barking dogs. They are clearly riled by the overhead presence of the flying car. She brings the dogs into closer focus and scrunches her face in disgust. They are mangy and bone hungry. Eenie leads the pack. What if she lands the skyLyft over on the pad and they find her? What if she gets stranded on the beach waiting for her mom to pick her up in the skiff? Muttering a few choice expletives, Amber turns the flying car back toward Addy's Wedgie.

She finds Mom heading toward the marina. She waves the note Amber had thrown out the window. Something is scribbled on the backside, which Amber enlarges with the camera: "DANGER! Eenie and his pack on new south island. Land at marina! Meet you there!" Amber gives a thumbs-up that she doubts her mom can see and heads back toward the marina.

She circles the marina's long abandoned picnic area from the state park days. Palmettos poke through the tall grasses surrounding lonely picnic pavilions. She enables free-landing mode, then sets the landing-coordinates to the wide, sandy place where the trail enters the picnic area. The hybrid electric "pods" rotate to vertical landing mode, and with her eyes pasted to the camera feed, she takes a deep breath. The flying car sets down a little rough. She checks the instruments. No dents on the skyLyft rental and no bruises on herself. Everything is copacetic. Well, except for her white-knuckled hand gripping the armrest.

◆ ◆ ◆

It is ninety degrees outside, and Amber drags out her rucksack and wishes for a cold beer. Instead, she drinks electrolyte water and heads down the trail. At about a quarter mile, her mom appears around a bend in the palmettos. Amber drops her bag and runs toward her.

They are soon trudging down the trail and chattering with such adrenaline-released abandon that gopher tortoises dive into their holes and an unwary armadillo jumps straight into the air in front of them and scurries back into the safe shade of a palmetto.

Amber relays the story of her journey, and, when she lets her mom get a word in edgewise, learns there is a warm loaf of coconut-rosemary bread waiting for them back at the house. Amber realizes she is famished. She takes her mom's hand and mentions the Bacardi Gold in her bag. That brings a smile to her mom, who tightens her hand's grasp. Around them, the heat rises in waves. They sip electrolyte water. Their shoes suck in the slop-land of Paradis. They talk about Mike and

Paradis

Gary and Cici and Dandi until they are standing beneath the archway of Addy's Wedgie. Amber looks around. Not much has changed. Maybe a little wilder. Her mom reminds her of some flowery piece of driftwood. For all their talking, Amber knows the same question is rotating silently in both their minds: *How long are you staying?*

● ● ●

After showering, Amber changes into shorts and a Cascadia tee and flip-flops. Aromas of spicy bean soup and warm bread permeate the wilderness, along with the scent of impending rain borne on the breeze. T-3 is out of his pen, roaming freely and adroitly digging despite his missing front foot. Amber picks up a gob of Spanish moss and brings it to him. He almost seems to smile as he gobbles it down. She inhales fresh air. All her senses are revitalized with the relief one feels after having completed an arduous journey. Laughter escapes her as she chases chickens into their coop.

Later, she stares hypnotically at the stream of rain filling a bucket her mom has placed under a leaky roof seam. The soup is how she likes it—hot with warm seedy bread to sop. Complete contentment in the present moment.

When the downpour ends, Amber cleans the dishes while her mom empties the bucket. They sit on the porch in the glow of the solar-powered overhead light from the front room and sip rum and listen to what exists nowhere else—the chorus of Florida wilderness. Late into the dark, they share tales of Kicklighters and wild dogs, of Richy, of father and husband and Cici and Snug Harbor mixed with the soft, white noise of mosquitoes and crickets and frogs. They debate the pathways of civilization. A cancer on the environment, her mom concludes, and Amber's thoughts turn to her mom's lack of any kind of medical care. Suddenly, she feels a great tiredness.

As Amber is setting the ladder to climb up to the loft, she notices the family photo on the shelf. "I remember this," she says as she picks it up. "I was fourteen, just in high school. I got so upset because I got taco juice on my new dress."

Her mom nods. "I couldn't recall how old you were."

Amber's eyes brim with tears. "That was a good day."

She returns the photograph to the shelf. She sighs and sniffs and continues up to the loft.

● ● ●

Up just before dawn, Amber stands sleepily at the top of the steps—flip-flopped and pajama-clad—and sees her mom already downstairs.

Her mom puts her finger to her smiling lips.

Amber pauses. The island trees rustle and chirp. She smiles back at her mom and heads down the stairs.

T-3 peeks from his burrow and yawns. Her mom unlatches the chicken coop. Dandi Too parades forth like a proud drum major leading forth his little band of hens and chicks. He trumpets his presence to the new day.

Her mom points her finger toward the glowing sky.

The chirping in the cluster of trees rises to crescendo, and mother and daughter marvel as a multitude of small birds lift and flock toward the beach.

Paradis

● ● ●

After bread and eggs, mother and daughter fill mugs with coffee before heading toward the beach where they sit beneath the archway of the two palms. The beach seems narrower than Amber remembered it. Plovers chase the gentle surf. Not yet 10 a.m. and the sun is brilliant on the white sand. The turquoise water glints blindingly. Time to engage sunglass mode on the iGlass.

"I've something to show you," her mom says. She unzips her pack and brings out a drawstring bag printed with tiny palm trees. She unties it and lets the contents fall onto the sand.

Amber thinks it's a joke at first. She picks up a gold coin and tries to check the authenticity on her iGlass before remembering there is no signal. Certainly, this Philippus V fellow must have carried some moxie to get his facestamp on a piece of gold. She takes off her iGlass and puts it beside her on the sand. She squints at the coin.

Her mom tells the story.

"The Paradis '*e*' restored."

"On Kicklighter land."

They both giggle.

"Will sure come in handy once we get back to civilization," declares Amber, flipping the coin clear up to a palm frond and managing somehow to catch it on its downward fall. The words spill out so naturally that Amber is surprised when her mom doesn't answer. Instead, her mom stares straight ahead. Amber contemplates. Mom could hurt herself; there is no one around to help. She will run out of drinking water. The island is sinking. She can't be thinking of staying. They will fly back to Issaquah together. Fight for survival together. Can't give up on civilization. It's all we have.

But Amber knows better than to say a word.

A tear slides from the corner of her mom's eye.

Amber places Philippus V gently on the little pile of silver and gold resting in the sand alongside her iGlass. In the sand, a tiny fiddler crab raises his fiddle. The breeze lifts grains of sand; small shells shine like gems. Amber raises her eyes to scan the narrow beach toward where the waves ebb and flow from the endless gleam of the Gulf of Mexico. Sanderlings chase the foamy broth that forms where the water meets the land. A flock of roseate spoonbills rises and settles. Baby thunderclouds hover at the horizon. When the small clouds pass over the sun, the water turns dappled as a loggerhead. A pod of porpoises eases on by.

The tear continues its journey, following a fold on her mom's sun-damaged cheek until succumbing to gravity. It falls, imprinting an ephemeral circle in the sand.

The women sit and ponder the horizon—a bold demarcation, a forever receding future. They are unity and division, resilience and struggle, parent and child. They sit juxtaposed upon the sands of Paradis—part of the landscape of an island fractured and incomplete. The sun rises higher. The fin tips of migrating rays etch the water's surface like blades on hot glass. The world is bright neon. White and teal and cobalt blue, the waves roll in.

Acknowledgements

First, I want to extend my deepest gratitude to my mom, this book's primary author, Mary Burke. I am honored to share your beautiful story with the world, Mom.

Next, I must thank my husband, Keenan, for being my ultimate support throughout the editing and publishing process. The years following my mom's death have been very challenging, and I cannot express enough how much your love and support meant in my time of grief. I must also thank you for your feedback, ideas, and brainstorming sessions that helped me finish this work for my mom.

I also want to thank my friends and family who read through my mom's manuscript and helped shape it into its final published version. Thank you to Carolyn Engelke, Peter Sieg, Joy Pollock, Alexis De Girolami, Janet Ung, and anyone else whose contributions I may not have been aware of.

Additionally, I am grateful to the editors and professionals who provided valuable feedback throughout the novel's creation: Peter (last name unknown), Jan Powell, and Bill Chamberlin.

Finally, a special thank you to editor Nicole Fegan, whose work was indispensable in bringing the novel to its final state for publication. Your edits and advice were crucial in shaping this work into a publishable quality.

Author Bios

Mary Burke lived in Florida for sixty-three years. After retiring from a career in education, she moved to Washington State in 2019, before passing away in 2021. She held a master's degree in Social Studies and Counselor Education and worked in a variety of positions teaching, writing health curricula, and guidance counseling. She has published articles in *The Social Studies* and in Tampa Historical Society's *Sunland Tribune*. *Paradis* is her first published novel. She was an active advocate for preserving Florida wildlife.

Natalie Burke has spent over a decade in the video game industry and is credited in multiple games, including Bungie's *Destiny* and Guerrilla Games's *Horizon Forbidden West*. In addition to her project work, she has lectured and consulted on storytelling in virtual reality at the University of Washington. *Paradis* is the first novel she has worked on. She currently lives in the Netherlands with her son and husband.

Printed in Dunstable, United Kingdom